The Twelve Dancing Princesses

Nancy Madore

The Twelve Dancing Princesses

Spice

Spice

THE TWELVE DANCING PRINCESSES

ISBN-13: 978-0-373-60516-3
ISBN-10:   0-373-60516-1

www.Spice-Books.com

Printed in U.S.A.

This book is dedicated to Cindy, Linda and Sharon—three women who provide a never-ending supply of material for a book like this.

PROLOGUE

LONG AGO, IN THE DAYS OF ROYALS AND WIZARDS, THERE LIVED A KING who had no sons, being instead blessed with twelve healthy daughters. The princesses were much admired throughout the kingdom, for each of them possessed dispositions that were at once curious and content, fun-loving and kind. The king held his daughters above everything else, and all of their activities were of interest to him.

When the princesses grew up, each in her turn took a husband, leaving the castle but none of them going very far, so the king continued to watch over them and fancied he knew all that concerned them.

One day a peculiar rumor reached the king's ears; a rumor that appeared to be known by everyone but him. It seemed that the whole of his kingdom was speculating over the princesses' shoes, or more particularly, that it took four kingdoms just to keep them in shoes. What was puzzling about this was that the princesses' new shoes were always worn to shreds the day after they were purchased. It little mattered how sturdy the material the shoes were made of, or how well put together they were, or even how little worn they had been when the princesses removed them in the evenings. Each and every morning the shoes would be found in tatters. And it seemed that the princesses were more baffled than anyone by this.

Immediately upon hearing of this oddity the king ordered the princesses to appear before him. They confirmed that the rumors he heard were true but could provide no clues as to the cause. The king, who prided himself on his problem-solving abilities, discussed the case with his daughters and their husbands in great detail. Could they have been sleepwalking during the night? Further debate proved that they had not. Could a third party be tampering with the princesses' shoes? This also proved to be impossible, as they had begun placing their shoes under lock and key. Were the shoes made of defective materials then, that perhaps disintegrated after so much time? On and on the king questioned his daughters but no new light was shed on the mystery.

The king was at first intrigued, as well as bewildered; but over time the mystery began to wear on his sense of logic and order. Each and every evening he would ride out to the homes of all twelve of his daughters to inspect their shoes. In almost every case the shoes were in pristine condition, only to be discovered the following morning thoroughly worn through, as if they had been used for many years, rather than only one single day. And every morning that he found the shoes in this condition, the king became increasingly frustrated and determined. He spent all his time between morning and night looking into the matter, and the poor man could find no peace until he discovered the secret of his daughters' worn shoes. These events took their toll on the king, and at length, he issued a decree that whoever solved the riddle would be awarded half his kingdom. This was not a challenge for the faint-hearted, however; for in order to discourage insincere applicants the king added the stipulation that anyone attempting to solve the riddle and failing would be put to death.

At first, there were a surprising number of brave men who came forward to accept the challenge, but each and every one failed to successfully solve the riddle and lost their lives in the bargain. During the period of time when proposals to explain this matter of the shoes were flooding in, the princesses opened their eyes each morning with dread, wondering if another innocent man would lose his life. Their carefree, happy childhood seemed a lifetime away. But after a while, the number of men willing to step forward and accept the challenge became fewer and fewer, and the riddle of the princesses' shoes became merely a topic of conversation—for everyone but the king.

Then one day from a faraway land, there came to this kingdom a wizardess called Harmonia Brist. She had traveled a long way from an unfortunate place, where her powers of perception and healing were not only unappreciated, but actually condemned. She left that place in search of a home where she could prosper from her talents. It was here that she paused in her journey to take food and rest.

The wizardess Brist was not long in the kingdom before the topic of the princesses' shoes caught her attention. She was immediately intrigued, and listened with great interest to all that the innkeeper and his daughters would tell her about the matter. When she was satisfied that she had heard enough, the wizardess stood up and said, quite calmly, "Kindly instruct me on the directions to the castle, for I would like to explain this riddle to the king."

Everyone present was astounded. They abruptly dropped what they were doing—and even the innkeeper closed up his shop—to personally escort the wizardess to the king's door. As they proceeded to the castle, the gathering grew larger, with bystanders stopping to inquire what the matter was, and then joining in when they heard what the wizardess was about. Each and every one of the townspeople virtually ceased all activity to follow the wizardess on her adventure to the castle, until there was quite a long parade down the middle of the street.

At last the procession reached its destination and the wizardess was received with much pomp and courtesy, as might well be expected. She was placed in a comfortable room high in a castle tower to await her appointment with the king. Invitations were printed, the princesses were notified and a great feast was prepared. It had been a long time since anyone had dared to attempt the riddle, and in spite of the gruesome outcome that was likely to result, everyone was filled with excitement and anticipation.

In a matter of days the night of the great feast arrived, but in spite of the festivities, drink and music, everyone present was impatient for the moment when the wizardess would have her say. Everyone, that is, except the king. He had, over time, given up hope of ever learning the secret of his daughters' shoes, wearied by the many deaths of those who had already attempted to solve the riddle. He did not wish to see another life lost, least of all the life of this woman. He watched in bewilderment as she calmly enjoyed the festivities. Even the bravest of men who had accepted the challenge had had the good sense to be nervous! He remembered how confident and self-assured she had been on the day when the townspeople presented her to him. He had not been able to stop wondering about her since then. He felt that he should not allow her to accept the challenge. He must dissuade her somehow. The possibility of her losing her life was not worth the risk. The likelihood that she would solve the riddle was impossible. Other wizards and learned men had tried and failed. And yet, all the while, he was as intrigued as everyone else to know how this Harmonia Brist—this wizardess—planned to resolve the mystery.

So the king delayed the awaited moment longer and longer while he debated what he should do. At last the hour grew quite late, and the wizardess approached him.

"A word, Your Highness," she said, addressing him as if she were the one who was royalty. The room was packed to overflowing and yet you could have heard a pin drop at that moment.

"By all means," he replied, astounded by her boldness.

"I am impatient to discuss the riddle," she told him matter-of-factly. "Is that not why we have all gathered here?" There was a collective intake of breaths, including the king's, and the princesses looked at each other apprehensively.

"I will be as forthright with you as you have been with me," said the king, liking her more and more. "I have begun to lose my appetite for the answer to this riddle in my grief over putting so many to death. It does not bode well for me to knowingly send another, especially a woman, to her grave."

"So you have withdrawn the decree regarding the riddle?"

"Well," admitted the king, "I have not officially..."

"Have you refused other contenders who have come forward?" she continued, interrupting him and questioning him in the same tone one would use with witness in a trial. His blood was becoming heated by her audacity.

"No," he replied, intentionally neglecting to inform her that he would have done so if it had been necessary, but no one had come forward to accept the challenge as of late. He had assumed that everyone else, like him, had given up ever discovering the truth about the shoes. But he did not like her tone and refused to explain himself to someone who was not even a constituent of his, and who had no better sense than to speak to him in such a way. Harmonia went on, seemingly unaware of his darkened mood.

"Aha," she exclaimed. "So this kingdom, too, is afraid to accept a challenge from a woman!" The silent room suddenly came alive with a buzz of voices, low, hushed and excited. Harmonia was too upset to notice. How was she to succeed in the world if she was never given an equal opportunity?

The king, as it happened, had always considered himself a great advocate of women. He had altered many laws to support women, at the advice of his beloved daughters. He had even, over the years, heard traces of whispers that perhaps he had gone too far on this score, causing an inequity for men. It did not bode well for him to be accused of discrimination against women.

The king stood up in order to look down at the wizardess, and regain his sense of authority. "Harmonia Brist," he thundered, "I will accept your challenge but it will be on my terms, not yours." There was silence in the great hall now as the king continued, somewhat grudgingly. "Your bravery is to be commended but I will not be coerced into agreeing to conditions which I now find objectionable. Past wrongs do not make a right." He took his time, deliberating as he spoke. He felt correct in withdrawing his original decree, with its cruel and unusual penalty for failure. However, in removing the high penalty he could not very well continue to offer half his kingdom; it would not be fair to those who had preceded her. He concluded, therefore, "If you still wish to solve the riddle, you may do so with impunity and, if you succeed where others have failed you may have any single thing from my kingdom that you desire."

Now it was Harmonia who was surprised. She stared at the king, momentarily speechless.

"Well?" prompted the king. "Keep us waiting no longer. What

happens to my daughters' shoes during the night that causes them to become so worn by morning?"

The wizardess recovered from her shock quickly, excited now by this new opportunity. She stood perfectly straight, looking the king directly in the eye as she accepted the challenge. She spoke out in a loud, clear voice. "The shoes are merely a symptom of the princesses' discontent," she explained. "They are nostalgic and adjusting poorly to their married lives. It is by the sheer powers of their innermost secret desires that they come together each and every evening to dance their cares away, right here in this very castle, just as they used to do when they were children."

There was silence. One did not know whether it was the simplicity of the idea that offended or the notion of the princesses' "discontent." Either way, it was clear that the king was not only disappointed, but annoyed. However, his voice remained calm.

"I suppose that is a clever reply," he said evenly, "since you begin by flattering me that my daughters miss living here with me. Oh, that I could have them here forever but it is better that they should leave me to marry. Yet you insult me sorely to imply that my daughters return here without my knowledge or that we have not already thought to monitor their nightly activities and established that they have not left their beds during the night!"

The wizardess was unperturbed by the king's demeanor and, in fact, smiled. "You will not see your daughters when they come here together in secret, because they enter through the doorway of their most secret wishes and remain through the power of their longing," she explained. "For some reason, these cerebral activities are being made manifest only through their shoes."

"You are not such a foolish wizardess after all," remarked the king. "You find an explanation that cannot be proven or disproved."

"It is proven by the worn slippers," replied the wizardess.

"You have given an unsatisfactory explanation that cannot be proven!" bellowed the king.

"Father!" exclaimed the youngest princess at that moment. All eyes turned to her.

"It is true!" she murmured. "I have dreamed it!"

Suddenly the room buzzed with lowered voices. The young princess turned to her sisters, who seemed very confused indeed, wearing expressions of their struggle to recollect memories that were just out of reach.

"I apologize if my explanation did not satisfy," continued the wizardess, raising her voice above the noise in the room. "But I assure you that the cure will be more to your liking."

The room became silent again.

"The cure?" asked the king. "Do you mean to say you can stop my daughters' shoes from being worn through during the night?"

"Of course," said the wizardess. "Would I have ventured forth if I could not?"

"If you can accomplish this, you will indeed have solved the riddle," promised the king. "So what is the cure?"

"It is different for each of the princesses. I must prescribe them individually. Within one week of following my recommendations, their shoes will cease being worn down during the night."

"So it shall be!" bellowed the king. "You have one week."

A cheer rang up in the room, for no attempt had been received so well thus far. The remainder of the night was filled with jolly celebration as hope sprung anew; until the next morning, when somber reality returned in the shape of twelve pairs of shoes worn clear through.

PRINCESS ATTENTIA

PRINCESS ATTENTIA WOKE UP THE MORNING AFTER THE GREAT FEAST FILLED with excitement. She was the only one of her sisters who had fully recognized the validity of the wizardess's claims. She knew it was true; for she could recall in vivid detail the dreams where she and her sisters gathered together in their father's castle each night, dancing away the hours. She also knew that she was not nearly as happy now as she had been in her childhood home. What surprised her was to learn that her sisters suffered similarly. They had all seemed, to her, so content and settled in their married life. No doubt she, too, appeared to be the same.

She was certain the wizardess could help. The fact that Harmonia Brist had identified the problem of the worn shoes gave her cause to hope. How wonderful it would be if she could become as joyful and content with her husband as she had been with her father and her sisters.

Princess Attentia put on her prettiest dress and sat down at her dressing table to style her hair. As she did so she thought about the wizardess. How beautiful she was! And oh, how Princess Attentia admired her. She wished that she were more like her.

Just then her husband's head popped out from under the blankets. "What are you doing up so early?" he asked.

"I want everything to be perfect for the wizardess when she gets here," she told him. "And you, too, should get up and make yourself ready."

"Isn't it a bit early?" he asked her sleepily.

"I don't know when she will arrive, but I'm sure she'll come here first since we are the closest to the castle." With one last adjustment to her hair she approached the bed and sat close to where her husband lay. "I do so want her to like us."

"How could she not?" he asked, reaching out to grab hold of her and draw her closer to him.

She smiled but pulled herself gently out of his grasp before he could rumple her dress. "I just want to be sure," she replied.

He looked at her speculatively for a moment. "You seemed genuinely moved by her theories last night," he remarked. "Are you unhappy, Attentia?"

"Of course not," she replied automatically. She looked at her husband and was instantly charmed by his appearance. His face had a childlike quality while it was still flushed from sleep that clashed delightfully with the masculine stubble on his chin. His gentle gaze and husky morning voice captivated her. She loved him so much. Shouldn't that make everything right? It seemed that it did not. She knew that he loved her, too, and that he wanted to please her. And yet there were times…

The door chimed just then, causing the princess to jump. "I knew it!" she exclaimed, running from the room.

Harmonia breezed in, looking exuberant and self-assured. She wore lovely bright colors that complemented her golden hair streaked with gray. She had a young, watchful expression, as her eyes took in everything around her. She carried with her a doctor's bag of sorts, quite large and stuffed to overflowing. Princess Attentia wondered what was inside.

Princess Attentia apologized profusely for not having any refreshments prepared as she led the wizardess into their kitchen and immediately set about the task of making coffee.

"I have breakfasted already," the wizardess told her, sitting down at the kitchen table. "What I would really like is for you to sit here next to me."

The princess dropped what she was doing and sat down immediately.

Harmonia smiled at the girl's eagerness to please. "Where is your husband?"

"Oh, he will be down in a moment. He didn't expect you so early."

There was silence a moment as the women looked at each other.

"Are you going to give us some kind of test?" the princess asked nervously.

"No, not really," replied the wizardess. "Usually I can identify the difficulty by observing symptoms in people. Sometimes I have to ask questions. But once I know where the problem lies I can often produce the appropriate remedy."

"So you're like a doctor."

"A bit," agreed the wizardess. "Except that instead of medicine I use a lot of intuition and a little magic."

"I hope that doesn't mean there's any chance of me being turned into a frog," said the prince from the doorway, looking perfectly turned out as he joined them.

Princess Attentia laughed cheerfully as she looked her husband over with appreciation. He gave her a wink. The wizardess was charmed by the pair. But where was the problem? Was the princess simply unknowledgeable in matters of sharing pleasure with her husband? Or was there something else? She watched them carefully.

"You both seem very much in love," she observed.

"Oh, we are," the princess insisted earnestly. Indeed it is so, thought the wizardess.

"And you no doubt find each other very attractive," she continued.

"Oh, immensely so," said the princess.

"Perhaps too much so," agreed the prince.

The wizardess stared at the prince for a moment. "Well!" she exclaimed at last with a look of satisfaction. "I have something here that will be of great benefit to you both." She set her overstuffed bag on the table and began to shuffle through it determinedly.

"Have you detected our problem so quickly?" asked the princess.

"Oh, it is not so much of a problem at all," the wizardess assured her. "You will by no means have difficulty in overcoming it. Ah. Here it is." And she pulled from her bag a most extraordinary leather contraption.

"What is that?" asked the princess.

"It looks like some kind of a…surely it couldn't be…" The prince stumbled over his words in stunned mortification. "A…*chastity* belt?"

"It is worn like a chastity belt," admitted the wizardess. "But it does not serve the same purpose. This belt is charmed, as you will soon find out. The inscription on the leather will tell you all you need to know." The wizardess set the belt on the table and stood up. "Wear it whenever your husband is nearby Princess Attentia, and all will be well. It is lightweight and as soft as skin, so it shouldn't trouble you overmuch."

"I don't know…" said the princess doubtfully. She looked at her husband, who was still staring at the device in horror.

"The king has decreed that my instructions are to be followed to the letter," Harmonia reminded them.

"Well…I suppose it couldn't hurt to try it," consented the princess. Her husband remained speechless.

"I must go now," said the wizardess. "I have the rest of your sisters to visit. Goodbye."

As the princess escorted the wizardess out, the prince picked up the mysterious belt from the table. It was indeed as soft as skin. He examined it closely.

"How does it work?" asked Princess Attentia, rushing back into the kitchen after having led the wizardess out as quickly as she could manage without being rude.

The prince squinted as he examined the inscription. "It says, 'There is no key. The belt will open of its own accord at the opportune time.'" He looked up at his wife. "What do you suppose that means?"

"I don't know."

"Well, put it on and let us see," he suggested. For the moment at least, his sense of curiosity was piqued.

Princess Attentia tentatively accepted the belt from him. It was lightweight and soft, just as Harmonia had promised. She took the belt upstairs into their bedroom, with her husband following close behind her. She went into her dressing room while the prince waited for her on their bed.

The leather contraption fit just like any ordinary chastity belt, with surprisingly soft yet sturdy straps that wrapped around her waist and thighs to hold it in place. Between her legs there was a delicate, yet sturdy barrier that fit perfectly over her opening; so perfectly, in fact, that she could still perform all bodily functions without its getting in the way. The feeling of the supple leather straps wrapped around her thighs and waist gave her a little thrill. She lowered her skirts and went to her waiting prince.

"Well?" he asked expectantly. She blushed. "Let me see," he insisted impatiently.

Nancy Madore

Princess Attentia raised her skirts. Another tingle shot through her as she bared herself for her husband.

The prince stared at his wife, naked except for the chastity belt from her waist down. Her little triangle of curls was the first thing he noticed. She was quite bare to his view except for the dainty straps that held the contraption in place around her waist and upper thighs. Upon closer inspection, which he immediately set to by kneeling before her, the prince noticed the little barrier that closed her off from him.

"The question is how we get it to open," he murmured.

"What?" she gasped, becoming excited to have him examining her so closely.

"The inscription said it would 'open of its own accord at the opportune time,'" he reminded her. "I'm just wondering when the 'opportune time' is."

"I don't know," she admitted truthfully, although she was beginning to wonder. Could this be the answer to the many nights of unfulfilled passion, where she was always so close but never able to find her release before it was all over? Perhaps there was something to there being an "opportune time." The princess was eager to find out. "Shall we test it to see?" she asked.

"I imagine we will think of nothing else until we do," he agreed, and with his usual enthusiasm the prince hastily removed his clothes. Then he removed Princess Attentia's dress. But as he stared at the leather straps that bound her and kept him out, he abruptly came to a halt.

Normally this would have been the 'opportune time' for the prince, but the chastity belt was still closed up tight.

The prince led his wife to their bed. She lay down on her back nervously, not sure what was expected of her. He stared at her for several minutes, taking in every detail of her body as she lay there waiting for him, wearing nothing but the chastity belt. This simple pause for contemplation was exquisite for the princess. To be looked at, studied and wondered over, like an intricate machine that had to be figured out, was in itself quite gratifying.

The prince approached his wife tentatively, trying to think of what she liked but realizing suddenly that he really didn't know. He decided it was high time he found out. He lay on his side next to her, leaning up on one elbow. His body was hardened with arousal, but he mentally checked himself, using self-control to hold back the urges that threatened to overwhelm him. He knew that he would need to concentrate on the task at hand in order to maintain that control. He would take his time, moving slowly and carefully, so as not to miss the secrets that his wife had so far kept hidden from him.

He leaned over her and brushed his lips very lightly over hers, teasing her with the hint of a kiss and then moving away to do the same along her cheeks, forehead and shoulders. She delighted in the feel of his warm breath on her skin as she waited and anticipated his next move.

While his lips covered her with feathery kisses from the shoulders up, the prince's fingertips began to lightly caress his wife's body from the shoulders down in the same teasing manner. He circled his fingers nimbly over her skin, not grasping or rubbing, but merely hinting at touches to come. As he traced over her form, he took the opportunity to admire the curves and bends in her flesh, and the silky feel of her skin. Each time his lips came back to brush over hers, he noted her increased breathing and little gasping noises, and from these little signs he measured her readiness for more. He had decided that each and every advance from him should be craved before it was received. As his hands circled lower and lower, lightly flicking over every part of her, the princess arched her body and moaned, telling him without words that she was longing for a more lingering touch.

Once he was absolutely certain that the princess was truly longing to be kissed, the prince took her lips thoroughly in a deep, penetrating assault with his mouth and tongue. He realized now what the chastity belt was all about, and he guessed that it would not open quickly or easily. But he did not mind this in the least.

The prince continued to kiss his wife passionately until she clung to him, trembling. He broke the kiss then and whispered huskily, "Now we will find out what you like. Will you tell me or will I have to try everything and see what works?"

She was speechless.

He laughed and kissed her again. The touch of his hands came steadier and firmer, tracing the curves of her body as if to sculpt them. As he brought his hands up over her breasts he lovingly molded them in his palms before abruptly pinching the tips. At this, Princess Attentia moaned loudly.

"Ah," he sighed with satisfaction. "There is something you like." And he pinched the tips of her breasts again, a little harder this time. She moaned again and writhed beneath him. He leaned in close to blow on the reddened tips. She shuddered. He continued to play with her breasts in a leisurely manner, trying one thing and then another, and gauging her responses to everything he did. She reveled in the attention, but more than that, a passion was building inside her that she had never felt before.

After a while the prince moved his hands lower in a very leisurely manner, pausing to caress her stomach before he moved even lower still, and circled his fingers down closer to the chastity belt barrier. She lifted her hips up to meet his hand, pushing herself into him but he wanted to maintain control over the pace so he circled back up and around over her belly again, causing her to moan in disappointment. He continued to circle his hand round and round, teasing her, and each time his fingers reached down below her belly button she lifted her hips up to meet them, showing him that she wanted to be touched. Still, he refrained from touching her there in order to build up her anticipation to the point that when he did at last touch her, she would indeed be truly ready for him. And even when he finally made contact there, he did it lightly and fleetingly, passing over and around the sensitive area, to heighten her anticipation and excitement even more. His patient efforts seemed to be working, for she was consumed with a desire to be touched, writhing and bucking beneath him without a thought for anything but his hand.

He caressed her with the same fixation on her pleasure, leaning in close to explore her with his eyes as well as his fingers. This is when he happened to notice that each time his fingers flitted over one particular spot the princess moaned a little louder and thrust her hips forward with more vigor. He decided he would like to explore that area further.

The tender little spot was located just above her opening, which was still sealed shut by the chastity belt. However, the place that piqued his curiosity was fully exposed.

With his fingertips he felt all around the area, taking his time, ignoring her moans for the moment, and simply becoming acquainted with her body. He spread her legs wider and leaned in between them as he performed this examination. He leaned in so close that she could feel his warm breath on her skin.

At length the prince became aware of a tiny bump beneath her flesh. He had never noticed it before. As he played with it, it appeared to become more pronounced, seemingly swelling and hardening under his touch. This now, was something he understood!

With further investigation, which the prince continued in a very unhurried and thorough manner that was driving his wife wild with desire, he learned that touching the underside of the hardened and inflamed little protrusion caused her hips to jump and jerk away from him, but touching her just the right distance over the top of it made her entire body melt under his fingers. It was very similar for him, he marveled. But he still had yet to learn the correct rhythm and intensity for handling the little mound of flesh for just the right effect.

The prince experimented with many different strokes and caresses over the tiny bud of flesh, using varying levels of pressure from his fingertips. At length he found just the right combination of tension and pace with which to stroke her, and he settled into a rhythm that had her hips dancing in perfect time with his fingers. As her excitement grew she gripped the bedsheets with her fingers. He watched in astonishment as the chastity belt slowly opened.

The prince's body ached to respond immediately to this invitation, but he forced himself to hold back just a little longer. He knew now, firsthand, how similar their bodies were, and he could relate only too well to how disappointing it would be for her if he were to stop his titillating caress. He could tell by the way she was writhing and moaning with such abandon that she was very, very close to finding satisfaction. Keeping perfect time with his fingers, he leaned in to kiss her where the chastity belt left her open and exposed for him. He let his tongue linger there affectionately, sliding up and down the length of her. Suddenly her hips stopped moving and she cried out loudly with pleasure. He could feel the pulsing of her inner body with his tongue.

He waited until he was certain she was thoroughly satisfied before rising up over her. Her eyes were shining and she appeared somewhat dazed. Her legs, which were still spread, trembled slightly. The chastity belt was wide open now and she reached her arms out to embrace him.

The prince slid easily into her body, and marveled at the way she felt. Her inner flesh was soft and swollen and soaking wet. He slid in and out of the thick, silky flesh, relishing in the way it clung to and around his hardness. The princess, fully satiated from the initial driving need that had previously consumed her, now found a new pleasure in the feeling that came from simply having her husband moving inside her body. She held him close with her arms and legs, kissing him feverishly. She felt all at once vulnerable and empowered. She savored her husband's every stroke, without, for once, fretting over how long it would last. When his thrusts came faster and his time drew near, she felt a new and distinct surge of satisfaction, milder to her senses but more intense to her soul. It seemed that they were moving in unison and, for the first time in their marriage, she felt that they truly were one.

Afterward they clung to each other in surprise and delight.

"I did not know," he said simply.

"I should have told you," she admitted.

"Why didn't you?"

"I thought there was something wrong with me," she tried to explain. "I thought maybe my body wasn't working right...or fast enough."

"So you never...?"

"Sometimes...afterward," she paused. "I would...finish."

He groaned. "Never again," he promised her. He kissed her face, ears, lips and everywhere. "I'm pleased with the belt," he said at last.

"You are?"

"Definitely," he continued. "It's not just better for you. It's better for me, too."

"It is?"

"Yes," he said, looking into her eyes. "I never knew it could feel like that."

"It was different?" She could not believe they were speaking so frankly. Somehow the deeper intimacy they had shared sexually was giving them the freedom to communicate more freely.

"It was…amazing. Everything seemed magnified—your body felt warmer, softer, wetter…it was amazing," he repeated, at a sudden loss for words. She blushed, delighted by what she was hearing. And then they were both silent. He was thinking about how loving his wife had been, and so eager to please him. He realized now that he had mistaken her eagerness for readiness. She wondered over how he had managed to learn her secrets so quickly and to satisfy her so expertly. If only she had known how easy and worthwhile it was she might have told him sooner.

Still, it perplexed her that his sexual satisfaction seemed to come from activity that was so separate and individual from her own. She had always thought that true love would bring about mutual fulfillment simultaneously. Had she been wrong about that?

These musings followed Princess Attentia throughout the rest of that day and into the evening. She decided this time to confide her thoughts to her husband.

"Do you think it is odd that we both get satisfaction from such different means?" she asked him pointedly when he came to her that evening.

"To be honest I was surprised to discover how similar we are in that regard." He took her hands in his and kissed each of her fingertips.

"Well, but what I mean is, don't you think we should come together in that way at the same time?"

"Oh, *that*." He thought for a moment. "I suppose we could try," he said at last with a grin. She laughed. "No, I mean it," he said, getting serious. "Now that I know what pleases you I will just have to find ways to do that while we're engaged together."

"Sometimes when we have been together…before…I have felt pleasure by rubbing against you a certain way," she began.

"But you never got the opportunity to find out where it would lead, eh?" he finished for her. "I must confess it is pure torture to feel you rubbing up against me like that. I will have to learn to exert more control."

"And there might be other ways, too," she mused.

"I am thinking of a few I would like to try right now."

"Well, but there is still the chastity belt to contend with," she reminded him.

"By 'right now' I meant some time in the next few hours, not this second," he assured her. "We're just going to have to accept that our bodies are different. Yours needs warming up, and I'm glad of that. It's fun warming you up."

With a giggle she pulled off her nightgown. She was naked except for the belt. They both looked at the dark leather contraption wrapped around her fair skin. There was something very sensual about the look and feel of it. Princess Attentia felt warm under her husband's gaze, and her skin began to tingle with anticipation.

Once again the prince used his lips and tongue and fingertips to tease his wife into readiness for him. This time she reciprocated, and they both experimented with new ways to excite each other. It became clear that he needed much less encouragement than she, and they proceeded accordingly. She was careful to keep him excited enough so that he did not lose his arousal altogether without causing him to lose control. She found that she could she do this by giving him little bits of attention, such as short strokes from her fingers or little flicks of her tongue. She also discovered that he became quite excited when she showed him openly how his attentions affected her. He loved nothing more than to hear her cry out or to see her body writhing in excitement. There was no good reason to hold her feelings inside, for not only did it enhance the experience for him, but it did so for her, as well.

Soon the prince was once again stroking his wife in just the way she liked best and, low and behold, the chastity belt slowly opened.

"Shall we attempt it together this time?" he asked her.

"Mmm."

He stopped stroking her and moved between her legs. "Let's try it this way," he said as he slid himself into her slick opening. Once he was settled nicely in her warm, wet body he slipped his hand between their bodies and resumed his stroking, carefully, with just the same tension and rhythm he had used before. It was only mildly awkward for him to do this; just enough, in fact, to keep his concentration on what he was doing to her instead of letting his body overrule his mind. At the same time he moved within her very slowly, so that he could enjoy it, too—but not too much. Soon her hips were gyrating wildly beneath his. Watching her beautifully flushed face thought-fully, he perceived that this position would, indeed, allow them both to find fulfillment, if not simultaneously, then close to it. But now that the prince had learned to reign in his own pleasure in order to enhance Princess Attentia's, he wanted to draw the experience out even further.

He abruptly stopped his caresses and pulled himself out of his wife's body, smiling tenderly at her look of disappointment. "I can't be certain if that was working well or not," he teased. "Let's try something else…turn around."

The princess moved herself somewhat awkwardly onto her knees, but her arousal soon overcame her inhibitions. Her husband helped to arrange her body in the way he thought it might work best. Then he slid himself back into her body from behind, holding very still for a moment, and reminding himself that these little exercises in self-control would prolong the pleasure and intensify his and her satisfaction. He reached his hand around her hips to the place she liked best to be stroked and discovered that he could pleasure her from this position, too. As could she; for her fingers were already there!

Before long Princess Attentia was once again reaching the precipice of her desire. The prince watched in fascination as her plump buttocks moved round and round in front of him. All he had to do was kneel before her and enjoy the view. He found himself caressing her buttocks gently as they wriggled about. The pleasure was intoxicating, and it was all he could do to continue holding himself at bay, but through sheer determination he managed it. Time and again he would hold back the surge that threatened to overwhelm him. And each time he held it off it came back the next time feeling even better—and harder to resist.

The princess moaned and writhed about, delighting in the freedom this new position offered her. From this vantage point, it was remarkably easy for her to stimulate herself while fully enjoying the exquisite feeling of her husband moving slowly in and out of her from behind. She leaned comfortably on one forearm while she used her other hand to pleasure herself. This position raised her bottom up higher than her head, considerably enhancing the feeling of having her husband inside her. And as for her husband, he was trying to find ways to not enjoy it quite so much.

But alas, the prince stopped her again, for he had become like a child with a new toy, curious to experience every aspect of it from every single point of view. This time he laid down on his back and had the princess mount him from the top. She gasped to feel him so deep inside her. She settled with her knees on either side of him, sitting straight up, but raised just a bit to ease the first bit of pressure. From this position also she could quite easily stimulate herself, and she slipped her hand down in order to do just that, but her husband's hand slid in first and took up the task, applying just the right amount of pressure and motion with the thumb and middle finger. This time she rocked back and forth as his fingers caressed her, rubbing herself ardently against his hand. She clung to the hand that caressed her with both of her hands, holding it firmly in place to prevent him stopping again. With his other hand the prince caressed her breasts, pinching the tips the way he knew she liked.

The prince watched in awe as his wife rode him. Her breasts jerked about as her body bobbed forward and back over him. She stared at his face as she moved over him. The leather straps of the chastity belt strained over her opened thighs. He could tell by her movements that she was getting close to her time. And he was ready for her. But he wanted to make sure he waited long enough, and he focused all his concentration on the timing of it.

The time was drawing near. Very carefully, without stopping his caresses, he took her hand and led it to where he was rubbing her. She immediately took up the rubbing with an expertise and vigor that amazed him. He grasped on to the leather straps of the chastity belt and held them firmly, waiting for exactly the right moment. He bit his lip in his effort to hold back the tide of his pleasure.

During this time of waiting for Princess Attentia, which was indeed challenging for the prince, he reached a point where he was able to observe the scene from a spectator's point of view. The intimacy they were sharing staggered him. It was not just that he found pleasure in being able to please his wife, although this was something he enjoyed very much. But more than that, he had developed a new awareness of his wife's needs that required from him attentiveness and self-control. His efforts in this regard bore fruit, strengthening his bond with her even as they strengthened her bond with him. How unexpected it was, to receive this kind of pleasure from giving. As the prince caressed his wife he marveled over these things. And she became more beautiful before his eyes as his hands helped bring her to life.

But alas, her time was indeed drawing very near. The prince watched his wife vigilantly now, gauging every movement and sound with a keen and exhilarating awareness.

At length he perceived a sudden change in the princess. Her body stiffened in an immense shudder, even as her fingers continued their frantic stroking. He felt his own excitement mount, barely contained as she cried out, and all at once he yanked on the leather straps of the chastity belt, pulling her forward and back as she had been doing but faster, and with much more force. He joined her cry with a deafening yell of his own. Then she collapsed over him with a sob. He held her firmly to stop her trembling until he realized that he was trembling, too. His body felt weak from the incredible pleasure of his release and he could tell that she felt the same.

Princess Attentia was motionless for a while, but all of a sudden she began kissing him. She kissed his lips, his cheeks, his nose and forehead. She was elated from the powerful emotions that had been released with her passion. "Oh, how I love you!" she exclaimed.

"And I you," he agreed when he could find his voice.

"It was so lovely," she cried. "I feel so happy right now."

He grasped her face in his hands and searched her eyes. "Do you think you might stay here with me tonight instead of slipping out to your father's castle in your dreams?"

She stared back at him. "I wonder...?" she murmured.

And sure enough, the next morning—and every morning thereafter for that matter—the princess's shoes showed no signs whatsoever of excessive wear.

Nevertheless, Princess Attentia and her husband have kept the magic chastity belt, and they use it to this very day.

PRINCESS CONSCIA

PRINCESS CONSCIA WATCHED HER HUSBAND FROM ACROSS THE KITCHEN table. He was so handsome that it took her breath away when she looked at him. She loved the time they shared together, and this time over breakfast was her favorite. With no pressure, she could simply enjoy his company without feeling she had to participate in things that were awkward or embarrassing in order to please him.

"I wonder what the wizardess will have to say," she mused as she sipped her morning coffee.

"I can't imagine," said the prince. "Perhaps she will wrap your sexy feet in gossamer to keep them from flying off each night in your dreams."

She smiled stiffly over this, wondering why the undercurrent of "it" had to enter into so many other parts of their life. Why was it so important to him? In the evening, when the lights were out, she could permit and even sometimes enjoy the sensations of it, but didn't he realize how discomfiting it was for her to talk about it outside their bedroom? It was so humiliating to think about it after the fact. She didn't think it was appropriate to reference those private matters during the day, especially not in the context of her shoes or feet. But there didn't seem to be any subject that failed to remind her husband of it, and he enjoyed making comments to that effect.

She particularly disliked speaking of body parts in the context of "it." What on earth was sexy about feet, for example? Even the parts used during the act, to her mind, were not especially sexy. She disliked the way they looked, in fact, which is why she insisted on doing it in the dark, if they must do it at all.

It was all just so bewildering. She supposed it was the price she had to pay to keep her husband happy, but still, she wished he didn't want it so often. There were, sometimes, little pleasurable sensations, but the awkwardness made it impossible for her to enjoy them. She felt the positions were degrading and most unflattering. The noises embarrassed her. She shuddered to think what she must look like in the midst of it. And some of the things he suggested she do left her so shocked she could not even respond.

But they had loved each other enough to adjust and had settled into an arrangement where he, for the most part, fulfilled his needs in a timely and conscientious manner, with as little embarrassment to her sensibilities as he could manage and she, in turn, submitted willingly. She did enjoy pleasing him, provided he was considerate enough not to take advantage.

If only he would not persist in these inappropriate comments outside their bedroom, insinuating things from every scenario; things that simply added to her discomfort over that particular subject.

And now here he was again, trying to interject the topic of "it" into their discussion about the wizardess, where it could not be more out of place.

"It is not my 'sexy' feet which are wearing out my shoes," she replied, trying to keep the resentment out of her voice. She did not want to appear frigid or distraught, but rather, preferred to draw him back to reality with dignity and common sense. "The wizardess has already explained that our shoes are being worn out by our thoughts, not our feet."

"Yes, but have you never considered what those thoughts might be?" he asked her.

"Why, of course," she replied. "The wizardess has as much as said that it is homesickness for my sisters and my father's castle. We had such wonderful times there. I do miss it."

"I don't think that is all there is to it," the prince argued. "You didn't forget that the wizardess also mentioned 'discontent' in your marriages."

She stared at the prince, shocked by his bluntness. "It does not seem so outrageous that our new lives should be a bit difficult to adjust to after such an enchanted childhood," she countered.

"Or perhaps it is something else," he said, with meaning and emphasis.

So here he was, referring to "it" yet again! She ground her teeth and asked, "What else could it be?"

"I'm sure I don't know," he lied. "But I am very interested to hear what the wizardess has to say about it."

She forced another stiff smile. "More coffee?"

Princess Conscia had been looking forward to the wizardess's visit, but now she was suddenly feeling nervous. Would the wizardess think her a failure as a wife? Or worse, would she be expected to humiliate herself even further to her husband? Surely he would not be so debased as to bring "it" up while the wizardess was here!

She struggled for the proper words to caution her husband while she poured his coffee. "I hope you won't impose your own ideas about this on the wizardess," she began. "I think it would be best to listen to what advice she has to give." A little blush crept up her cheeks as she said this.

"What ideas are you speaking of that have you blushing so, my darling?" he asked her with a teasing smile.

"I don't have anything in mind," she lied, wishing she had held her tongue. There was no stopping him anyway, so why had she bothered to ask?

He took her warm, flushed face in his hands and held it until her eyes met his. "I, too, wait anxiously for the wizardess's advice," he admitted in a low voice. They were both silent a moment, until the front bell rang out shrilly, causing them both to jump.

The prince went to the door to admit the wizardess while Princess Conscia regained her composure. A moment later the wizardess entered their kitchen, observing the princess carefully.

"Do I smell coffee?" she asked casually, but she noticed everything as she spoke, from the blush on Princess Conscia's face to the slightly gloomy yet determined expression of her husband.

"I hope I did not interrupt anything," she said with a sly smile.

The prince and princess looked at the wizardess; he with surprise and her with horrified embarrassment.

"Oh, heavens, no," Princess Conscia insisted quickly. "We were simply finishing up our morning coffee."

"Actually," her husband divulged, "we were trying to guess what you had concluded about the shoes."

"Indeed," laughed the wizardess. "That is good."

"Really?" asked Princess Conscia. She had feared her husband's bluntness might have offended the wizardess. She poured them all a cup of coffee and sat down, feeling a bit more relaxed. She did not, however, want the wizardess to inquire further about where their conjectures had led, so she attempted to divert this by saying, "Have you questions you wish to ask about my...um, shoe problem?"

"My observations thus far have, in fact, been sufficient for me to identify the problem," replied the wizardess.

"But, you have only just arrived," the prince objected. "Perhaps you have missed something important."

"Oh, I have missed nothing," the wizardess told him with a smile. "Everything you will need is right here." She shuffled through the contents of her bag and finally pulled from it a long, brown cylinder. "There it is," she said, handing the cylinder to the prince. "I think its best if you delay the treatment—or even discussing it—until late in the day, when you are both ready to retire. Please follow the instructions to the letter," she admonished him firmly, "and its magic will not fail." She swallowed the last of her coffee and stood up.

"But..." objected the princess.

"You may see me out, Princess Conscia," interrupted the wizardess.

With an anxious glance at the mysterious object in her husband's hand, the princess reluctantly walked out with the wizardess.

"I don't understand," she murmured.

"You will in time, my dear," the wizardess assured her. But the princess was not reassured.

The prince, meanwhile, had opened the tube and removed from it a roll of white parchment and a paintbrush. The parchment was made of a mysterious substance that shimmered as it caught the light. Several sheets were stacked together on a roll. As he unraveled the parchment he noticed that there were instructions on the back of each sheet, and he began to read. A low whistle escaped his lips.

"How strange," Princess Conscia remarked, returning to the kitchen.

Her husband made no comment as he quickly put the parchment back on the roll and slipped it and the paintbrush back into the tube.

"May I see that?" she asked him.

"No," he replied.

"What?" she cried in shock. "But I wish to see it."

"I think not," he replied.

"Do the instructions say that I can not see it?" she asked.

"No," he answered.

"Then for heaven's sake," she said, "allow me to see it at once!"

"I will show it to you when the time comes," he replied with a note of finality that made it clear he was not going to give in.

"Do you mean later this evening?" she asked.

"Yes," he agreed.

"When we are 'ready to retire,'" she quoted from the wizardess.

"Exactly," he confirmed.

"Not before?" she pressed.

"Not a moment before."

What a long day that was for Princess Conscia! Whatever was in the strange, brown cylinder must not be to her liking, she mused, for her husband to have refused to allow her to even look at it. And yet how objectionable could it be, when it was recommended by such a dignified figure as the wizardess? It was impossible to imagine that Harmonia Brist, who commanded so much respect, would suggest something inappropriate.

And yet, why was her husband keeping it from her? He would not do so unless he had reason. The princess quickly deduced that the cylinder must contain something to do with "it". That was the only plausible excuse she could come up with that would explain her husband's behavior. He knew that would upset her. But why would the wizardess recommend anything to do with that? And what could it have to do with her shoes?

She now regretted her promise to her father, the king, that she would do exactly as the wizardess instructed. But having given her word, she supposed all she could do now was to submit to whatever it was until the week was over. She was not pleased by it, even though she still didn't know exactly what it was. But she was certain that it must have something to do with their activities in the bedroom. She had glimpsed the paintbrush and the white roll of parchment. Obviously the paintbrush was for painting on the white paper. No doubt it was her who was to be painted. This would not be something unappealing to her, unless...so that was it! She was to sit nude for her husband to paint. The more she thought about it the more convinced she became that this was the case.

Once she accepted the situation, Princess Conscia realized the best way to deal with it would be to prepare for it. She would surprise her husband by being ready and uncomplaining. He no doubt expected her to object, which is why he did not want to tell her about it until the very last moment. She smiled when she recalled that he had not gloated or even shown pleasure over the contents of the cylinder. She knew how much he must love the idea of having her sit before him without clothing. She was grateful to him for not only accepting her as she was, but doing so with kindness and discretion. Thank goodness it was him who she was obliged to go through this with.

She contemplated the matter all day, and by the time her husband was due to arrive home she felt almost as much excitement over the event to come as apprehension. She had slipped into their bedroom twice during the afternoon and removed her clothing so that she might find the most appealing angle at which to position herself for the painting. The body was so impossibly horrible without clothing in her opinion, but there were ways to make it seem less so. The first visit to her bedroom was hurried and frantic; the second more relaxed. She was glad she had gone the second time, as she was able to enhance the position in which she planned to pose for her husband. She adjusted the candles all around the room so that the light would be more flattering to her skin, especially in places where it tended to bunch up into those horrible little clusters of fat. She disliked that intensely. But between the lighting and the posing, which by now she had perfected, she felt certain that the prince would be properly impressed.

Even so, the beating of her heart was almost painful as she finally joined her husband in their bedroom that evening, wearing nothing but a robe. He looked at her skeptically.

Thinking to surprise him, she removed her robe calmly and perched herself upon the divan in the pose she had practiced earlier that day.

To her shock, he laughed with genuine amusement. "You certainly are a sight," he said.

She reluctantly turned from her perfect pose and faced him. "Do you mean to say I don't have to be painted in the nude?" she asked, almost disappointed.

"Oh, yes, you have the 'painted' and the 'nude' parts correct," he said, becoming more serious now.

"Well?" she prompted, unable to even conjure up further possibilities without his assistance.

"The position you are in is not exactly right," he told her. He paused a moment, allowing her to absorb this.

Her lips pursed slightly. "Should I show more of my backside?"

she asked, perturbed. She had not practiced ways of making that look good.

"No, not your backside tonight," he replied, trying hard to remain aloof so as not to alarm her. Any moment now she would likely be fainting or something equally dramatic, and all he could hope for was that his own calm demeanor would have the effect of making the situation more palatable for her. He casually opened the tube and unraveled one of the parchments. It seemed much larger than she had remembered. He examined the directions a moment. "You are supposed to lie down on your back..." he began cautiously.

To his surprise she did not object. She was thinking this might be even better. Lying down could be more flattering. She propped the pillows just so and lay demurely down on her back upon the bed.

The prince approached Princess Conscia, holding up the parchment and doing his best to keep his expression firm and serious. "Just a few little adjustments," he explained, as he turned her head a little so it faced up, placed her arms out flat and then pulled her legs up toward her body. She resisted this last and sat up.

"What are you doing?" she asked.

"I am placing you in the position outlined in the instructions," he replied.

"May I see?" she asked.

He paused another moment before turning the parchment over and holding the instructions up in front of her face. Her breath caught in her throat as stared at it. She was silent and still for several minutes.

"Shall I help you with the position?" the prince asked her at last.

"No," she replied. "I will do it." But she could not seem to make her body move. "Look the other way," she implored him.

The prince had brought with him a bowl of water and now he

brushed some of the water onto the sheet of parchment and placed it carefully on the wall beside the bed. When he was satisfied with its location he smoothed the parchment out over the wall. Next he arranged a nearby chair just so.

Meanwhile, Princess Conscia lay back down on the bed. Taking a deep breath, she bent her legs and brought them all the way up until her thighs touched her shoulders. She clasped her arms together behind her knees just as the instructions indicated. Her feet rested on the headboard behind her. She breathed out and in deliberately, trying her best to rest comfortably in the awkward position, but even her limbs were rejecting the unfamiliar pull on their ligaments as every part of her struggled to stay put and await the approaching events. A tingling sensation prickled sharply within her.

"Ready," she said at last in a strangled voice.

The prince turned toward her and stopped. He stared openly for several moments, causing a rush of blood to engorge her exposed area. She could feel it beginning to warm and swell, even as she fought against her embarrassment.

Sensing her discomfort, the prince suddenly moved into action. He adjusted the light over her exposed flesh, warming her with the comforting heat of it. Her genitalia felt prickly and engorged. She continued to breathe in and out forcibly, achieving some degree of calm from the fact that she had given her word to do everything as instructed, and, too, possessing enough curiosity to want to find out where all of this might lead. If truth be told, it was not the end of the world to be laid bare in such a way under the deliciously warm lights, especially when the person she was exposing herself to was as kind and gentle as her husband. She knew that this would be especially pleasurable for him. Wasn't he always longing to see more of her? Although she could not really see his face from her position, she imagined she could feel his eyes upon her and it caused her skin to tingle.

"You are beautiful," she heard him murmur. "It will truly take magic to capture on the parchment what I'm seeing here." His husky voice sent vibrations throughout her body, beginning in the exposed area between her legs and from there coursing through every single vein and artery.

Princess Conscia felt as if she were in a dream. The moment did not feel like an actual part of her life, and it was almost as if it was someone else entirely who calmly replied, "I didn't even know that you painted."

"I don't," he admitted. "But it seems this is a magic brush that allows me to recreate an image I see by visualizing it on the parchment."

"Oh, my," she remarked. "What an amazing thing!"

"Yes," he replied absently, concentrating wholeheartedly on the task in front of him. "The most remarkable thing is the colors. I simply dip the brush in water and it creates the exact color of whatever I am painting. I think I have an aptitude for this."

Princess Conscia was as relaxed as she was capable of being in her situation, except for the spine-tingling vibrations that here and again assailed her senses. It seemed that all her awareness was focused on that part of her body that she spent most of her life trying to avoid. She was wondering what she looked like in this most unusual position, and tried to visualize the image that presented itself before her husband. All aspects of her consciousness were concentrated on the small amount of flesh that rested between her legs; even her heart seemed to be steadily pounding, pounding, pounding…from within that place. And with each pounding beat she fancied she could feel the flesh there becoming more and more engorged, swelling to enormous proportions until it seemed to be absorbing the rest of her body. Her breathing was becoming more and more rapid. She tried to focus on something else but could not.

The prince noticed his wife's discomfort and was amazed and delighted that her response was so similar to his own. He had thought she would hate every minute of this, but he saw now that he had misjudged her. Perhaps her previous anxieties in the bedroom were not caused by a lack of desire, but something else entirely. As he painted he could not help noticing her laborious breathing and the flushed and engorged flesh between her legs. His own body was steadily growing and hardening, and his breathing, too, was becoming more labored.

Princess Conscia wondered that her husband did not touch her. She had been thinking about the different ways he had stroked her before and how he might caress her now. Mostly she was just aching for the feel of his hands on her. Why didn't he touch her? What would it feel like when he finally did? She had never wanted to be touched so badly. Her flesh seemed to be rising up into the air with its desire for contact. All her senses waited, alert, for him to touch her. While she waited she could almost imagine that she felt each individual ray from the warm light as it met her sensitive flesh. It was all she could do not to reach her hand down and stroke herself. What would her husband think if she did that?

The prince noticed that his wife seemed to be becoming more and more agitated. Every now and then her hips would jolt ever so slightly upward, causing his own body to surge forward in a similar manner. He longed to touch her, but concentrated on his painting.

Suddenly, the princess became aware of the moisture that had been accumulating inside her since the moment when she had first removed her robe for her husband. The pressure had been building until it seemed that she could hold no more inside and so, ever so stealthily, a single droplet began to push its way out through the thick fleshy walls. And she could feel it! She held her breath, trying to keep it in, but it continued its agonizingly slow descent. The thought of her husband noticing it, too, caused another surge of excitement in her that brought even more of the silky liquid to the fore. At length the little droplet squeezed its way out through the nearest exit point, where it sat precariously balanced on the warm, tender flesh. The princess expelled her held breath with a small, involuntary moan.

The prince heard her moan and his paintbrush stopped in midair. He noticed the little droplet then and stared at it, mesmerized as it sparkled and enticed in the warmth of the light. The instructions had been firm and clear in their edict that the painting be completed before anything else, but how could he resist that little drop of moisture and all that it signified? It seemed to be communicating something to him; something that he had been longing to hear since that very first night they had spent together as man and wife. He knew she loved him but he had doubted her need for him—until now. In that little droplet he seemed to find everything he had been searching for in his wife. And he wanted to respond to it. He wanted to touch it—and taste it. And yet he knew he must capture this moment first. He must finish the painting, if only to show his wife what he had seen. She would understand everything, he was certain, if she could just see what he was seeing. With a groan, he dipped his paintbrush in the water, trying with all his might to capture the exquisite beauty and all it meant with the strokes of the magic brush.

The princess was hovering somewhere beyond reality and fantasy. Nothing seemed real. She had never felt such longing. She hardly cared anymore what she looked like or how she appeared. She was a sensual being. She was, at that moment, like a flower that was open wide with its stamen exposed, and with nothing to do but wait. In a gesture she was hardly aware of, she slid one of her hands slowly and caressingly down along her leg and thigh, stopping just short of where the little drop still sat, trembling.

The prince groaned again. He would never finish the painting if she kept giving him more material to paint. He feverishly dipped the paintbrush into the water, altering the portrait adeptly to reflect her new position.

The last few minutes that it took for the prince to complete the painting stretched out for both of them like hours. The princess was in a highly excited and agitated state, and the prince was so hard that his body ached. At last, with a sigh of relief, he threw down his paint-brush and moved toward his wife, holding her legs in position now while he kissed her swollen flesh repeatedly, devouring the seeping wetness and burying his tongue deep within her. She cried out loudly, actually tightening her arms around her legs and even further exposing herself to him, terrified that he might stop. She gave herself over com-pletely to the incredible pleasure she felt in at last being touched, no longer caring whether he touched her with his hand, or lips or tongue, just as long as he continued to touch her. The longing ache she had been feeling subsided a bit in relief from his touch, but behind the relief rushed a new tide of sensations that were building inside her with equal intensity. It seemed she was awash in pleasure, and she allowed the tide to take her to places unknown. Her heightened desire had diminished her consciousness of decorum and appearance. She was conscious only of the pleasure that her husband was giving her, and her growing need to follow where it would lead.

Her husband's tongue was doing incredible things to her, and she was stunned by the pleasure it gave her. All she could do was murmur the word "yes" over and over again. She didn't know how he happened to find the little spot he was massaging with his tongue or how he knew how just to rub it in just the way she wanted him to. All she knew was that she would die if he stopped. But then he did suddenly stop, and although she didn't die she gasped in horror.

Before Princess Conscia could move or speak, the prince was inside her. He was kneeled before her bent body, leaning over her as he entered her. With one hand he held her legs in place—in the same position she held for the picture and which now felt to her like the most natural position she could imagine—and with the other he resumed the rubbing motions he had begun with his tongue. He moved slowly within her, pulling himself very nearly all the way out and then pushing himself back into her until their bodies touched.

The prince leaned his head back and closed his eyes. His wife's body had never felt so deliciously soft and wet, but then, she had never wanted him this much before. Always something had held her at bay but tonight she was his completely. He relished in the feel of her and wanted to enjoy it for as long as she remained so receptive to him. He stroked her with care, wanting her to find satisfaction as badly as he wanted his own.

The princess was shocked to know that having her husband inside her could feel so utterly amazing. She thought she had found some pleasure with him before but now she realized that she had never come close to enjoying the full measure of that pleasure. In the position she was currently in, her legs still covered most of her view of the prince, and this small measure of concealment sufficiently shielded her from her usual timidity and self-consciousness. She clung to her legs and shut her eyes tight as she moaned and writhed with abandon. Her moans grew louder and she uttered little words in between, such as "yes," and "please," and "I love you"; not extraordinarily bold words, but little admissions, nevertheless, of her utter surrender and loss of control. She had always carefully held all such utterances back, so hearing them now had the effect of stoking the fire that already burned so hot in the prince. He bit his lip to maintain control as he stroked and caressed her.

At last the princess felt an amazing surge of agonizing ripples of pleasure rush through her. In an involuntary motion her arms collapsed to her sides and her legs fell open. There, between her spread legs was her husband's face, staring down at her as she cried out, completely overwhelmed by the intense sensations. Seeing her face and knowing her pleasure was the prince's undoing. He grasped one leg in each of his hands and spread them wider apart as he thrust himself into her one last time. He let out a loud yell. She stared at him wide-eyed, realizing suddenly that they had never made love with the candles lit before this.

Princess Conscia was astounded that she did not feel the embarrassment she had imagined she would under such circumstances. What she wanted was to hold her husband in her arms. He seemed to read her mind, for he carefully put her legs down and embraced her. They clung to each other for a long moment. He realized he had not even kissed her yet, and he did so now. They kissed with all the passion of forlorn lovers. Then the prince looked into her face with a grin.

"Aren't you even interested in seeing the painting?" he asked incredulously. He thought that would have been her first consideration the moment he set down the paintbrush.

Princess Conscia gasped. "I had forgotten all about it!" she exclaimed, equally surprised by herself. They both laughed as they got up to look at the painting. When she saw it she let out a little cry.

The prince watched her carefully. He could not tell if her expression was one of horror or delight. "I should warn you that one harsh word could cause me to give up painting for good," he told her.

She laughed halfheartedly, and reached out her arm to touch him. She could not take her eyes off the painting. Was that how she looked? She could not believe it. The woman in the painting exuded sensual vulnerability. She held her legs lifted high as she bared herself for the painter. Her eyes were dazed, her lips were parted and her expression was one of utter abandon. Her fingers rested shameless in the curly nest of hair between her legs. A small pearl of liquid picked up the light as it squeezed its way through her swollen flesh. It was terribly revealing, and incredibly lifelike. It took her breath away to see it.

"Is that how you see me?" she said at last.

"It is," he said. He tried to lighten the moment by adding, "On the rare occasions I get to see you, that is."

"I never thought of myself in that...way." She still couldn't draw her eyes away from the portrait.

The prince drew Princess Conscia to him and kissed her. He said nothing, simply allowing her to stare in amazement at the painting. He still wasn't sure whether she was pleased or disappointed by it. When she finally turned to face him there were tears in her eyes.

"I love it," she told him. And he pulled her down with him onto the bed and they slept very well indeed that night.

The next morning, Princess Conscia was first to wake. She smiled when she looked at her sleeping husband. Slowly, the memory came back of their lovemaking the night before and then she recalled the portrait. She turned toward the wall and there it was. In the daylight it seemed even more graphic and a bit unseemly, but even so, the princess felt a little twinge of pride and desire curling up within her at the sight of it. Was she really that woman?

She felt her husband move and she turned to him. He was watching her. She was still unclothed and she blushed.

"It's all right," he told her. "You will get used to it."

"I still can't believe it's me," she admitted.

"It's only one part of you," he told her. He rose up and she noticed he was aroused.

"Perhaps…" she faltered, and bit her lip.

"Perhaps…?" he prompted.

"Perhaps…we should have pancakes for breakfast," she finished with a little smile. She glanced at the painting one last time before dressing. She felt sure that if she truly was the woman in the painting she would have known how to say what she wanted to say. But even if she had known what to say, she was not entirely certain that she was ready for that kind of intimacy in the bright light of day.

Throughout the day, Princess Conscia repeatedly found reasons to return to their bedroom and look at the painting. Each time she did this she felt terribly excited about the evening to come. In what position would her husband paint her this night? She imagined several scenarios and each left her breathless.

At long last the evening came and her husband with it. She rushed toward him as he entered their castle, a little blush coloring her cheeks. He was delighted by the change in her.

At dinner the princess barely touched her food and once again the prince wondered at her behavior. It was almost as if she were anticipating the events to come. He had barely lifted the last bite of his food to his lips when she scooped up his plate and whisked it off to the kitchen. She was out of breath when she returned only a moment later.

"All cleared away," she announced. Her voice had a slightly shrill edge to it.

"No dessert?" he teased.

She didn't smile. "I, uh…thought with the heavy dinner…" her voice trailed off.

"Never mind," he said. "I am well-satisfied."

He was astounded by the wizardess's astuteness. She had been perfectly right when she told him that she had missed nothing. All it had taken was a little push and his wife was quickly becoming the sensual creature he had always known she could be. He took her hand and led her wordlessly up the stairs to their bedroom, where she rushed into the bathroom to disrobe while he arranged the bed and candles, and set up a new piece of parchment. Daylight was just beginning to dim, and dusk was following closely behind her. There was a strange excitement in their bedroom, giving the air an electrical charge very much like it did before a storm.

Princess Conscia took deep breaths in an effort to remain calm. Even the preparations for the event were bringing about the most delightful sensations of excitement. Earlier that day she had trimmed the hair on her body and now she patted her flesh with scented powder. When the princess had arranged herself to her satisfaction she joined her husband in the bedroom. The lighting was spectacular and her eyes shone with excitement. She noticed that he had moved the bed to accommodate a new panel of blank parchment on a different wall. She glanced again at the previous evening's painting and bit her lip.

"Ah," said her husband, "here is my subject at last!"

She walked over to the bed. "How shall I...?"

He handed her the instructions for the night's painting and watched her while she read them. Her face was pink when she handed them back to him, but she approached the bed bravely and removed the silken robe she had been wearing. His body hardened at the sight of her.

Princess Conscia's heart pounded as she approached the bed. She had never known that women assumed such positions to be admired in. Of course she had heard mention of such decadence in hushed tones of mockery and had even succumbed to that position once or twice in the dark, when her husband had been quite insistent. But this was different. It was hard to control her breathing, but somehow she managed to gracefully kneel in the center of the bed with her legs spread far apart. She arranged the pillows just so and then crossed her forearms just below them. Then she lowered her head onto the pillows. She felt her back arch as her head touched the pillows, causing her hips to spread wider. She gasped at the feelings this position evoked.

At the sight of her the prince could have wept. He did not want to paint. He wanted to make love to her. And yet, he told himself, by painting her like this he would be able to enjoy the image many times over. With that he picked up his brush and repositioned a candle. A little groan escaped his lips as he began his task.

The princess heard his groan and knew well how he felt. The intimacy of it all was overwhelming. And yet, even as it overwhelmed her it also seemed to quell her inhibitions. She basked in the warmth of the candles as their gentle heat penetrated her flesh and radiated inward, imbuing her with a sweet anticipation for the moment when her husband would appease her. She knew he would take her exactly as she lay, just like he had done the night before.

The thought of it made her breath catch in her throat. The illumination upon her sex had the effect of accentuating this part of her life with her husband, underscoring the beauty and necessity of this aspect of her being. For this moment, at least, she was created for this, and she could not call to mind a single reason to shy away or abstain from accepting the pleasure that their bodies offered them. She knew that he, too, eagerly anticipated that moment when he would have her.

The prince marveled at the mastery of the enchanted paintbrush as he adeptly reproduced the extraordinary image before him. There was almost a supernatural quality to his wife's appearance as she posed for him, which was awe-inspiring as well as exciting. He felt new and intense emotions overwhelming him before he could even identify them. He was completely disarmed by the sight of her, and struggled to concentrate on the task ahead of him.

The overall effect of this lingering delay in consummating their desire was an increased awareness and intimacy that would not only enhance their pleasure, but also draw them closer in other aspects of their life together.

Princess Conscia's wetness was causing her body to open further to her husband's gaze. Her hips seemed to reach out toward him, further extending the arch of her back. Every now and then an impatient sigh escaped her lips, and in her expression was a look of wanton abandon. The prince duly noted each of these little modifications to her appearance as he attempted to capture every detail on the parchment. He, too, sighed, impatiently, aching for the feel of her in spite of his absorption in completing the painting.

At long last the prince applied his final stroke, and he noted with delight that, with the help of the brush, he had captured his wife's image so perfectly that the parchment appeared more like a mirror's reflection than a mere likeness.

The prince set down the enchanted brush and approached his wife. Very slowly, he raised his hand and stroked one finger gently along Princess Conscia's open slit, feeling her wetness. She gasped and moaned, thrusting her hips toward him so that she was pressed more forcefully against his hand. He reached down farther beneath her and found the sensitive part of her that he wanted to caress. Meanwhile, he resumed rubbing up and down the length of her open slit with his tongue.

Princess Conscia cried out with bliss. The pleasure was so intense that nothing else could penetrate her consciousness. She focused on her husband's tongue and what it was doing to her with every bit of her awareness. Her hips pumped up and down as she rocked herself absently against her husband's hand and lips and tongue. She was losing herself fully as she sought after the exquisite pleasure that she now realized she could get from him.

The prince did not want to disrupt the princess's pleasure, but he felt he must be inside her or die. Her newfound excitement increased his own arousal tenfold, and so he, too, was finding something new and amazing in their intimacy that he had not felt before. He quickly and efficiently mounted his wife from behind. Her body seemed to draw him in and clutch at him, causing him to moan loudly. He forced himself to go slowly as he reached around her hips and resumed his caressing of her. He realized how much harder it was for her to become satisfied than he, and so he used self-restraint and diligence to support her. It was, after all, just as much to his benefit as to hers to do so. He had been astounded to find how much more intense his own satisfaction became when he put it off time and again. He was certain that this was no coincidence; he knew his increased pleasure was a direct result of his consideration for his wife. He wondered that he could have remained ignorant of the connection between the two for so long.

He was, in fact, becoming more capable in holding off his own pleasure in order to satisfy his wife. He could feel his command over his body strengthening. He stroked and caressed his wife leisurely, enjoying every exquisite sensation without concern for time. When the pleasure came close to being too much to bear, he slowed even more in his movements to hold himself at bay. With his new knowledge of his wife, it would be unimaginable for him to allow any weakness on his part to thwart her. He was determined that she be satisfied.

As he watched his wife's hips wriggling around his hardened flesh and listened to her cries, the prince found it harder and harder to withstand the temptation to let the pleasure overtake him. There were a few times when he had to turn away from the luscious sight of her, and close his ears to her enticing cries. Pleasing her brought the most intense sensations he had ever known. It seemed to soothe all of his broken places and give him strength.

Princess Conscia rocked her hips instinctively. The pleasure was incredible. Her husband's slow, measured movements were exactly what she needed to remain focused and keep her rhythm. They moved together in perfect harmony until suddenly the princess stiffened and shuddered, crying out convulsively. She closed her eyes as the waves of pleasure rushed over her.

The prince took one small moment to languish in the sweet satisfaction of satisfying his wife and the exquisite anticipation of fulfillment to come. He moved his hands over his wife's backside, delighting in the soft feel of her and then, settling his fingers halfway between her hips and waist, he grasped her securely and thrust himself into her violently.

Princess Conscia was suddenly filled with a new and strange exhilaration that was at once thrilling and poignant. She had always wanted to please her husband of course, but never so much as she did while under the effects of this mysterious afterglow. Throwing the very last of her inhibitions to the winds, she opened her legs even wider and arched her back to thrust her hips up as high as possible, opening herself to her husband even more absolutely and completely, and willing his pleasure to be as wonderful as hers had been. Noting his groans of delight when she moved, she accelerated the rocking of her hips in the manner she thought he liked best. How delightful it was to be able to excite and please the one you loved best!

The prince half thought he must be in a dream. His wife's response was so unrestrained and enthusiastic he hardly recognized her. That she wanted to please him he could clearly see, but his heart leapt at the fervor of her desire to please, and the pleasure she was deriving from it. All of this he perceived from her behavior; although he noted it unconsciously, for it was beyond his capabilities of self-restraint to resist such wanton surrender. His whole body quaked from the power of his release as he at last gave in to all of the pent up desire and stimulation. He let out a loud cry of satisfaction that caused the princess to tremble. He clung to her hips after the initial rush of ecstasy, momentarily dizzy from the intensity of it.

At last they collapsed together, entwined as closely together as they could get. She clung to him and he clung to her. They remained quiet, for words were not necessary. Princess Conscia wondered that she felt not the slightest uneasiness or embarrassment over her behavior.

Quite the contrary in fact; she felt positively joyful and self-possessed. It seemed to her that she had learned something new about life and what she wanted from it. No more would she look backward for simpler pleasures. She had grown up.

The paintings continued throughout the years, although the need for them disappeared after that very first night. The exceptional artwork covers their bedroom walls completely, with erotic images of the princess in every imaginable position. Often the princess will find herself alone in that room, staring at the walls in amazement. The images never fail to arouse her. And needless to say, the princess no longer dreams of escaping her bedroom to rush away to her father's castle and dance holes in her shoes with her sisters.

PRINCESS DEVOTIA

Princess Devotia put down her bible and rose up to get her husband more coffee.

"My dear," said her husband. "I can get it for myself."

"I know," she replied. "But I enjoy getting it for you."

It's too bad, he thought, *that my devoted little wife doesn't enjoy doing the things I want her to do for me.* But alas, she was zealous to please him as it pleased her—not him—to do. He sighed in frustration and she looked at him.

"Are you still hungry?" she asked.

He was not sure how to answer that question. "Yes and no," he said with meaning. But the doorbell rang before she had time to respond to this.

In truth, Princess Devotia wanted very much to please her husband, and she knew full well what he referred to in his little innuendos. It was just that the things he was always pining for did not always feel appropriate to her. For one thing, his desires were far too concerned with the gratification of the flesh. Surely that had nothing to do with love; for the heady sensations they evoked led to the kind of abandon that felt more like lust and greed. Love, she believed, had more to do with self-control and restraint.

The prince returned to his wife with the wizardess in tow, and Princess Devotia eyed her with a mixture of curiosity and distrust. She was wary of thoughts and activities that could undermine the beliefs she had collected since childhood about right and wrong.

Harmonia duly noted the princess's prim appearance, the bible on the kitchen table and her guarded approach.

The wizardess was a spiritual woman also, but she had learned to rely upon her own inner conscience for guidance, rather than what certain men had set down before she had even been born. However, she had a deep respect for all fellow humans who were aware enough of their spiritual needs to seek guidance, provided they did not follow that guidance too blindly, to the detriment of themselves and others.

More importantly, she could see the glaring discrepancies between the husband and wife as she watched them, and she suspected she knew the reason.

"I could not help noticing that your castle overlooks the ocean," the wizardess began conversationally. "I would dearly love to have a closer look at the view, if you would be so kind as to escort me," she said to the princess.

"I would be delighted to," replied the princess eagerly, for there was nothing she loved better than to be near the ocean, which to her mind was one of God's most delightful creations.

"Wonderful!" exclaimed Harmonia. "You don't mind if we leave you here, do you?" she asked the prince, making it clear she did not wish for him to accompany them.

"Of course not," replied the prince courteously. But he was disappointed.

"Shall we go then?" asked the wizardess, effectively dismissing the prince so that she might speak more candidly with the princess.

The ocean was like a living thing as the women approached it, with full white waves pushing their way onto the shore. The princess's mood visibly improved as they came closer to the beach. The gulls screamed overhead. The sun was quite bright, but the air was cool.

"How glorious it is," exclaimed the wizardess.

"It is awe-inspiring," agreed the princess.

"What did you think of my conclusion regarding you and your sisters' shoes last night?" the wizardess asked her, believing the princess would respond best to a direct approach.

"I think you may be correct about the 'discontent'," she admitted, surprising herself and the wizardess. "But I think my husband may be the discontented one more so than I."

"You don't say," replied the wizardess, shocked by the girl's honesty even while she admired and appreciated it. "Then perhaps it is his discontent that is causing yours?"

"I think you may be right," Princess Devotia agreed. "I would be perfectly happy, I think, if only my husband would understand my position and be content, too."

"I take it there is a difference of opinion over one matter in particular?" encouraged the wizardess.

The princess blushed, but she looked directly into the wizardess's face. "Yes," she said. "It is rather delicate."

"I don't need details," Harmonia assured her. "I am more interested in the opinions and beliefs that are guiding your feelings. I think I may understand already, but I would like to be certain."

The princess paused to think about it. "It seems that I am forever feeling guilty. If I resist the temptations of the flesh I disappoint my husband, but if I give in to my husband I worry that I am being unfaithful to my beliefs. Either way, I end up feeling that I have failed."

"By 'give in to,' are you referring to being intimate with your husband?" asked the wizardess.

"No, not exactly," replied the princess. It was harder to explain than she had expected it to be. "I know that it is permissible for me to have relations with my husband. That is how children are conceived. But I am uncomfortable with some of the things my husband wishes me to do and the…feelings and images that it causes me to have."

"These feelings and images make you uncomfortable because they seem…sinful?" inquired the wizardess.

"Yes, exactly," said the princess. "I know it sounds prudish but it is just how I feel."

"My dear," began the wizardess, "there is much in life that is so exhilarating as to appear sinful. That feeling of indulgence bordering on wrongdoing can be found in many things, from a lustful embrace, to a decadent dessert, to a glass of wine, and even to the intoxicating smell of this ocean." She breathed in deeply as she said this.

"So how does one know for certain when these things become sinful?"

"That is for each individual to decide," replied the wizardess. "I personally believe sin comes into play when a person hurts themselves or another. In the case of the decadent dessert for example, an overindulgence could mean the violation of one's body through excess weight that could cause health problems. That would hurt the person indulging and those who love him or her. That, to my mind, is a very great sin."

"And in the case of the…lustful embrace?" asked the princess.

"It is the same. To be able to give and get pleasure from another person in this way is a very special gift that should be celebrated and honored. To criticize or condemn the gift simply because it is so utterly indulgent and pleasurable is terribly rude and unappreciative. And to deliberately abstain from it or withhold it from one's partner, without reason, I think, is quite unkind. Who of us has the right to put limits on any of the gifts we share here on earth?"

Princess Devotia was astounded by this speech. She had felt so pious in her struggles against the flesh that she had never even considered the origin of these struggles.

"Do you have a source for guidance, Princess Conscia...that is, do you base your beliefs on one resource in particular?" continued the wizardess.

Princess Devotia provided the details of her faith.

"Very well then," said the wizardess, pulling a little black book from her bag. "Here is a little devotional, containing many verses from your chosen source of guidance. A word of caution though—beware of being too dependant upon the writings and interpretations of mere men. You cannot be certain that they are all speaking for our creator, and you would not want to follow an imposter."

"How will I know?"

"Another of our many gifts is logic and a conscience," replied the wizardess. "It is high time that you take responsibility for yourself, and use these gifts that you have been given."

The princess stared at the wizardess. She had been taught by her religious teachers to be leery of anyone questioning their teachings and yet, wasn't it true that she had the ability within her to decipher right from wrong? She knew that her conscience was indeed willing and able. Yet, wasn't it her conscience that was most troubled when she succumbed to certain sensual pleasures with her husband? Or was it just an idea that had been put into her head?

"Walk me back, won't you?" Harmonia said with a final look at the captivating ocean. The roar of the waves filled her with hope. So far, her day had indeed been exhilarating. She was doing what she loved to do, and doing it well. It filled her life with meaning to be so engaged. Furthermore, she enjoyed the challenges the princesses presented for her. Each of them held great promise of something wonderful in the palm of their hands that, with a little guidance, could easily bring them success in their endeavors and lead them to happiness.

When the wizardess had left her, Princess Devotia opened the little devotional booklet and began to read. It opened with a verse that read; "There is no fear in love, but perfect love throws fear outside, because fear exercises a restraint. Indeed, he that is under fear has not been made perfect in love."

Princess Devotia read the verse several times over, pondering. Was it possible that fear was behind the guilt and shame, and not wrong-doing? She continued to read another quote from the little devotional. "And rejoice with the wife of your youth, a lovable hind and a charming mountain goat. Let her breasts intoxicate you at all times. With her love may you be in an ecstasy constantly."

Well! That certainly echoed her husband's opinions. This was advice from a prophet...why? She rushed to find that same verse in her own personal translation in order to discover its context. She located it easily enough and read the material that was put forth before and after the amazing little verse. Throughout the material there was much discussion of avoiding the sin of adultery. This she had never even considered; that in giving her husband pleasure, or "ecstasy" as the verse put it, she could actually help prevent sin, not to mention the horrible pain it would cause them both should temptation arise.

The princess was stunned. But why then did the most religious and pious always give this type of pleasure such a negative intonation? Well, as the wizardess had correctly said, the princess had a functioning mind of her own, and from this day forward she vowed to use it. With a renewed desire to seek out and find the truth, Princess Devotia continued to read, coming upon another interesting verse that read, "Let the husband render to his wife her due; but let the wife also do likewise to her husband. The wife does not exercise authority over her own body, but her husband does; likewise, also, the husband does not exercise authority over his own body, but his wife does."

Princess Devotia contemplated this. It seemed to indicate that her husband had every right to do all of the things he wished to do with her. The thought of this gave her a little thrill. The thrill was immediately followed by a twinge of guilt. But this time she contemplated the guilty feeling instead of allowing it to automatically control her thoughts. She asked herself why a sensual thrill should bring about an automatic feeling of guilt. Was it conscience or habit that was the cause? She had been thinking about pleasing her husband when the thrill came over her, and there was certainly nothing sinful in that. Was it the thrill itself then that felt sinful? Was she afraid of pleasure?

Princess Devotia continued to read and think and examine her feelings in this way, until her mind could absorb no more. But she was quite recovered by the time her husband came home that evening, and willing to open her mind to him, as well as her feelings. She was prepared to accept the gifts her creator had seen fit to bestow upon her and, in fact, to embrace them without fear. With her usual zeal, she approached the marital bed with the objective to not only accept these gifts, but to enjoy them with an eagerness that would actually bring glory to the giver.

When she joined her husband in their bedroom that evening, she was groomed and dressed for his pleasure. That it titillated and excited her beyond her wildest imaginings to present herself to him this way, she refused to feel penitent for. Taking pleasure in giving surely did not make the giving less meaningful. In fact, she suspected her husband would also find joy in knowing that she, too, was getting pleasure; for hadn't he been struggling to get her to accept that pleasure since the very first night of their marriage?

The prince immediately noticed his wife's revealing attire with a little start of surprise. She approached him with anticipation; for once excited by the prospect of giving him the "ecstasy" described in the verses she had read earlier that day. She almost felt that in serving her husband she would be serving their creator.

Lowering her filmy gown timidly, Princess Devotia exposed her upper body to her husband's gaze, recalling with a little tremble the advice she had read that said, "Let her own breasts intoxicate you at all times." Yes, she thought, let them intoxicate him to the fullest!

The prince gasped when he saw her. His eyes drank in the sight that to him was beauty itself. He could not stop his fingers from reaching out to touch the full richness that she presented to him. At his touch she did not shrink away, but actually seemed to move toward him, reveling in the exquisite feel of his hands as they caressed her breasts so lovingly. He could not account for this change in her demeanor, but he would not question it, either. He lowered his mouth to taste of her flesh, and suckled eagerly at the tip of her breast, causing a ripple of pleasure to shoot through her and sending a surge of moisture between her legs in preparation for her body to receive him. And she could not help but reflect upon how faultlessly perfect it all was!

But her husband was in no hurry to take her. Whatever the cause of this little godsend, he intended to enjoy it to the fullest extent that his wife would allow. He continued to suckle one and then the other of her breasts, pushing her nightgown farther down with his hands, until it fell silently to the floor at her feet.

As her husband was savoring his exploration of her body, the words Princess Devotia read earlier that day rang in her ears—"Likewise, also, the husband does not exercise authority over his own body, but his wife does." It was the same for her then, she realized. Just as she was surrendering her body over to him, he was obliged to do the same for her. Her hands began to trace over his sinewy muscles, delighting in the male strength of him. Her curious touches quickly led her to the object of her interest, and she grabbed hold of it; for it was standing proud and eager, pointing out at her from between her husband's legs. The prince jumped at her touch, but he did not interfere with her hands as they continued to explore and touch. He seemed to possess the same desire as her, to own and be owned by the other. She imagined their creator watching as she stroked him, and suddenly it occurred to her that He would be pleased.

There was one thing in particular that her husband had always wished she would do, but without ever giving it much consideration she had dismissed it as too indulgent and therefore immoral. Now she could not recall why she had felt that way. What particular teaching or verse had validated that opinion? She did not know. All she knew for certain was that it was a way to give her husband pleasure, and wasn't it within her rights to do whatever she wished with his body, short of hurting him?

She had been kissing the warm flesh over his chest and stomach and so she simply moved her kisses lower, until she spread her lips over his hard shaft and took him all the way into her mouth. This simple act of putting her mouth on him sent thrills of pleasure through her. Her husband responded also, nearly jumping out of his skin as she engulfed him in her mouth, and gasping loudly with his obvious pleasure. How lovely it must feel, she mused, for him to respond so. She licked and sucked his fleshy appendage with vigor, and every little moan of delight that escaped his lips made her quiver with satisfaction. She felt that by loving her husband so fully and fearlessly, surely she was embracing all that was right and good. The old guilt was nearly completely gone; replaced with a new fervor to "do onto others as you would have done onto you." He had fulfilled her expectations of a husband in every way she had allowed; shouldn't she, too, do the same?

Princess Devotia's husband seemed to be thinking the same thing at that moment, because he stopped her suddenly to pick her up in his arms and place her lovingly on their bed. He kissed her hard on the mouth, passionately, and then asked her in a hoarse whisper, "May I, too, my love, partake of your banquet?"

"Indeed," she replied, delighting in the knowledge that he wanted to please her, too. "I am yours to do with as you wish."

His eyes widened and his head shook in amazement as he heard this, but he did not linger long in confusion. He lay beside her, facing in the opposite direction, so that both could enjoy the other at leisure and however they wished. He explored her with his fingers and tongue, using the little noises of pleasure that escaped her lips with the trembling responses of her body, to determine what she liked best. In short time he learned a great many of her secrets.

The princess, too, was quickly discovering the best ways to give pleasure to her husband, using her lips and tongue and hands. Suddenly it had all become clear, and his body no longer seemed illicit or depraved. On the contrary, it was as if he was an extension of herself, and she remembered vaguely an admonishment she had heard in their marital vows that "the two shall become one." In accepting her husband and pleasing him, she was accepting the handiwork of her creator and pleasing him. In giving her husband more than the minimum service, more in fact than what was expected of her; she felt that she was honoring life. She delighted in this service and performed it to the best of her abilities.

On the other hand, the princess also assigned to her husband all rights to her body, splaying herself wide open for him to do with her as he wished, hiding nothing, and withholding nothing, and thereby allowing him to give her the pleasure he, too, had been instructed by their creator to give. If there had been shame in their marital bed before, it now occurred to her that it was the shame that she herself had brought in through the sin of self-righteousness, pride and apathy. She had been following the advice of charlatans, who had the impertinence to speak for their own creator.

Indeed, if any spirit had looked down at them in that moment, they truly would have appeared to be one flesh; for their embrace was absolute in its love and benevolence and passion, and they had reached that stage of ecstasy that visits the body and mind directly before the thrill of release and its subsequent exhilaration.

But the prince stopped abruptly, desiring all of a sudden to hold his wife within his bosom and taste her sweet moans when she reached the height of her passion. The princess acquiesced to the adjustment quickly, clutching her husband to her so earnestly that she practically absorbed him into her flesh. She perceived immediately that her munificence with him had already paid back div-idends, not only in her own heightened pleasure, or even the pleasure one gets from truly pleasing another, but, rather, the completely unforeseen bonus of having strengthened the bond that she had previously shared with her husband, and even creating a new, more genuine intimacy between them. Until that very moment, she had not even realized how desperately she had needed the intimacy.

All of these ruminations were rather fleeting and faint, like little epiphanies that hover unseen behind one's consciousness, but have much impact on their behavior.

Meanwhile, with her body, the princess focused all her effort and energy on pleasing her husband and accepting the pleasure he offered. She was determined that they should find the ecstasy that was de-scribed in the verses she had read—the ecstasy that their creator had made available to them if only they would take advantage of it.

Without guilt, shame, pride, fear or any of the other negative emotions that had been preventing her from fulfilling her obligations as a wife and, indeed, as a human, she was able to not only accept the pleasure, but seek it openly. She moved her hips, and used her hands and anything else she could think of that might please her or her husband—they were both truly one and the same in her mind while thus joined.

The prince, meanwhile, accepted all these changes in his bride un-questioningly. He had always been aware of her inner struggles over conjugal matters, but he had not fully understood all of the challenges she had faced. Even so, he was filled with admiration and respect for her, and for him their sudden intimacy was accompanied with newborn trust. He had always known that his wife loved him, but now he was beginning to know that she was willing to grow and change with him, and not remain a child forever.

And although the sensual pleasure they found that night was beyond what the prince had ever dreamed of having with his wife, it paled in comparison to the love and intimacy they were only beginning to share.

It surprised neither of them when Princess Devotia's shoes ceased being mysteriously worn in the mornings.

The princess was no longer afraid of the pleasures marriage offered, and it was a good thing, too, because over the years she and her husband never stopped learning new ways to please each other, in and out of their bedroom. With every new pleasure their intimacy continued to grow, and with it their love, too, so that when the time came for their union to be tested—and it did, time and again—their feelings were strong enough to endure the most difficult of tests. And so they lived, for the most part, happily ever after.

PRINCESS DOITALLA

PRINCESS DOITALLA FLEW THROUGH HER CASTLE, PICKING UP THIS AND dusting that in preparation for the wizardess's visit. The children were napping at last after a trying morning, but at least she had not had time to worry over what the wizardess would counsel. Whatever she prescribed the princess was obligated to do, since her father, the king, had decreed that they follow her instructions to the letter. It was just one more thing she would have to attend to.

Any moment the wizardess might arrive and yet where was her husband? As usual, it was she who had to be concerned over the preparations for the event, for she knew that her husband could barely be relied upon to remember to be there. It was little wonder that she could not wait to close her eyes each night and escape from the tiresome everyday responsibilities of her life, doing heaven knows what in her dreams that wore her shoes to ribbons; but how could the wizardess understand that?

She mused over these things as she continued to scurry about until the room was the picture of order and cleanliness. She glanced in the mirror then to fix her hair, and at last her husband came strolling in as if without a care in the world. She sighed as she faced him.

"Are you going to wear that shirt?" she asked him.

He smiled. "No."

She sighed again. It was just like him to make jokes when she was being serious. "Darling, please change into something a little more agreeable," she begged, thinking to herself that the very least he could do was turn up looking presentable. She had managed to entertain, feed and successfully nap their children, clean the entire castle and still look fashionable and pretty. What had he been doing?

Before he could respond there came a knock at the door. Princess Doitalla jumped when she heard it, forgetting her husband's shirt for the moment as she rushed to answer it.

With just a single glance around her, Harmonia took in the princess's nervousness, the sparkling clean and orderly room and the prince's discomfort.

"Please be seated and put yourself at ease, Princess Doitalla," the wizardess told her. The princess sat straight-backed and rigid on a chair, feeling a bit chastised and embarrassed by the wizardess's take-charge attitude. The prince and the wizardess sat down, too.

"Tell me about your day, princess," said the wizardess without preamble.

"Well…it was unusually chilly this morning," she began, desperately struggling for something interesting to say about her day.

The wizardess smiled. "What did you *do* today?" she asked her.

"Oh, um, let me see," Princess Doitalla began, irritated about being put on the spot. But she was quick to recover, for this was her favorite topic, and it was not often people were interested in hearing about all the many things that she did. "This morning I dressed and fed the children, and next we played tiddlywinks for a while. Then I folded laundry while sitting with the children as they played. After a while, I brought the children back to the kitchen for their morning snack, and while they sat at the table I cleaned away the morning mess. Shortly after that—"

"I see," interrupted the wizardess. The princess was far from finished with the long list of things she had already done that day, which were even exhausting to think about, let alone to actually have done, but Harmonia was already turning toward her husband and asking him the same question. The princess's face turned pink as she silently fumed. The wizardess had not been even slightly impressed— or supportive for that matter.

"I was out slaying dragons early this morning, like every other," the prince said casually. "And now I am here with you."

"Exactly as I thought," said the wizardess. She reached in her heavy bag and took out a little pad of paper. She tore out the top page and handed it to Princess Doitalla. Then she tore out another page for the prince.

The wizardess stood up. "Please contact me immediately if in three days from now the symptoms have not changed," she instructed. "And do not delay, for my success depends upon it!"

The princess and her husband looked at one another. Then they looked down at the paper in their hands.

"Uh...is the message in invisible ink?" asked the prince.

The wizardess laughed. "Not at all," she replied. "The note should be a blank sheet presently."

"Presently?" asked the princess.

"Yes. You see, I've given you each a very special 'to do' list. Things will appear on the list as needed to balance out your activities. Please do everything just as it appears on your list, without exception. You may carry on with your daily activities that are not on the list of, course, but when the list beckons you must obey. Please check it periodically and keep up with it as best you can." With this Harmonia wished them luck and shortly after that she was gone.

"How strange!" exclaimed Princess Doitalla. "I wonder what she meant by 'as needed' to balance our activities."

"I'm sure I don't know," he replied. But there was a strange light in his eyes as he looked thoughtfully at his wife.

The couple was exceedingly curious and they repeatedly checked their lists throughout the rest of the day. But it wasn't until that evening, after dinner, that the first instructions appeared on their "to do" lists. Around that time, there suddenly appeared on Princess Doitalla's list of instructions "at precisely seven o'clock drop everything and leave the castle for one full hour," while the prince's list said, "at precisely seven o'clock assume your wife's role for one hour, spending that hour exactly as she would do."

They glanced at the clock. It was six thirty-two. Princess Doitalla jumped up with a gasp. There were a million things she still had to do that night. She set immediately about the kitchen and she was still rushing around when her husband approached her at seven o'clock.

"It's time," he said.

"Oh, dear," said Princess Doitalla. "I have not quite finished here yet."

"Never mind that," he told her. "You must drop everything to follow the instructions on the list."

"Yes, but first I must just tell you about the children," she began, but he interrupted her.

"You must go *now,* Doitalla," he said firmly. "I will manage my part."

She paused a moment as if to argue the matter further, but at last she sighed and gave in. She left the kitchen and pulled the little "to do" list out of her pocket to read it again. "At precisely seven o'clock drop everything and leave for one full hour." Where was she supposed to go, for heaven's sake? What was she supposed to do? She stepped outside and stood on the stoop wonderingly. How on earth was *this* supposed to prevent her shoes being worn out?

She stepped off the front stoop and began walking as she contemplated the wizardess's instructions. It gave her an unsettled feeling to simply walk away when there were still so many things left undone. Yet it was strangely exhilarating, too. She pondered what all this had to do with her marriage, and even more puzzling, what it could possibly have to do with her worn shoes. It was certainly true that the worn shoes had begun appearing in the mornings soon after she had married. Could it be that the prince was the wrong man for her? She thought about her husband, and wondered what he was doing at that moment.

The prince looked around the kitchen. He was supposed to "take the place of Princess Doitalla for one hour, spending that hour exactly as she would do." He was pretty sure he could manage this; for she was forever listing the things she had to do every day. He knew, for example, that she had been hurrying to finish tidying the kitchen so that she could put the children to bed. After fighting dragons all day he was fairly certain he could handle these tasks.

Princess Doitalla walked more briskly through the cool night air. She thought it was rather strange and pleasant to simply wander around as if she had nothing else to do. She couldn't remember the last time she had extra time to do nothing—certainly not since she was a young girl living at home with her father and sisters. Wonderful memories of those times came flooding back. She remembered how she and her sisters would sit around on old tree stumps in the woods, wondering what in the world there was for them to do.

"I've already read you three stories," the prince was saying. "Why won't you just go to sleep already?" But his children just kept on jumping on the bed. How on earth did Doitalla manage to get the children to settle down? He did not recall her ever having as much trouble as he was having. She was so good at everything that it was indeed difficult to do things exactly as she did them.

But at last the children did fall asleep and the prince tiptoed out of their room. From there he proceeded to pick up stray items as he went, just like he had seen his wife doing on previous nights. She seemed to think she had to be doing something every moment, and he wondered why it bothered her so much to just let things go sometimes. He heard her footsteps outside and hurriedly finished his tidying. He knew she probably would have accomplished more than he had with that hour, but even so he felt he had done enough so that she would not complain that he had set her back.

At precisely eight o'clock Princess Doitalla came home and looked around the quiet and tidy house in surprise. "Are they asleep?" she whispered.

"Of course!" her husband replied, as if it had not been a difficult thing. "You know," he added honestly, "I rather enjoyed it."

She laughed, giving him a dubious look. "I can arrange it so you can enjoy it every night," she told him.

He laughed, too. "What about you?" he asked.

"I rather enjoyed it, too," she admitted. "Though for a few minutes there I wasn't sure what to do with myself."

"Sometimes doing nothing is the best thing you can do for yourself," he said. "But this isn't one of those times." He waved his "to do" list as he added this last.

"Oh, I almost forgot!" She pulled out her own list and read it. The earlier message was replaced with the word *shower*. "Hmm," she said. "What does yours say?"

With a self-satisfied smile he showed her his list. It, too, had just the one word, *shower,* appearing on the otherwise blank sheet. "I'm enjoying this more and more," he remarked.

She couldn't help but smile, too, even though she was not sure she was in the mood for a shared shower with her husband. However, she had agreed to follow the "to do" list and was obliged to do so wherever it led her. There was, she had to admit, something very comforting in merely following directions.

She undressed quickly and slipped into the shower to get a head start on her husband but, alas, there he was, stripped of everything but his grin.

"We're going to have to squeeze in close in order to get equal shares of water," he told her. She laughed. His overjoyousness over the situation forced her into a better frame of mind about it. "Here," he said cheerfully, "I'll wash your hair for you." He splattered shampoo onto her head before she had time to protest, leaving her just enough time to close her eyes so she wouldn't be blinded by the soap. Whistling cheerfully, he rubbed the suds into her head vigorously with his fingertips. In spite of her reservations, and the sloshing of soap everywhere, she had to admit it felt nice having her hair washed by another pair of hands. And he was actually doing a thorough job. She told him so.

"Well, I should be good at it by now," he told her. "I just finished doing each of the kids."

"You bathed them, too?" she asked.

"Well, not bathed exactly," he replied, tipping her head back in order to rinse her hair better. "I just lined them up in the shower and scrubbed them down, one at a time."

"And they went for that?" she asked.

"They loved it," he replied smoothly, adding under his breath, "Once they got the screaming out of their system." He emphasized this last with a low whistle.

Princess Doitalla threw her head back and laughed heartily. The prince stopped scrubbing her hair suddenly to watch her. The sight of her laughing so happily delighted him. It seemed that his jokes, of late, antagonized instead of amused her. Yet here he was, in the shower no less, and making her laugh! Impulsively he kissed her. Her laughter caught in her throat. She wrapped her arms around his neck, savoring the delightful feel of his hard body against her own softer one.

"It's so wonderful to hear you laugh," he whispered close to her lips, and then kissed her again. She could feel his body getting harder and she pulled away.

"Shall I wash your hair now?" she asked him.

"Sure," he agreed, dipping his head so she could reach it. She lathered his hair, scrubbing his scalp with her fingertips. "Mmm…" he murmured. "Feels good."

"It is amazing how nice it is to have this service performed," she agreed. "It feels totally different when someone else does it."

"Does that mean I get to wash your hair every evening from now on?" he asked.

"Maybe," she laughed. But she resumed her ever-efficient manner with him, managing the proceedings of their shower as she might have done with the children, while he now and again attempted to amuse or touch her. At length they were washed, rinsed and dried.

"Let's see what our 'to do' lists say now," the prince suggested hopefully. He was beginning to think that the lists would have to literally state, "make love to your husband" before she would get the idea. But as it turned out the lists were not that specific. "Go to bed" was all his list said. He looked at his wife's list, which had the same message, but with an added instruction beneath it that said "massage prince's injured foot."

"You injured your foot?" Princess Doitalla asked him, concerned. He had made no mention whatsoever of the injury that she could recall.

"Oh, it is nothing," he replied with a note of dismissal, surprised that it should have turned up on the mysterious list.

"Well, apparently it could use some massaging," she replied, and he realized suddenly that his foot was indeed aching. "Get comfortable and I will be there in a minute." She put on a nightgown before joining him.

"It's this one," he told her, putting the foot in her lap as she settled herself comfortably at his feet on the bed. She picked up his foot and inspected the swollen and bruised ankle, wondering that she had not noticed it before.

"How did you do this?" she asked.

"Oh, you know," he replied, with his usual casual air that was belied by his wince as she tentatively touched the injured area. "I must have twisted it or something."

"You don't want to talk about it?" she asked.

"I simply doubt that it would interest you," he replied honestly. Then, seeing her shocked expression he added, "I mean, I know how many things you have on your mind already."

"Is that how I seem to you?" she asked, horrified.

"Well…yes, actually. Besides, you've made it very clear that you don't wish to discuss my activities during the day, or the significance of them."

"I have?"

"Haven't you?"

"No!" she replied defensively. "I have merely tried to get you to realize that my job here with the children is important, too."

"Is that what you have been trying to do?" he asked. "Here all this time I thought you were trying to put me down a peg." He said this lightheartedly enough, in his usual mocking manner, but there was also a serious note to his expression as he looked her right in the eyes.

"How can you say that?" she said, fully on the defensive now.

"Because it's true," he replied quietly.

She did not feel like touching him suddenly but continued massaging his foot nevertheless, reminding herself that she was compelled to do so by order of the wizardess. They were both silent for a moment. She spoke up first, trying once again to defend her previous actions. "I simply don't think you understand how difficult it is to stay home with…"

"The children," he finished for her. "I know. I've heard this over and over. You don't have to do it, you know."

"That's not what I'm saying!"

"Then what are you saying? Are you saying you like what you do or that you don't like it? Do *you* even know what you are saying?"

"I know that you are being extremely difficult!"

"Ah, there it is," he sighed with satisfaction.

"What?" She stared at him.

"When I question you," he explained, uncertain why he was confronting her at this particular moment. "You simply change the subject with a derogatory remark about how I, a man, cannot possibly know what you are talking about and furthermore that I am intentionally being difficult about it. The truth is, my dear, you simply are not making any sense!" Finally his anger emerged.

"That's ridiculous."

"Okay, then, princess, let us go over it again." He was now angered to the point that she was, in his mind, an adversary to conquer. "Let's get to the bottom of this once and for all, shall we? I am not an idiot, after all, so perhaps if I struggle hard enough I will finally comprehend what you are trying to tell me. Now, the original topic was how we can never discuss a single thing that I do during the day without you producing your speech about how much more difficult your day was. Correct?"

"I don't want to argue like this," she said with tears in her eyes.

"Oh, no you don't," he said, too geared up for battle to accept this too-easy defeat. "You always do this when you are losing an argument, only to bring the subject up another time when I am less inclined to take you up on it. Not this time, princess. This time, we will settle this now!"

"What do you want me to say?"

"I want you to be honest with yourself and with me. Don't play the docile little innocent now that we are getting close to the issue. Since the day we were married you have been resenting me and complaining about your life. Admit it!"

"I have not been complaining," she denied. "I just want you to know what it is like."

"Why?"

"Because I don't think you appreciate all I do."

"What exactly have I done to make you think that?"

Princess Doitalla was flabbergasted. She had always thought she would welcome this conversation but now she was completely lost for words. However, in the conversations she had envisioned, she would be leading the topic and it would merely focus on how she felt, not how she came to feel that way. That was harder to explain.

"Well?" he prompted.

"I don't keep track of every little thing in order to list them for you," she said.

"Oh, really…don't you?" he asked, incredulous.

"Not things like that," she added, blushing. This was definitely not going in the right direction.

"The truth is that I have not done a single thing to make you feel that way, have I?" he persisted. "In fact, I have completely stopped mentioning the events of my own day so I can show my appreciation to you for all you do by listening night after night to the details of your day."

"That…isn't true," she stammered.

"Really?" he asked. "You tell me what I did any day last week and then I'll tell you what you did." She was silent. "So why, princess," he continued, more determined than ever now, "do you complain about your day so much?"

"I…" She paused again. "I don't know," she admitted at last. The tears returned to her eyes.

"Why do women always have to argue the importance of what they do?" he mused now. She was still massaging his foot dutifully and he absently picked up one of her feet to reciprocate.

"I don't know," she said again.

"And why," he continued, "do women refuse to put an end to their workdays?"

"That's just it," she said, jumping in with new vigor suddenly. "We can't. Our workday never ends."

"Nonsense," he told her. "You make that choice in an attempt to add undue importance to your job. Look at tonight. You would have stayed busy until late in the night if the wizardess hadn't ordered you to do otherwise. And the sky is not falling because you stopped."

"What if one of the children wakes?" she pointed out. "Or becomes ill?"

"When is the last time that happened?" With her silence he continued, "I just think that if you come to terms with your life, or change it—it doesn't make any difference to me—you will not have to defend it so fiercely by talking about it all the time and criticizing everything everyone else does."

"I had not realized that that was what I was doing!" she said huffily, and even more tears gushed forward. She did not like to hear these things but could not find the explanation to deny them, either.

"I think the first thing you should do is set a time each day when you stop working," he suggested, feeling better now that he had at last gotten his point across. "After that, just walk away...like I do."

"I can't just walk away," she insisted.

"Neither of us can, literally, walk away," he agreed. "But mentally you can tell yourself that the time of day has come when you will stop your workday. If something happens with the children to force you back into it we will handle it together, but otherwise, you will be on your own time."

She wanted to find something wrong with his suggestion and reasoning, but could not. He made it all seem so simple. Why was she still so resentful? Was she unhappy? Should she find something else to do with her days? Her husband's warm strong hands rubbing her feet were having a soothing influence on her. Still, she was feeling a bit restless, unused to retiring so early in the evening.

The prince had won the battle and now he wanted to take on more. He liked the way it felt to challenge his wife. Perhaps he had been wrong to allow her to command all aspects of their relationship. He did not want to be an ogre husband, but he realized he was no longer willing to just follow her knowingly in the wrong direction, either. Somewhere in between there had to be a balance and he was determined to find it. Princess Doitalla was clearly too immersed in her own personal issues to properly take the lead and so he would have to take the reins from her.

First on his agenda was the issue of their celibate marital bed.

"If you want something really important to do," he said, intentionally goading her, "I have something right here you can tend to." As he said this he grasped her legs with his strong hands and pulled her toward him.

She was outraged. "That is not funny!"

"Indeed it is not," he agreed, quickly maneuvering their bodies so that she was flat on her back and he on top. It was not easy to do with her struggling under him but he managed it, and for good measure he raised her arms above her head and held them there in a firm grip.

"How dare you," she hissed, but as he inspected her more closely he noticed her breathing was more rapid and he could see she was aroused.

"As your husband I dare," he answered. "Shall I take my demands elsewhere?" He was purposely antagonizing her, perhaps because of the frustrating months without sexual contact, but he was seeking any response he could evoke as long as it came out of passion. His wife struggled against him as he held her down.

"Tell me, princess," he murmured, kissing her with deceptive gentleness even as his hands held her arms in a viselike grip. "Shall I take my demands elsewhere?"

"Oh, you animal," she cried, enraged by his threat. But he did not back down. How could he, once he had begun?

"I did not marry to become celibate," he insisted. "What shall I do then, princess?"

"I don't care what you do!"

"Be careful," he told her. His voice, although still low and gentle, had a hard edge to it. "Or perhaps I should not pay attention to your words. It seems you don't really know what you feel." During this condescending speech he pulled her arms together and held them with one hand while his other hand moved over her body, leisurely stroking her breasts and stomach, and then moving lower.

The princess was coming alive with a variety of sensations in one tumultuous jumble of emotions, from outrage to exhilaration, and was assailed with strong desires to both fight and surrender. She at once loved and hated her husband's behavior and it occurred to her that perhaps he had a point in accusing her of not knowing her own mind.

The prince's hand had reached down below her nightgown and, slipping underneath, began its ascent up her thigh. She gasped as his fingers pried gently between her legs, stroking her moist opening a moment before pressing further into her hole. His lips captured hers in a triumphant kiss.

"Apparently, you are not as unmoved as you pretend," he laughed in between kisses. "So what is it to be, wife? Will you perform your duties and pleasure us both or will you push me into the arms of another?" He was determined that she would surrender to him this night.

Princess Doitalla could not answer his question without painting herself in a corner. If she answered that she wanted him, which her body seemed to do whether her mind did or not, she felt she would be humiliated somehow. Yet how could she justify turning him away when she wanted him as much as he wanted her? She remained silent, biting her lip.

"You know," he whispered at last. "You really are a spiteful bitch." He said this with remarkable gentleness, stroking her lips lightly while murmuring the harsh words. His fingers still slid in and out the length of her silky wetness. Tears sprang to her eyes and he saw them as he watched her. Still, he continued on. "I think this is really about power with you," he guessed. "Instead of managing your own life you use your frustration to torment and lord it over others."

"That's a lie!"

"Is it?" He was at his most ruthless, because he had suddenly realized how much he needed her to tell him, right now, how she felt about him. That he was making it extremely hard for her to do so did not seem to occur to him. He simply continued to goad her. "Whether I talk about it or not, I actually do work damn hard to protect and provide for you and the children. And whether I mention it or not, I don't get appreciation, affection or even honorable mention for my efforts. You seem to think your activities, thoughts, desires and feelings are the only ones that matter. Well, I'm tired of begging for your forgiveness and affection, Princess Doitalla. Either you want me or you don't. Which is it?"

"I can't talk to you when you're like this," she cried, angry with her body for responding to his touch and frustrated, too, by her inability to give in to him.

"Oh, but you can," he argued, kissing her again. And with his fingers he continued to stroke her! "Which is it, Doitalla?" he asked again, mockingly.

She did want him, more than ever. If only he would be his nice, usual self. Suddenly it occurred to her that it was always him that compromised. He backed down and gave in continually for her. Why was it so hard for her to do it for him? Was she really just a spiteful bitch, like he said? "You know I want to be with you," she conceded finally.

"Not good enough princess." He kissed her lips again and she felt his warm breath on them as he raised his lips mere centimeters from hers to continue. She was beginning to like the way it felt to have his hand firmly gripping her arms over her head. And she could also get used to his fingers gently stroking between her legs. "I want to hear you tell me that you are willing to perform your wifely duties."

"You know that I am willing," she whispered.

"Try again," he insisted, kissing her neck, shoulders, breasts.

"I am willing," she said.

"I'm not convinced."

"Please," she whispered.

"Slightly better. Maybe you can show me what you have so much trouble telling me," he said, releasing her and raising his body up suddenly so his hardness was poised over her lips. "Are you willing to show me?"

She hated the way he was acting, so antagonistic and unreasonable and yet she found herself opening her mouth to him. It was true; with words she could not say the things she could show him with her actions. She took him as far into her mouth as she could and back out again. She bobbed her head up and down as she tried to express everything with her lips, tongue and throat.

"Mmm...yes, that's much better," he murmured. She blushed with a mixture of mortification and excitement, knowing he was saying these things to ensure her total submission, and realizing suddenly that she wanted that submission as much as he did. In response to his words she sucked harder and with more vigor, knowing she had never pleasured him so well, and finding a wonderful new stimulation in that knowledge. Her whole body trembled with expectation and desire. She tried her best to communicate her enthusiasm by caressing him most lovingly with her mouth, licking up and down the length of him as he moved in and out of her. A moan escaped her as she welcomed all of him that she could hold in her mouth, and she relished the amazing rigidity of him as he attempted to push himself in deeper. His sighs of satisfaction sent thrills right through her.

"This is what I married you for," he told her in a husky voice. "Not to run my life."

Her face burned and she felt an automatic rush of anger from his words, even as yet another alarming thrill surged through her, causing her sex to swell and ache. A tumult of emotions raged within her, bringing more tears to her eyes. She looked up to see that he was watching her eyes as he spoke, and when her eyes met his, he seemed to be silently challenging her. She stared up at him, unable to look away. She felt a tear slowly slip its way down her cheek. Her face burned hotter, but she continued to please him with her mouth, even more vigorously now in fact, for there was an oddly liberating element in her absolute capitulation. She stared up willingly into his eyes, letting the tears flow, as she bobbed her head even faster, determined to give him more pleasure from this experience than he had ever received before.

The prince was amazed by the sight of his wife. He had never felt so aroused by her, nor had he felt so much love. Seeing her submit in this way was something he had never expected. He had always felt that he would draw her closer to him by accommodating her in her every wish, but he now realized that there had to be a balance. While he would always elect to please her, he would no longer feign agreement simply to avoid displeasing her. She was not a frightening creature to be condescended to but an intelligent being who was capable of dealing with the truth. He fought dragons all day long; why should the sound of a female voice, raised and upset, intimidate? He knew now that she could and would accept the truth from him, just as he would do for her. He would not always be right, perhaps, and it certainly would never be easy, but he felt a new intimacy emerging in the knowledge that she really would accept him, even if she did not accept all that he said.

This new awareness caused the prince's confidence and trust in his wife to soar.

The prince felt a surprising surge of tenderness for his wife and he pulled away so he could take her face in his hands and kiss her ravaged lips. She clung to him, kissing him back wholeheartedly. With her response he suddenly became even more urgent, bombarding her with kisses all over her face and neck, tasting the tears on her cheeks.

"You are mine," he told her, again and again, as he opened her legs. She trembled in anticipation, wrapping her arms and legs around him. He took her tenderly, reveling in each and every stroke. Her body was warm and soft and willing. She was not performing a task now; she was loving her husband with her whole being. They whispered endearments to each other in between solemn kisses.

"I love you," she murmured, over and over again.

"I love you, too. And I need you," he admitted.

They were words of surrender, sweet to hear. Both delighted in the

intense exhilaration they felt from the heady combination of full submission amid absolute victory.

Their intimacy gave way to a new abandon. Princess Doitalla responded to her husband without reservation, undulating wildly in his
embrace. And as for the prince, he withheld only his climax, and that
for the sole purpose of satisfying her. He kept his strokes slow and
easy, kissing her and coaxing her with words of love and adoration.
He remembered how she had responded when he had held her hands
firmly over her head earlier and he did it again now, pulling her arms
high above her head and holding them in a viselike grip. She seemed
to like this, and the rough play appealed to him, as well, so he bent
his head down to suckle vigorously on her breasts, plucking aggres-
sively on the tips with his mouth. She cried out and thrust her hips
against him faster and harder. This made him suckle her all the harder,
although he was careful not to actually hurt her.

Princess Doitalla rubbed her hips fiercely against her husband in
order to further stimulate herself. Her behavior seemed foreign to her
and yet, she knew she had never been more true to herself. She loved
what her husband was doing and cared nothing for the control she had
lost. Perhaps she would think about that tomorrow, but for now she
virtually swooned under the power of her husband's strength as he
held her down and ravished her. Before long it became more than she
could bear and she bit into his shoulder to avoid screaming. Her whole
body shuddered in a release that was more intense than any other she
had experienced.

With a low chuckle the prince pulled his wife's arms together so
he could bind them with one of his hands. He had fully subdued her
but he was still in the mood to dominate. With his other hand he
caressed her face. Her head was turned to the side and she was staring,

as if spellbound, at the wall. He was still moving slowly in and out of her. He stroked her hair ever so gently at first, while kissing the side of her face, but ere long he pulled on it firmly, forcing her head to turn and face him. This brought her out of her trance and she opened her mouth to receive his kiss.

Princess Doitalla luxuriated in the exquisite feel of being pinned down beneath her husband. She was suddenly and remarkably aroused all over again. His forcefulness, so all at once antagonizing and enticing, had her body yearning and pining for more. Although she would never admit it, she thrilled to the strength of form and character he established with his gentle domination of her. Had he loved her less, perhaps it would not have been so, but in the circumstance of his tender purpose to forge a stronger intimacy she found it irresistible. She had never felt so safe and cherished. And she had never before felt so aroused. It seemed her husband had kindled a flame within in her that was burning out of control. She once again allowed the flame to build up inside her, encouraging it even further by rubbing her hips just so against her husband.

The prince restrained the princess even more securely in response to her renewed arousal, so that her arms were stretched high over her head and her face and breasts were his to ravage. She clung to him with her legs as she ground her hips against him. Her breath came quickly in little gasps and cries as she was carried away by the rapturous emotions and sensations that overwhelmed her. Her mind whirled with a plethora of stimuli that left her unable to focus. She was first and foremost aware of her husband's superior physical strength as he pinned her ruthlessly to the bed. His slow strokes spoke of control; control that she could tell—from the sweat that trickled along his skin—took real effort and love. She was aware that he chose to first please her and this knowledge sent her senses reeling. Soon another rush of pleasure shivered through her.

Upon feeling her shudder the prince finally let loose. He suddenly drove into her with a force that made her cry out. Her cries caused him to grip her all the tighter. She clung to him, bearing up under his strength as best she could, kissing his face and encouraging him with all the endearments that were in her heart. Suddenly he stiffened and threw himself all the way into her with a loud yell. And her body yearned for him still!

The prince stayed atop the princess for several moments, shifting his weight so as not to crush her. At length he perceived that she was crying. He looked down at her with concern.

"Did I hurt you?" he whispered, kissing the tears on her cheeks.

She remained silent, trembling violently beneath him. He became alarmed.

"Princess," he said more urgently. "Did I hurt you? Tell me."

She still couldn't speak but she shook her head to quiet his alarm. She could not say why she trembled and cried. How could she explain that she was filled with too many emotions to identify, much less articulate to him? Who was she? What did she want? Was she strong or weak? What did she desire from her husband? These were questions that she could not begin to answer. All she really knew for the moment was that she felt safe in her husband's arms. And he did not ask her any more questions that night.

The next morning the princess awoke from a deep slumber, feeling inordinately content. The loss of time from her schedule on the previous day should have set her behind but she felt somehow quite the opposite. Many of the daily duties that previously tormented her now seemed rather empty. Things that usually worried her appeared trivial. Aggravations failed to bother. *What is happening to me?* she wondered.

She wished she could talk to her husband about it. Perhaps she would later that night. He was, no doubt, already out slaying dragons again.

As for her, what would she do today? She looked down at her shoes and noted with surprise that they were in nearly new condition. She laughed in surprise. Perhaps she would have to wear them out in the ordinary way from now on.

And that is precisely, from that day forward, what she began to do.

PRINCESS DREADIA

PRINCESS DREADIA SMILED TIMIDLY AT HER HUSBAND FROM ACROSS THEIR luncheon table. She had served him a midday meal that would delight even the finickiest of palates and satisfy the heartiest of appetites in her attempt to please him, hoping that would make up for any deficiencies she might have as a wife. She loved him dearly and wanted so much to be a worthy mate. Why did she suffer so? Life had finally given her what she wanted. Why couldn't she forget the past and enjoy the present? What would her husband think of her if he knew about the things that really went through her mind? What would he think of her if he knew how she really felt?

He must never find out. Princess Dreadia jumped up from her chair at the mere thought of it and went to get her husband more coffee. She nearly spilled the coffee when the doorbell rang.

"That must be the wizardess," said the prince cheerfully. "This should be interesting." He had been at first bewildered by the wizardess's words at the king's feast, but he did not let it concern him overmuch. He had seen firsthand how happy his doting wife was, even if she was a bit skittish in the bedroom. That would be remedied in time, with patience and effort, he had no doubt. For his wife loved him, he knew, and he could not miss how devotedly she tried to please him. He believed that she would warm to him in due time. Besides this, he had never been one for mystical things. No doubt this was some kind of scheme on the part of the old woman to gain the king's favor. Even so, it would be a curious thing to see what she would have to say.

The prince was surprised by Harmonia's effervescent beauty. From a distance, one only noticed her graying hair. A closer inspection revealed intelligent, alert eyes and lips that turned up on one side in secret amusement. Her skin glowed and her white-blond hair fell in waves around her face. The prince was impressed and intrigued by the unusual woman.

Now the wizardess had been inspecting the prince just as closely as he had been eyeing her. She noticed his approval of her and smiled her secret smile. He was obviously a kind man who was not threatened by a strong woman, so what was the problem here? She followed him into the kitchen to meet the princess.

Princess Dreadia was also impressed by the wizardess. *Oh, to have her self assurance,* she thought wistfully, *truly here is a woman who has full command over herself.*

Harmonia approached Princess Dreadia carefully. There was something in the princess's eyes that put her on alert at once. She grasped both of the princess's hands in hers and held them for a moment. She was simultaneously startled and filled with compassion by the pain she felt emanating from the young woman. The princess, too, seemed startled and was silent.

"She's exquisite, isn't she," remarked the prince, misunderstanding the wizardess's response to his wife. "One can't help but love her."

The wizardess remained quiet for a moment, then she let the princess's hands drop.

"Come," she said. "Let us all sit for a moment."

The prince led them to an exquisitely decorated and immaculately kept little sitting room that had been prepared for this occasion, with a cozy fire burning heartily in the grate. They sat around each other in a circle so that they were facing one another.

The wizardess spoke first, addressing the prince. "I hope I do not underestimate you," she said. "For I will certainly need your help."

The prince stared at the wizardess. He hadn't the slightest idea what she meant. Was she confessing that her status as wizardess was a sham and enlisting his help in duping the king in the matter? "Help with what?" he asked warily.

"With the princess's dilemma," she replied. Then finally noticing his confusion, she said, somewhat surprised, "Oh, well, of course, you have no idea!"

"Now just a moment," said the prince, rising.

"Oh, dear," said the wizardess. "We haven't time for this." But she recovered herself quickly and said, "Please sit and allow me to finish."

The prince sat and Harmonia now addressed the princess. "Do you wish to get better, Princess Dreadia?" she asked.

The princess glanced at her bewildered husband. She, too, felt confused, but it was not over the wizardess's inquiry. She was wondering how the wizardess had learned her secret. No one, not even her sisters, knew about it. The thought crossed her mind that the wizardess might actually have some magic, and that even perhaps she could help with her "dilemma," as she called it. She blushed deeply and, avoiding her husband's eyes, she answered the wizardess, "Yes."

"Better from what?" demanded the prince.

"You will learn soon enough," replied the wizardess, grasping his hand for a minute to reassure him. Then she turned back to the princess. "You must trust your husband," she advised, "for you, too, will need his help." She fished through her bag and retrieved a strange little bottle that was decorated with shimmering beads. She handed this to the princess. "When you are ready to begin your journey, you must give this to the prince," she said. "And do not delay." Then she got up and looked at the prince. "Your husband will walk me out," she said.

Princess Dreadia remained frozen on the sofa, waiting for her husband to return. He lingered with Harmonia for what seemed like forever. What was she saying to him? How much did she know? The princess looked at the little bottle in her hand. What was inside? How was her husband going to be able to help her? What had she gotten herself into? She felt all at once terrified and exhausted.

When the prince returned to the sitting room at last, he looked quite ashen. However, he sat next to Princess Dreadia and smiled. He searched her eyes for a moment and then took her hand in his. "We *are* going to make this better," he told her firmly, and her heart suddenly soared. Perhaps—?

"I have no idea what I am to do," she admitted.

"We will figure it out together," he promised with assurance. He was disgusted with himself for not having noticed that his wife was suffering with any conflict. He realized now how hard she must have been trying to please him, and he was determined to try just as hard to help her. "Perhaps it would be best if we put this aside until this evening," he wisely suggested. "Getting today's business behind us will likely help." He hugged and kissed the princess, holding her pressed tightly to him for a moment before letting go. Then, with an encouraging smile he left her to go about her day.

Princess Dreadia took her husband's advice and kept busy. Throughout the day she felt a sense of dread about what might happen, even while she harbored a secret hope that perhaps things would work out after all. The wizardess seemed remarkably capable and she was surprised by the kindness and determination her husband had shown so far. Dared she hope? She must hope, she decided. All three of them had too much at stake. She might have suffered forever rather than cause such distress to her husband, but now that it was out, she would only cause him more distress if she did not put forth every effort to fix her problem. And she did not wish to cause the wizardess to fail in her endeavor, either. No, she must address this challenge with courage, just as her husband and the wizardess both had.

At last the day came near its end, and Princess Dreadia and her husband were eating their dinner. They had only exchanged polite conversation so far, but at last the prince said to her, "I trust you are willing and ready, my love, as am I, to resolve this matter between us?"

The princess answered her husband with a whispered "yes," even as her heart began pounding heavily in her chest. She was terrified and filled with anticipation all at the same time.

The prince captured her cool hand with his warm one, holding it gently but firmly as he led her to their bedchamber. His attitude of absolute, unbending determination filled the princess with confidence.

In their bedroom the prince put out his hand to his wife. "You have something for me?" he reminded her. She handed him the little bottle, which sparkled radiantly in the evening candlelight. Her hands were trembling.

"You will feel better shortly," he assured her. He set the little shimmering bottle down on a nearby table and approached his wife. Slowly he began to remove her clothing. The princess looked surprised, and froze a little, hesitating to cooperate with him fully. He took her face in his hands and looked into her eyes. "Will you trust me?"

The princess continued to stare into her husband's eyes as she acquiesced. He undressed her completely while she stood by mutely and watched him.

When he had the princess fully unclothed the prince groaned inwardly. This was truly going to be difficult. However, he knew that it would be worth the effort if it helped her to get over her fears. With much restraint, he kissed her forehead gently and said, "Now lie down on the bed."

While Princess Dreadia arranged herself on the bed her husband picked up the little bottle that the wizardess had given them. He opened it cautiously, so as not to spill a drop of the precious fluid. Very carefully he poured a very little puddle of it into his palm. Immediately upon doing this he could feel a tingling sensation penetrating his hand and arm. He gained hope by this, thinking perhaps this really was magic fluid after all.

The princess watched him from the bed as he approached. Immediately his hands were on her skin, warm and caressing, firmly massaging the oil into her tingling flesh, beginning with her arms and shoulders and neck, and moving down over her torso to massage her breasts and stomach and hips. The tingling started at the outer layer of skin and seemed to work its way down into her very bones. Her husband, meanwhile, massaged more oil in vigorously and conscientiously and, in spite of her earlier nervousness, the princess felt herself giving in to the oil and her husband's strong hands, and at length, she felt her tension easing away.

"That's it," her husband coaxed. "Let yourself completely relax. You are safe with me." His own body was tense and hard, but he ignored the painful yearning he felt and focused on his wife. He noticed that she was quite comfortable. His hands continued to rub the mysterious oil into her skin, making it glow.

"There's something you've been hiding," he said at last, when he was certain the oil had had time to take effect. He said it in a very matter-of-fact manner and with kindness, not accusing her, but rather speaking conversationally. When she remained silent he came closer to her and whispered into her ear, "Can you hear me, princess?" She nodded that she did.

"Something happened to you," he continued. "Tell me." This, too, he said in a very matter-of-fact but determined tone.

"It was…" She stammered a bit and then said, "I'm afraid." In the meantime, the oil had reached her very brain, it seemed, for she suddenly did want to tell him everything. Still, it had been inside her for so long that it was difficult to find the words.

The prince continued to massage the oil into his wife's body as he patiently encouraged her to tell him all about the incident that had traumatized her so absolutely that she could not be touched without thinking about it. Gradually the oil and the prince's encouragement had the desired effect and the event was brought out into the open, from the furthest depths of Princess Dreadia's memory for the very first time.

The princess's first thought upon the telling was that, bad as the event had been, it did not deserve such influence as to alter her entire existence.

The prince, on the other hand, was greatly disturbed and enraged to hear of his wife's suffering. But as the wizardess instructed him, he kept these emotions from his face and voice as he continued to massage the magical fluid into her skin. Now that he knew the substance of the event, he remembered that he must get her to speak about even the minutest of details. It would be extremely unpleasant for them both, but it would ultimately free her to think and speak of it while being completely comfortable and safe, and show that it was not something that she should continue to be afraid of. It was a memory and it was over.

With this in mind the prince asked the princess many specific questions. The more the object of his interrogation upset her, the more questions he put to that object. At one point his hand went between her legs and he asked softly, "Is this where he touched you?" And when she replied that it was, he assured her, "He will not touch you there again."

To speak of it in such matter-of-fact detail seemed inappropriate at first, but it soon became obvious to both of them that, uncomfortable as it was to revisit the event, each detail that was exposed and released brought yet another degree of relief, and the longer they spoke of it, the smaller it seemed to become.

So they talked about what happened to Princess Dreadia in great detail, leaving out none of the particulars, and without hastening to get to an end to their task; in fact, on the contrary, with the thought to keep it out in the open air for as long as was comfortably possible. The prince exhausted his imagination to conjure more questions, not only about what had happened to the princess, but what she thought about during the episode, what she wished she had in her power to do at the time and what she might do if threatened with the possibility of facing a similar event in the future. On and on the discussion went, with the prince rubbing the oil into his wife's body all the while, and having the effect of further minimizing the importance of the horrible memories with the much more pleasant experience of being loved.

With the help of the magical oil, they both came under a spell that brought forth truth without censure and provided comfort for pain.

At last they were too tired to speak anymore. Any hysteria the princess experienced during this ritual was done—passed all the way through and presently forgotten. Confident that much had been accomplished this night, the prince ran his wife a bath and carried her into the tub. There he bathed her very well and shortly after tucked her into their bed, holding her in his arms until she slept.

At length the prince rolled away from his sleeping wife and stared at the ceiling, unable to find sleep himself. He thought about many aspects of their life together and the problems that he had not even been aware of until now. He did not like the things his wife had told him that night, but in his heart there grew a new, stronger desire to protect her now and always. Furthermore, he had gotten a glimpse inside the mind and heart of the loving woman he had married, and he knew that he would always see her differently from that day forward.

The next morning, Princess Dreadia woke up alone. The prince had left her; was it to save her embarrassment or to avoid having to look at her? She had told him everything! In a wave of anguish she suddenly felt all the shame she had feared she would feel if anyone found out about the incident. Even through the shame and mortification however, she still felt a solid relief of having gotten it out in the open. She remembered the words of the wizardess, telling her she must trust her husband. Perhaps she should do just that. Hadn't he proven trustworthy so far? But what if…? No, she would not think about what-ifs. She would not let what-ifs run and destroy her life!

With determination she dressed and went to find her husband. From now on she would face her fears head-on, come what may.

As it happened, the prince was waiting for her in the kitchen where, for once, he had prepared breakfast for her. She again felt shame and unworthiness over his kindness but she resolutely brushed these negative thoughts away. He smiled at her when he saw her.

"Come and eat," he told her. "You are going to need your strength."

She was curious. "What, pray, will I need my strength for?" she asked, amazed inwardly that they could speak so comfortably with each other after the night previous. She was also delighted and relieved to find that she still felt the same pleasure in being with her husband and curiosity and excitement over what they might be doing.

"We have something very important to do today," was all he would say. And try as she might, she could not get him to tell her more until she finished all of her breakfast. They ate together cheerfully, with him changing the subject every time she tried to pry that day's events from him.

When at last she had eaten all she could, he took her into their large living room. All of the furniture had been moved into a corner. "Now princess," he said. "You are a woman and cannot hope to be as strong as a man, but there are still some things you can do to protect yourself from an attacker. I am going to show you these things today."

She was at once on the defensive. "So you do blame me," she said, immediately angry at him with a velocity that surprised even her.

The prince tried not to show his frustration as he faced her unreasonable accusation head-on and with determination. "Listen princess," he told her matter-of-factly, "I do not believe you are at fault any more than I believe it is appropriate for men to attack helpless women. However, I do believe that the more positive action you take on this matter, the more you will gain your confidence back." He paused for a moment to let this sink in. "It certainly couldn't hurt," he added.

For some reason she wanted to be angry and did not want to hear logic. Why should she even have to do this? He saw her obstinate look and he took her by the shoulders and forced her to look at him. "For whatever reason this has happened," he said firmly, "we must try everything we can think of to solve the problem."

She sighed grudgingly. "What would you like me to do?" she asked reluctantly.

He was careful not to smile. He proceeded to point out to her every man's weakest points and ways that she might take advantage of those in a struggle. Before long, Princess Dreadia found herself quite intrigued with the things he was showing her, and she began to think that this new knowledge could indeed help her if she found herself in an unfortunate situation with a man in the future.

Aside from all of this, the close contact with her husband combined with the exhilaration of learning new things felt to her more exciting and intimate than anything they had done before. She allowed herself to feel protected and cherished.

At length, their lesson became more playful and she found herself teasing him as they tussled, now in fun.

Suddenly the prince took her firmly in hand and before she had even realized what was happening she found herself pinned beneath his rock-hard body. She stared up at him as he breathed down at her, serious now. "You must understand, princess," he continued, "these things I've taught you today are tenuous at best if you come up against an assailant. You must also take great care to avoid any circumstances that might put you in danger."

This speech tore the smile from her face. She once again felt the rush of indignant anger brought on by injustice. "Are you saying I was reckless before…?" She did not want to elaborate. She had gone over the event hundreds of times in her mind over the years. She had conjured up twenty or thirty ways she might have avoided the circumstance. Always, though, a little voice in the back of her head kept crying out, "It wasn't my fault!"

"I am saying that you can take control of the matter, in your mind at least, if you take the precautions now that you wished you had then. It will make you feel safer in the present if you do. It may not even make a difference in your safety but it will help your peace of mind. I know this because I face dangers and have fears, too. Implementing ways of preventing your fears from happening, even if only in your mind, combats worry."

The princess thought about this for a long moment. She sighed. "Okay," she consented. "As a matter of fact, I have been more careful since my...accident." She still had trouble talking about it.

The prince kissed her on the nose. "Good girl," he remarked, and then released her.

The hardest thing, the princess thought, was not letting every remark and action anger her. Where did all the anger come from? Well, however it came about, her love for her husband would help her push it out and away from in between them. Perhaps after enough effort expended over the matter, her anger would not appear so often. She noticed her husband had become aroused during their little scuffle. Yet he was struggling against it, and she knew it was so that she could have time to heal. She really did have a lot to be thankful for, she mused.

The princess got up, renewed with energy from these realizations. "What next?" she asked.

"Nothing more for the moment," he replied. "Tonight we will repeat last night's ritual."

"What?" the princess gasped. "Why?"

"Because the wizardess says so," he answered. "That's why. And frankly, I agree with her," he added. "I, too, think a person should face their terrors, repeatedly, until they are no longer afraid of them."

"Meaning I should not be afraid of such a thing happening?" she choked.

"I do wish you would stop turning everything I say around," he said with exasperation. "No one can say what is going to happen in the future and, in truth, we are even somewhat limited in what we can do about it. But what I am referring to is the unrealistic terror you still have of this memory and everything that reminds you of it. Not to mention what it is doing to you. It is over. It is only a memory now. I will not allow the memory of that horrible ordeal to dictate the rest of our life together."

"*You* will not allow!" she echoed, succumbing once again to the easily instigated anger.

"Look, princess," he reasoned, "you promised to try. Stop fighting and arguing against me every step of the way. You have more than an obligation to the wizardess and to me. You have an obligation to yourself. Do you want what that man did to you affect you and me for the rest of our lives?"

"No!" she said indignantly. "Of course not."

"Well, then, my dear, one would hope that *you,* as well as I, are not going to allow it to consume our lives." And with this final retort he left her.

She huffed in frustration. This was indeed going to be harder than she thought!

But as it happened, when the time actually came for her to submit to the ritual, she found that it was not so hard after all. She certainly did not approach the event with nearly so much trepidation as she had the night before. In fact, she realized she was rather looking forward to having her body plied with the magic oil by her husband's warm, firm hands. That part, at least, was something to persuade her.

The prince rubbed her body enthusiastically with the oil, until his own body was tense and fully hardened. He found his mind wandering to the things he would like to do to her once this problem was fully behind them. He did not want her to ever equate their intimacies with that other invasion again. To learn that that was what had caused her hesitancies with him in their marriage had been indeed hard to swallow.

He waited until she was fully relaxed before he determinedly broached the subject and once again encouraged her to talk about the event.

The princess was surprised to find herself answering her husband's inquiries mechanically and with much less emotion than she had felt the night before. She felt little, in fact, except an intense hatred for the man who had violated her. The nerve of him! What a coward he was. She would like to see him dare to face up to a man like her husband and she told the prince this.

"I, too, would relish the opportunity of making his acquaintance," her husband remarked in dangerously low voice. This comment sent a thrill through the princess, even in her present highly relaxed state. She had never felt safer or more cherished.

So once again they talked until late into the night and she could speak no more, and then the prince bathed her again and held her until she slept. As for himself, he did not sleep easily or well, but not because of his own fears or doubts as in the case of the night before, but because his body ached with a great need that could only be satisfied by Princess Dreadia.

On the days following, the prince continued to instruct the

princess in more methods of protecting herself, and during the nights they repeated the wizardess's ritual with the oil. By the fourth night, however, the princess was becoming bored. The massages she loved, but she was frustrated with the topic. At some point during the days that had passed, she had come to realize that the old memory was not worth the effect she had let it have on her life and, even more importantly, it was not worth this precious time they were spending talking about it. Surely they could be doing something far more enjoyable!

These thoughts brought the princess to the present with a start. Over the course of her treatment she had learned to trust her husband as never before, and the trust, in turn, had created a new intimacy between them that she would never have imagined possible. But more than that, she was becoming aware of a new emerging playfulness seeping into the space inside her that had previously been occupied with dread. Where before there had been fear and avoidance there was now curiosity and responsiveness.

What she wanted to do about these new emotions she was not certain; for her growth had been stunted altogether by the untimely misfortune of her past. It would remain for her to discover these things with her husband.

The mysterious oil seemed to be massaged into her very being after all this time, by her husband's skillful hands. As her mind wandered over these revelations, she had been mechanically answering her husband's questions. Now the magic took effect and she confessed in between inquiries, "I feel quite tingly between my legs."

The prince's hands stopped short when she said this. He was momentarily stunned by her statement, but at length his hands moved between the legs in question and he touched her there, asking huskily, "Do you mean here?"

"Oh," gasped the princess. "Yes!"

The prince was not sure what to do next. He was overwhelmed by a strong conviction that if he proceeded incorrectly all would be lost, even as he fought a fervent urge to plunge one of his fingers into her body. He decided to be as honest with the princess as she was being with him. "I want you more than anything," he told her. "But I need to know what you want."

"I don't know," she confessed. "I'm really not sure how to make the most of this." She sighed in anguish as she wiggled herself against his fingers. "What shall I do?" she asked him, confused and frustrated. "How can I get the same thrill from it that you do?" Declaring her innermost thoughts to her husband had now become as natural as speaking casually to him, so it did not even occur to her that she had just confessed another deep dark secret. Furthermore, her genuine agitation over the strong yearnings of her body and her ignorance about how to satisfy them were overriding any embarrassment.

But embarrassment would have been as ill-advised as it was a deterrent. The prince's adoration for his wife soared upon hearing her truthful declaration. And even though the prince did not know the answer to her question he was nevertheless delighted by it. Truth be told, he very nearly got his "thrill" right then and there when he realized that he would be the one helping her find the solution.

With this in mind he asked her, "Where does it feel best to be touched?"

"There is one little place," she began shyly.

The prince kissed her lips as his hand continued to stroke her. "Show me," he whispered into her lips.

Tentatively the princess moved the prince's hand to the place she had been telling him about. She pressed his hand into the little bud of flesh that when brushed against would send little quivers trickling through her, foretelling an even greater pleasure that might be developed.

The prince rubbed the nub of flesh carefully, allowing his wife's responses to guide him as he did so. Both of them seemed to be truly under the spell of the magic oil, for they approached the task of finding the princess's secrets with the candor and sincerity of children. "I want to taste you," he moaned.

"Oh, my," the princess replied, in such a tone that the prince had no qualms about interpreting the comment for consent. Suddenly his warm breath on her swollen flesh melted away the last of her inhibitions. She sucked in her breath as she felt his coarse tongue delving its way into her, deeper and deeper, licking her with long and deep strokes. Meanwhile his fingers were becoming expert in their gentle encouragement. He surmised, correctly, that the continual stroking of that little nub of flesh that she had led him to would bring about a conclusive and pleasurable release, much like the repetitive rubbing of his own flesh, done in precisely the right way, brought about his own release.

The prince's tongue continued its wriggling up and down along his wife's slit, pausing to dip inside as he wished it, taking her with his tongue and forcing her to accept, and even delight in, this intimate invasion of her body. She was engrossed with the thought of him using his tongue on her in this way, and the only distraction was the rhythmic caress of his fingers. He was determined to keep her much too preoccupied with pleasurable sensations to backpedal into disparaging scrutiny of the liberties he was taking with her body. His fingers kept steadily coaxing her toward the longed for release. It heightened his excitement tenfold to feel her writhing beneath him, and to hear her little cries and moans of pleasure. He knew he would work on her all night if that was what it took to solve the puzzle; for to fail now would be unimaginably cruel.

Therefore the prince kept on, with increasingly renewed vigor. He allowed not even the smallest faltering of will. For each and every pause or hesitation in her excitement, he doubled his efforts. Later, once she knew she was capable of enjoying this part of their life together, he would find numerous and varied methods of satisfying her. There was nothing he would not try; their new awareness of each other would exceed their inhibitions.

Thus the prince replanned the whole of their life together as he taught her about pleasure, and it was the most pleasurable commission he had ever taken up.

Now it is a very real truth that any objective, if approached thoroughly and resolutely, will most definitely be achieved, and it was no different with Princess Dreadia and her husband.

With a sudden, swirling rush, an intense wave of exquisite pleasure flowed through the princess, causing her to shudder. The wave seemed to begin where her husband's fingers held her and spread out from there to every part of her, diminishing in strength as it went. For a moment she was caught up in the dizzying surge, and the next it was gone. All that remained was a feeling of exhilaration. She could have wept.

The princess looked at her husband. She felt like she had been unlocked and opened. She was soft and wet, and wanted to feel him inside her. What pleasure! What bliss! Her husband poured himself into her, and now she knew exactly how he felt. She felt a brand-new delight in pleasing him.

That momentous evening proved to be the beginning of a very different life for both Princess Dreadia and her husband. The prince's plans progressed exactly as he had determined they would that night, so that finding new ways to please each other became both of their favorite past times. It was never again necessary for either of them to revisit the unpleasant event that brought the wizardess to them in the first place.

And in case you were wondering, the princess's slippers were never again worn out from an evening at home with her husband.

PRINCESS FEMINA

"IT'S YOUR TURN TO MAKE ARRANGEMENTS FOR DINNER TONIGHT," Princess Femina reminded her husband.

"Certainly," he agreed cheerfully. "What would you like?"

"I don't know," she said. "You decide." She stared at the clock and sighed. "If I had known the wizardess would be arriving so late in the day I would not have wasted my whole morning waiting for her."

"She has twelve of you to visit," he reminded her.

"All that talk about 'discontent' in our marriages," she scoffed. "How can a married woman not be discontented? The whole institution of marriage is arranged for the benefit of men...no offense." She made this little disclaimer automatically, without, in truth, the slightest realization of how offensive this statement was to him. But he remained silent, knowing from past experience that she was far less open-minded when others were as forthright with their opinions. She took his silence for agreement and continued. "I do hope she isn't one of those old-fashioned types who will expect me to further subjugate myself to this male-dominated world when I have fought so hard to come as far as I have."

The prince sighed. He wondered that she could so easily correlate her own personal beliefs to so many of the tired old platitudes. He resisted the urge to strangle her, and ventured to say, "Perhaps we should hear the wizardess out before we jump to conclusions."

"I just know from experience how this is likely to unravel," she insisted, settling herself into the defensive posture he was so accustomed to seeing her in with everyone who presented a new idea about anything. It was strange to him that she could be so adamant about having her views heard without ever attempting to hear anyone else's.

"She is a woman," the prince reminded her. "A *career* woman who has made her way in life by perfecting her talents as a wizardess."

"Yes, well, we shall see," said the princess, unconvinced. She was always certain that things were going to go against her, despite the fact that she almost always got her way.

"Yes, we shall," he agreed. "Presently, in fact, for I think I hear someone approaching." And sure enough, the bell rang just then. He left her to answer to the door.

The prince greeted Harmonia with much respect and honor, whereas the princess was suspicious and haughty. Within moments of arriving the wizardess had already assessed the situation to her satisfaction.

Now Harmonia was a woman who had fought hard to gain independence and respect, just as the prince had wisely surmised with his wife earlier. However, in the course of her struggles she had discovered that everything comes with a price and that with power came responsibility. Having paid the price and accepted the responsibility, she found herself disliking those who made claim to the same power simply on the basis of their gender or race. Choice and opportunity were indeed things that everyone deserved; power was not. Power, in the hands of the irresponsible, could be quite oppressive to everyone, and the wizardess could clearly see that this was the case with Princess Femina.

The wizardess reached in her bag and pulled from it a shiny green apple. "This will be just the thing for you both," she said, holding it out to them. The princess, of course, reached for it first.

"An apple?" she asked, curious in spite of her suspicions.

"A *magic* apple," corrected the wizardess. The prince stared at the apple with interest. How could a magic apple...unless it was a *poisonous* apple? No, he shook his head with the absurdity of such an idea. That only happened in fairy tales. Still, the image of his wife sleeping peacefully...

"Is one of us supposed to eat the apple?" he asked.

"Both of you must eat from the apple," instructed the wizardess.

"May I know what kind of magic this apple possesses before I bite into it?" he asked.

"Of course," said the wizardess. "Upon the moment of your both eating the magic apple your spirits will exchange bodies, so that the princess will reside inside your body while you reside in hers."

"What?" both the princess and her husband exclaimed at once. They looked at the wizardess in shock, but then slowly their gazes moved to each other.

"I would have thought that you, at least, would be delighted by the prospect, princess," remarked the wizardess.

"Well, I am, of course, but...how long would we stay like that?" she asked.

"Forever, if you like," replied the wizardess. "However, if you decide you do not like being in the other's body, the spell can be reversed by both of you biting into the apple a second time."

"I don't know," the prince said doubtfully. It was impossible to imagine his wife living his life for even a single hour. And yet, what better way for her to see his point of view? At any rate, it could be reversed easily enough.

"I'm game if you are," he told his wife.

The princess had been thinking along the same line as her husband. "Okay," she agreed.

The princess raised the magic apple and held it up between them. Both moved forward simultaneously, staring into each other's eyes. Together they bit from the magic apple.

No sooner had the princess swallowed the bite of apple than she found she was staring into her own eyes instead of those of her husband. How strange it was to view herself from this perspective. It was quite different from looking into a mirror. The prince, from inside her body, stared back at her with the same astonishment.

"Oh, one more thing," the wizardess now added. "You must wait at least twenty-four hours before biting from the apple again, or you could be stuck like this forever."

"What?" they both exclaimed again.

"Good luck, my dears," she said with a little giggle. And she saw herself out. The prince and princess hardly noticed her leave as they continued to stare at each other in amazement.

"I can't believe it!" said the prince.

"Could it be true?" wondered the princess.

After gaping at herself for a few moments the princess suddenly became aware of the body she was in. Did she imagine it or did she feel stronger? A strange sense of calm seemed to permeate her.

The prince, too, was becoming aware of the body he inhabited. The first thing he noticed was that he seemed smaller and lighter. There was something else, too, which he was unable to identify, except that it made him feel more edgy.

"It is truly remarkable," Princess Femina admitted, and her husband had to agree. "What do you suppose the wizardess hopes will happen?"

"I don't know," he confessed. "But it looks like we will be spending the next twenty-four hours, at least, finding out. It should be interesting."

"I wonder what we should do," she mused.

"I suppose we will, for the next few hours at least, go about our day as usual, with each of us taking the other's place."

"You mean me go to work for you?" she asked, horrified.

"Yes," he replied. "That is exactly what I mean. I cannot just take the entire day off. I promised to be in by midday. Besides, you've stated enough times that you wish you had my life...so this should prove enlightening for you."

"But I don't even know what you do," she protested.

"Interesting," he replied. "I actually know what you do. Does that tell you anything?"

But she was too upset to answer his question. "Don't you think it would be better if I—I mean you—were to beg off sick?"

He sighed and tried to speak calmly. His new voice sounded exceedingly high-pitched and whiny to his ears, but he couldn't seem to help it. "Although I rarely argue with you during your incessant ramblings about how much more difficult and important the things you do are than the things I do, the reality is that I can't just 'beg off sick,' and put things off the way you do. I actually have to be there or forfeit my position. You will just have to make your best effort...watch what the other fellows do."

"I ca…I mean, I don't think this is going to work at all," she said.

"Now listen here," he told her. "If I lose my position we lose everything we have. Remember how what you earn is yours and what I earn is ours? That means it pays for all of this!" He waved his arms around to emphasize "all of this."

"Ah," she said, "there it is. You earn more so your work is more important than mine."

"Look," he said. "Aren't you the least bit curious about what I do all day? Or are you afraid that you won't be able to do it?"

"I can do anything you can do," she insisted.

"Fine," he cut in before she had a chance to say more. "It's settled then. I'll see you tonight." He kissed her as he led her out through the front door, then he promptly slammed the door in her face.

Princess Femina turned back toward the door, fuming. Now what was she supposed to do? If she went back in the house it would be admitting defeat. At length she realized that if she did not go to work in place of her husband today she would never live it down.

The truth was that she actually did know enough about what her husband did each day to know that she did not want to do it. Oh, well, it was only one day, after all. What harm could it do?

Twenty minutes later the princess groaned. The work was physically difficult and monotonous and the conversation was insipid. Her husband's peers spoke solely of methods for constructing thing-things that she merely took for granted as being there. There was nothing to intrigue or stimulate her interest. Her muscles, or her husband's rather, protested in spite of the fact that they were doubtless used to the abuse. She hated every movement and longed to stop but the other workers were already giving her funny looks and one busybody had actually asked if she was sick. She sincerely doubted she would be able to finish out the day. Each motion had to be forced; and she wondered that her husband never complained when he got home. Was it possible that he liked it? No, her mind could not conceive of that. How did he do it then? She remembered suddenly a conversation they had once, when she had used the word impossible.

"Nothing is impossible," he had said. "You're using the word *impossible* when what you mean is undesirable."

She had argued the point then, but was he right? If he could do this, day after day, shouldn't she be able to do it, too, given that she currently possessed the same strength of body? Was it more than superior strength that enabled him to do this arduous work?

She realized that physically she probably could do this work all day. In fact, mentally she could probably do it, too. The truth was that she did not *want* to do it. She didn't like doing it. This realization made her feel better. It wasn't that she *couldn't* do it, it was that she didn't want to. She even went so far as to convince herself that, if she had wanted to do it, she could probably do it better than her husband.

Now that she had settled all this in her mind she needed to figure out a way to get out of working the rest of the day. She mentally ran through her usual list of excuses and realized that none of them would work for her as a man. She could hardly claim, for example, that she was having "feminine problems." Nor would it work, she reasoned, for her to say her child was sick, for it would be expected that her "wife" would manage that. What excuse did a man use to get out of work? She tried to think of the last time her husband had taken the day off and realized that she could not recall a single instance. Her mind could not accept the possibility that this substantiated anything other than her husband must simply love his job. Why else would anyone subject themselves to this day after day?

"I need one of you men to deliver a message to the main office," she heard the foreman call out suddenly.

Princess Femina nearly fell over herself to get the man's attention, throwing down her tools and yelling a bit too loudly perhaps, "I will. I'll do it. Over here. I'll go!" She did not care that everyone was staring at her. She smiled happily at the foreman as she approached him. "I'm your man," she said with a giggle. "Happy to help!" She was so glad not to be laboring anymore that she was giddy.

And so Princess Femina was well on her way to getting through the remainder of her husband's workday.

The prince, meanwhile, had arrived at Princess Femina's office with genuine curiosity. It would be interesting to see how she spent her time there. As he walked into the workplace he was immediately swarmed by three females who grabbed at him excitedly, even as they all spoke at once.

"You will never believe…"

"I can't wait to tell you…"

"Let me tell her…"

"Whoa," he said, putting his hands up in alarm. "What's happened?" His heart stopped for a moment, preparing for the worst.

"He said it," said one of the women solemnly. They all stared in expectant silence at Princess Femina.

The prince stared back at them uncomprehendingly. "Who said what?" he asked, determined to get to the bottom of this seeming emergency.

The women laughed. "Come on, silly," said the one who had spoken before. "I'll give you all the juicy details."

They pulled the prince along with them into a room, where they immediately began fixing coffee and snacks.

"I took your advice to the letter," the woman continued. "And last night, finally, he said the 'L' word!"

"The 'L' word...you don't mean...love?" The prince was aghast.

"Yes!" she continued, not noticing his discomfiture. "It was so romantic. You should have seen how shy he was about it."

"I do not wish to hear this!" the prince interjected. He found the communal sharing of intimacies between these women distasteful. But he was even more disgusted by the way every little sentiment he felt seemed to reflect itself into his voice, causing it to unexpectedly rise into a higher-pitched tone without any warning. It seemed that it couldn't be helped. The thing automatically changed with his moods. And that was another thing; he was beginning to feel as if he were a raging storm of emotions. It was clouding his judgment. Even so, he still had enough of himself left to know that he was not interested in hearing these women speak so frankly about the poor sap who had confessed his love, no doubt believing he was having a private moment. He was glad he didn't know who it was.

"What?" all three women exclaimed in unison, their voices sounding very much like his own had, only a moment ago.

"I think you women are shameless to discuss such a private moment as if it were an anecdote," he told them. "I have too many important assignments waiting for my attention to sit here and listen to this foolishness," he added, having heard his wife mention her "important assignments" enough times to realize she could not possibly have time for these women's nonsense.

The women stared openmouthed as Princess Femina left the room in a huff. When she had gone they turned to each other. Could it be that time of the month again already?

The prince shook his head and went into Princess Femina's work room. He immediately noticed the pictures of him and their children strewn about and smiled. He would try to accomplish as much as possible for his wife today, so that she might have it easier when she returned. He reached into her assignment box and pulled out the top page. He had to read it twice to believe it. Suddenly the strange emotions that had been building within him throughout the morning exploded. How dare they? He could clearly see why his wife complained.

He marched down the hallway to the office of Princess Femina's employer.

"A word," he said as he stepped inside and sat down.

"Of course, Femina," said her employer. "Anything for you. How are the children?"

The prince waived his hand, causing the eyebrows of the man he addressed to rise in surprise as he said, "They're fine. Listen, I want to talk to you about this assignment."

"Oh, you do not have to run any ideas by me," he said. "I trust you completely."

"A monkey could be trusted with this assignment," replied the prince. "Surely you have something better than this."

"I disagree," said the man with a tight smile. "This assignment is extremely important to us." The employer looked away as he said this and for the first time in his life the prince understood the frustration of being condescended to. He actually felt the same outrage he had heard his wife express so often.

"Look," said the prince, meeting the employer's eyes. "I can't presume to know what your position is—I don't. But I give you my

word that if you let me have a chance with something more important you will not be disappointed."

Princess Femina's employer looked away again and sighed. He was
obviously uncomfortable. "We have had this discussion before," he said
slowly. He seemed increasingly nervous. "I'm trying the best that I can
here to be fair, but I am the one who is liable for assignments that are
not completed."

"Of course," said the prince. "And I give you my word that I will
not let you down if you will just give me the opportunity."

The employer looked skeptical. He seemed a nice enough fellow.
"All right," he said after a long moment. He shuffled through a large
pile of papers and pulled a page out from among them. "Have a look
at this assignment and see if it appeals to you."

"Thank you," said the prince, pleased.

"I have never doubted your ability, Femina," said her employer.

The prince took the new assignment into his wife's workroom.
Upon review he noted with satisfaction that it was much more interesting and challenging than the previous one. Princess Femina would
be pleased. He had managed in a matter of hours to accomplish what
she had not been able to do in months. Perhaps this would show her
that the opportunity was truly there if only she would commit to it
and apply herself more fully. Didn't her employer himself hint at the
very same thing?

With this in mind the prince resolved to tackle Princess
Femina's assignment with the full extent of his abilities. He had
suddenly replaced his desire to please his wife with the even
stronger desire to put the little complainer in her place. He hoped
that by succeeding so fabulously where she had failed he would be
able to quiet her continual rumblings of how unfair life was. In

short time, he was fully absorbed in "her" assignment, and he felt certain he would in one day make a name for her forever in her career. But ere long, there came an interruption from one of the women who had accosted him moments before. She approached him coolly, apparently still grudging his behavior toward her news. It was for his wife's own good he reminded himself; this woman could only drag her down.

"You have a visitor," she said haughtily.

"Who is it?" the prince asked, but she had left as quickly as she had come. With a sigh of annoyance—he did not like being interrupted when he was just getting into his project—he followed the woman out of the workroom. She led him to a room where he saw his youngest child with her governess.

"What is it?" he said in alarm.

"It's another attack of the lungs," said the governess.

"Yes…?" he prompted.

"So I will see you tomorrow and we will try again," she concluded, preparing to leave.

"Hold it," said the prince. "You can't just leave. You've got to take her with you."

"I thought I made it quite clear that you must manage on your own when your child is ill," said the governess firmly. "I cannot be expected to risk my own health."

"Of course not," the prince agreed. "But I don't believe this is catching." He knew his daughter had a minor ailment that plagued her lungs but he was fairly certain that it posed no real danger to her or those around her.

"Nevertheless, my policies must be strictly adhered to," said the governess. "I do not see why we must have this discussion every week."

"Every week?" repeated the prince. "We have this discussion every week?"

"Your daughter has these flare-ups quite often, as you know. It seems we end up having this conversation each and every time."

"I see," said the prince. He looked at his little daughter then and his heart leapt at the sight of her, listening quietly to their conversation. She had never looked so adorable before. He had the urge to squeeze her very hard. He knew that he was seeing her through his wife's eyes and with her emotions. The feelings he experienced were staggering. "Thank you," he said to the governess. "You may go."

He took his little girl by the hand and led her to his wife's workroom. "Well," he sighed. "It looks like you're stuck with me today."

"We aren't going to stay here?" asked his daughter. "You promised you wouldn't make me stay here anymore."

"Just sit still for a little while," he told her, giving in to his urge to kiss her at last. He held her for a moment. He was suddenly filled with a horrible feeling of shame and remorse and he abruptly released his daughter. What was the matter? He examined his daughter's face. It revealed the usual combination of guileless innocence and sharp curiosity. There was nothing in her expression that condemned him, and yet…there was a lingering culpability that shrouded over him. Thinking about making his sick little girl stay here while he worked made the feeling more intense. But when he thought about going to Femina's employer to try and explain why he could not complete the assignment he was filled with even more dread. What was he to do?

"You know you're not supposed to have her in here," he heard from the doorway. It was the dreaded female again. She seemed a little more sympathetic now however.

The prince wondered what Princess Femina did when this happened. Perhaps this woman would know. He decided to take a chance. "I'm not sure what to do," he admitted. "I specifically asked for this assignment and now I have no choice but to finish it."

"I thought you had finally given up on all that," the woman said. "What possessed you to put yourself through this again, knowing what would happen?"

"This has happened before?" he asked.

She laughed and shook her head. "Some people never learn."

"I don't want to cause her to lose her job," he said.

"What?"

"I mean me. I don't me to lose my job."

"What's gotten into you?" asked her friend. "You know that can't happen. Our positions are protected here, being women." The prince stared at her in shock. He was beginning to feel sick from the strange and unwelcome desire to cry. How foolish he had been. But in fact, hadn't it all been just a little too easy?

"Anyway," continued the woman. "He probably knew this would happen and had someone backing you up, just in case."

The prince nodded, not trusting himself to speak. He looked at the assignment he had begun. It was just the kind of thing his wife would have loved. Just the scraps of information he had gathered about her work from her ramblings had been enough for him to have done very well with the assignment. She could have done it in her sleep. But alas, another, more important duty called. He glanced at his daughter. She was looking at him to see what he would say. He suddenly felt ashamed to be discussing this in front of her. He knew that Princess Femina would not have allowed her daughter to feel bad in this circumstance. He was suddenly filled with love and compassion for them both.

"Stay here for just one more minute," he told his daughter and he made his way back to the office of his wife's employer. He stood in the doorway instead of entering this time.

"Problem?" the employer asked, kindly enough, given the circumstances.

"I, uh…my daughter seems to be feeling a bit under the weather," he said sheepishly. He felt profoundly humiliated and subjugated. Yet surely taking care of one's sick child was not something that should be a cause for disgrace.

"I see," said the employer. "I understand, and hope your daughter is feeling better very soon." The words were spoken kindly enough, so why did they sound so judgmental?

"I'm sorry," the prince continued. "I really was starting to enjoy the assignment. Perhaps whoever takes over would like to use some of my notes…."

"That won't be necessary," the employer replied. "But thank you." And the prince realized he was dismissed. His face burned as he left.

"Come with me," he said to his daughter, and they left the building. He was profoundly happy to be out of there. He mused that to try and build a career while raising children was just setting oneself up for failure. With a shock he realized that that was precisely what his wife always said.

"We are going to play a game," he told his daughter, putting the miserable experience behind him. "You are going to pretend that I am the sick child and you are the mother."

His daughter giggled. "Why are we going to do that?" she asked.

He could hardly explain to her that it was because he hadn't the faintest idea of what her mother did with her while she was sick, so he said, "Because it will be fun." And as it turned out this was a sufficient explanation for a small child.

"Okay," she agreed easily.

And so the prince spent the rest of the day learning how to care for a sick little girl.

At about this time Princess Femina was arriving at the destination of her errand for the foreman. She entered a tidy office where she was greeted by a woman with a pinched face. The woman looked at her as if to say, "What now?"

"I have a message for you," Princess Femina explained, handing the woman the missive and then plopping down into a nearby chair. Perhaps she could strike up a conversation with the woman, and thereby delay her return to the work site. She watched as the woman read the message.

"Great," said the woman with annoyance.

"Bad news?" Princess Femina asked her.

The woman looked up with annoyance. "I hardly think it is any concern of yours," she said snappishly.

Princess Femina was instantly offended. "Well!" she exclaimed. "There is no need to be such a bitch about it. I was just trying to be friendly."

The woman glared at her.

As unpleasant as the woman was, Princess Femina loathed the thought of going back to the wretched work site. Still, it was terribly discomforting to be stared at with such open disdain. At length Princess Femina got up and left the woman alone.

Several hours later, just when Princess Femina thought the day could not get more unpleasant there arrived to the work site a man she recognized as her husband's employer. And he was heading straight for her.

"What did you say to Ms. Hardgrave?" he asked without preamble.

"Who?" replied Princess Femina.

"My secretary," said the employer.

"I hardly said a word to her," replied Princess Femina. "She was so unpleasant I was obliged to leave there as quickly as possible."

"Well, she has filed a complaint against you and the company," said the employer. "And she has left the office, claiming abuse and harassment."

"What?" exclaimed Princess Femina. "Why that——!" She tried to pull down the sense of rage and injustice that was rising within her, and added more calmly, "She was rude and unprofessional and I told her so. That is all."

"I know that Ms. Hardgrave can be extremely difficult to work with," said her husband's employer. "But need I remind you that since the king's decrees about women's rights, as encouraged by his daughters and your own wife in particular, we are obliged do as they wish and pretend that everything is fine."

"I don't believe that!" she said, even more outraged than before. It was as shocking as if he had told her that she had two heads. Was that really how the men of the kingdom viewed women? Was all of their deference merely pretended, in an effort to patronize them as if they were spoiled children?

"Enough with the jokes," said the prince's employer. "You more than anybody else know how to keep your opinions to yourself, being married as you are, so why in god's name would you have said such a thing to Ms. Hardgrave?"

Nancy Madore

"I said it because it was the truth," raged Princess Femina. "And I will smash that bitch in two if she does not admit it."

The prince's employer stared at him in horror. "Are you ill?" he asked. "Perhaps you have gone mad?"

Princess Femina felt sick. "I must speak to the king," she said.

It was very late when Princess Femina finally arrived home, thanking heaven her father, the king, had been able to clear up the horrible mess with Ms. Hardgrave. It had been difficult convincing her father that it was really her in her husband's body, and even more difficult to explain the encounter with Ms. Hardgrave. What would have happened to her—or her husband rather—if she had not been the king's daughter? She was so tired and hungry…she had never before felt so hungry…and she dropped herself down on her favorite lounge chair. Her eyes drooped as she dozed off to sleep.

"You're here," she heard her own voice say.

"Mmm," she murmured.

"I don't suppose you remembered that it was your turn to provide dinner?"

She wondered suddenly how it was possible that he had not strangled her. She felt him collapse next to her on the divan. She looked up to see her own face staring exhaustedly back at hers. She laughed. "You, too?" she asked.

"Let's just say I got a new perspective on things today," he told her.

"Me, too," she admitted.

But neither one elaborated.

"I'm starving and I did not even think to bring dinner," she admitted.

"I figured you would be tired and hungry so I made dinner. I was only teasing you a minute ago."

"Really?" she asked.

"Well, as it turned out I spent the day at home nursing the little one, so…"

"Is she in bed?"

"Yes."

Princess Femina stared at her own face, searching for her husband somewhere in the expression. She wondered if she would have made dinner for him had she been inside her body today. It was amazing how satisfying it was to be treated with kindness after such a trying day.

"Thank you," she said, meaning it.

He smiled. How nice it was to be appreciated! His day had been difficult and emotionally exhausting but he realized this was what made it all worthwhile. He wondered if he had ever remembered to thank his wife for all the times she had pulled herself away from her daily interests to care for their child and provide him with a warm inviting home and a delicious dinner. Perhaps she would not feel the need to point these things out so often if he would show a little appreciation.

Pulling herself up with difficulty, Princess Femina went into the kitchen and ate like a horse. It was incredible to be able to eat without a thought to her weight. She spied her husband eating with equal relish and raised her eyebrows.

"You are not planning to eat all that, are you?" she asked him.

He laughed, and then forced a serious face. Imitating her as well as he was able, he said with mock severity, "Just what are you implying?"

She laughed. "I am not insulting you…or me…I'm merely trying to keep from becoming a blimp."

"You could never be that," he told her.

"Yes, well, that is nice of you, but if you eat all that I will leave you in my body until *you* lose the weight."

"Okay, okay," he agreed, pushing away the plate. He could not live with that for all the food in the kingdom. "You know," he said after a moment, "it must really be awful to have to watch everything you eat."

"Well, women generally gain weight faster than men for some reason," she told him. She forgot to add that in his case it might be that he was burning more calories, too.

She ate to her satisfaction and then pushed her plate away.

"I'm going to bed," she announced.

"Me, too," said the prince.

She went to their bedroom and took off her clothes with her husband following the same routine behind her. She looked up suddenly and caught sight of her former body, fully stripped. She suddenly felt a dizzying surge as she became almost immediately aroused. The feeling was overpowering. "Oh, my!" she exclaimed.

The prince looked up and noticed her predicament. But to his surprise, there was no immediate surge of anything happening in the body he inhabited. There were some confusing emotions and very mild sensations, but other than that he might have been dead below the waist. In spite of this, he was curious.

"We'll never get another chance to see how it feels from the other side," he told her.

"I agree," she said. She, too, was curious, but more than that the body she possessed was taking over everything, forcing her to move toward the naked body that stood before her.

They went to the bed. The prince lay down and she heard him laugh nervously. "I'm not sure I'm operating this body correctly," he admitted. "Is there a button you push or something?"

But the princess was too preoccupied to explain anything to him about how her body worked. She could feel the blood rushing into her lower body and she suddenly found that she cared very little about anything else. She mounted her former body and thrust herself instinctively inside; once, twice and the third time she cried out as a searing rush of heat surged through her and she felt the hot liquid shoot through the shaft. "Oh, my god," she said.

"What the——!" she heard her husband gasp. "Well, my dear, I do think you've made a new record for me."

"I couldn't help it," she said, trying to recover. Now she wanted to sleep.

"Uh, actually, you *can* help it," he corrected her. "But now if you would be so kind as to tell me how this body works so I can have some enjoyment, too."

She groaned. It was only fair, she supposed. She leaned up on one elbow. "Open your legs," she told him. He obeyed and at last he felt some twinges of excitement. They were infinitely more subtle than what he was used to, though. It suddenly occurred to him that these sensations would need to be encouraged and stroked so they could build into something larger, unlike his own arousal, which came on like an eruption that needed to be contained.

Princess Femina settled between her husband's open legs and stared with new perspective at her private area. How lovely it appeared to male eyes! It reminded her of an exotic flower, whose scented blossoms curled forth to entice its prey in closer, tempting him to delve between the delicate petals for the promise of nectar. She stared at it for several moments, causing the prince to feel more twinges of excitement and a meandering yearning for more. The sight of his wife from within his eyes, staring at her own body with such desire, conjured thoughts of fancy that sent waves of pleasure and anticipation through him.

The princess suddenly moved out of her stupor to tentatively place her tongue on the soft pink flesh that was so very familiar and unfamiliar all at the same time. The smell of her was earthy and sweet, and the taste was imperceptible. Overall, her first impression was that the experience was much like a kiss. The fleshy pink slit reminded her of lips, soft and moist, and the flavor and feel was not dissimilar to the inside of a mouth. She could faintly taste the flavor of her husband, and she recalled with a start that it had been her who had put him there. But alas, she knew her body well, and after a moment or two of getting used to it from this vantage point, she immediately wriggled her tongue up above the slit to where the little pleasure bump resided. She flicked over it expertly with her tongue.

"Hell!" exclaimed her husband in surprise. She did not allow him time to recover, assailing him instead with a steady onslaught of flicks from her tongue, in just the manner that she knew her body liked best. She was well aware that her woman's body would need continuous stimulation in order to reach satisfaction, so she set out to provide just that. She could feel the body she inhabited becoming aroused again, seemingly of its own accord, and she marveled at the ease with which it functioned. She tried to remain focused on her husband though, hoping to give him the opportunity to see what this experience felt like for a woman.

"It's as if you've done this before," he murmured.

She realized that this idea probably excited him, and she knew from her own experience that a little bit of fantasy went a long way in helping a woman achieve satisfaction so, in order to help him along, she asked in between licks, "Would you like to see my face buried between a woman's legs like this?"

"Yes," he admitted.

"Licking another woman like this?" she asked, twirling her tongue masterfully up and around the pleasure area.

"Yes," he moaned again, breathing heavily.

"And touching her like this?" she asked, slipping a finger inside as she continued to massage the pleasure spot with the tip of her tongue. He was very close, she knew, but if he lost concentration it could all vanish. Impatience came over her for him to hurry it up and she suddenly realized how odd women must seem to men. Men probably thought women were just being difficult, intentionally prolonging the experience in order to gain control or extra attention when, in fact, they had to work very hard to achieve satisfaction. On the contrary, men seemed to have to work to keep from reaching it. How strange it all was!

"Yes," her husband was saying. "Yes, yes."

She worked her tongue vigorously and slipped another finger in. She marveled at how soft the inside of her body felt to a man's finger. "It might be your tongue I'm using," she told him, "but it is me doing the licking."

"Yes," he moaned.

"It's me doing the fingering," she added. She used her lips and tongue as she spoke to keep up the steady prodding.

"Yes."

"It's me who is giving your woman's body pleasure." She continued in earnest, stimulating her husband's mind, as well as the body he inhabited. Finally she felt the telltale shudder and she smiled with satisfaction. Now that her task was done she wanted once again to feel that exquisite release from her husband's body. No wonder men wanted sex all the time when it all happened so easily!

She rose up and slipped inside her woman's body once more. This time it felt infinitely better, softer and readier, and she even got a few more than three strokes in before her man's body erupted in delightful pleasure.

"I can't believe how easy it is for you," she murmured after.

"I can't believe how hard it is for you," he admitted.

She wanted to sleep. "Mmm."

But he, for reasons he could not fathom, needed something more. He snuggled up against her, wanting to talk or to touch. "Honey…" he grumbled.

"What?" she said with exasperation.

"I just thought we could snuggle," he said.

"Snuggle?" she asked. Suddenly she sat bolt upright in bed.

"What is it?" he asked.

But she was laughing. "Of course you want to snuggle," she laughed. "You want to talk, and cuddle and be close, correct?"

"Well…would that be so bad?"

"Yes, actually," she said. "I'm tired. But seriously, is this how it always feels afterward? I have no desire whatsoever to even kiss you now."

This time he laughed. "That does sound about right."

"But we often cuddle together after sex," she objected.

"Well, yes," he agreed.

"Do you hate it?" she asked him, mortified.

"No!"

"But you obviously don't need it," she said.

He could not lie; she was literally feeling what he felt. "I don't need it as you need it," he amended.

"Then why do you do it?" she asked.

"To please you," he explained.

"Oh, god," she moaned.

"No, wait. Hear me out," he said. "A man needs to be needed. That fulfills his needs. When you need me to hold you, for example, my doing so serves a need in me to please and comfort you. A man wants to believe he is solving problems. Do you see?"

"Sort of," she said. "But why don't you need it?"

"I don't know that, but I do know that it has nothing to do with my love for you."

"You know," she said, musing, "I think this was the best thing that the wizardess could have done for us."

"I agree," he said.

"I'm not going to take advantage of you anymore," she promised.

"I'm not going to take advantage of you, either," he said.

"Even though the sex is easier I don't want to be a man," she said emphatically.

"I don't want to be a woman."

"Well, if you'll be quiet and let us get some sleep, morning will come faster."

They both laughed before drifting off to sleep.

And needless to say, Princess Femina and her husband faced the rest of their lives together with a new awareness of the other, ending not only the saga of the worn shoes for the princess but also the discontent she had felt about being a woman, wife and mother.

PRINCESS HYGENIA

PRINCESS HYGENIA SWALLOWED THE LAST BITE OF HER LUNCH AND immediately got up to start collecting the dirty dishes into an organized pile.

"That was delicious," her husband said, rising from the table and taking her into his arms. He leaned closer to kiss her.

"I'm glad you enjoyed it," she replied, turning her head quickly away to prevent his lips touching hers. "We had better get this mess cleared away before the wizardess comes," she added to explain her avoidance of his kiss. It seemed that she was always looking for reasons to evade his caresses, even when she craved them. It was all so horribly awkward. And yet, how could she help it? He had just eaten a hearty lunch and the thought of tasting it, second-hand, from his lips nauseated her. But it was always the same, no matter what time of day; there was something she could detect on him that repelled her senses and made it impossible for her to enjoy the taste of him. In fact, she had never tasted *him* at all; for it seemed to her that he carried with him, at all times, a hint of something else, something musty or, even when he cleansed his teeth—which he did hurriedly and without any real purpose—there still lingered that certain staleness, only now it was mixed with the horrible taste of tooth cleanser. That was almost worse than if he had not bothered at all.

It was the same with other matters. She knew how he longed for her to kiss him in more intimate places, but it was extremely difficult and unpleasant for her to do so after he had performed his normal bodily functions all day without being cleansed. She wondered why he would shower every morning before going to work, and yet not bother to shower in the evening before coming to bed. Surely no one in his workplace would be nearly as intimate with him as she, and yet he did not seem concerned at all about how he presented himself to her. And even on the rare occasions when he did shower before coming to her—she was very excited when this first happened—she was later dismayed to find that he had not rinsed properly, so having him in her mouth was like sucking on a bar of soap. She barely got through the experience without gagging.

In the long run it had become easier to simply find excuses to avoid all intimacies involving her senses of smell and taste. When her husband made love to her, she turned her face away from his, or chose a position where she was not facing him at all. And she simply stopped pleasing him with her mouth.

Princess Hygenia compensated for this lack of control over her husband's personal hygiene by keeping the environment around her as sterile as possible.

The prince was merely confused by all of these manifestations in his wife, and assumed his wife was reserved.

Princess Hygenia mused over these discomfiting matters as she scrubbed the dirty dishes. Her husband knew better than to help her; for she was quite fastidious about things and would more than likely find fault with his efforts.

It was during this time that the wizardess arrived at their door. The prince went to greet her while his wife hurried to finish the dishes.

The wizardess observed the prince's laid-back demeanor and slightly unkempt appearance as he led her through their home into the kitchen. She noticed that he seemed somewhat out of place in the spotlessly clean environment.

Now Harmonia approved of a tidy home, but here she detected disorderliness in the extreme order, which indicated frustration in other matters. Princess Hygenia greeted her warmly, clasping her hand firmly, but there was sorrow in her eyes. The wizardess noticed that her hands were red and quite warm from the piping hot dishwater. And the princess was as tidy as her home. As the wizardess observed the setting all around her, she realized suddenly that the prince stood out like a sore thumb. And that, of course, was what causing the princess so much distress.

"It smells wonderful in here," the wizardess remarked. "What is that smell?"

"Oh, that," replied the princess. "It is a scented candle that I just love. It takes the other odors out of the air."

"You are quite sensitive to smells, I suppose?" questioned the wizardess.

"Oh, yes," sighed the princess. "Quite!"

"I think I have something here that will work wonders for you in that case," said the wizardess. She sifted through her bag and retrieved from it a little black bottle and a double-ended brush. "This bottle contains magic bubbles," she continued, turning to the prince and handing him the items. "Listen very closely. The bubbles will activate the most appealing scents from within you, making you irresistible to your wife. It is all natural and quite healthful to use. You may use the bubbles to wash any part of you that you wish to make desirable to Princess Hygenia."

The prince and princess both blushed. "And the brush?" asked the prince.

"That is for inside your mouth," she replied. "See, this side is to brush your teeth with, and the other side is for your tongue."

"My tongue?" asked the prince.

"Oh, yes," replied the wizardess. "You do want your tongue to be irresistible to the princess, too, don't you?"

"Yes, of course!" said the prince. He had never before even thought of such a thing.

"Well, then," continued the wizardess. "Use the brush and the magic bubbles on your tongue, too. Oh, and one more thing. Be sure to rinse very well when using the liquid, as it will not be good for Princess Hygenia or you to actually ingest any of it." So saying, the wizardess picked up her bag and went on her way.

"Good luck!" she called out with a little giggle.

The prince and princess looked at each other. The princess was doubtful. She was not sure that her husband simply using some good-smelling bubbles was going to help the situation but she was certainly hopeful. To her surprise, he said, "I think I'll try this brush right now!"

She waited anxiously to see the result.

"Okay," the prince said when he returned. "Let's see if the wizardess's magic potion has made me irresistible to my wife." He said this jokingly as he whisked her into his arms and swept her backward so that she would have fallen over if he had not held her so securely. She laughed at the romantic gesture, causing her to take a quick intake of breath as his lips approached hers. For the first time in her memory, there was no odor at all that she could detect in his breath, except the very mild smell of his flesh. She inhaled the pleasing aroma and it sent her senses reeling. This is what she had been craving.

For once it was her prince, and only her prince, that she kissed. There was not a single thing to distract her from the intimate moment when his mouth took hers. His lips brushed ever so lightly over hers for a moment, teasing her, before his tongue slipped out to taste the sweetness of her mouth. She inhaled his breath, warm and sweet and pleasant as it lingered over her lips and nostrils, adding a heady influence that weakened her at the knees. Her tongue, almost of its own accord, crept out to meet his, licking at him tentatively at first, but then curling around his tongue in an intimate dance. At her response his arms tightened around her and his kiss became more demanding. This was exactly how she had always dreamed a kiss would be. The prince kissed her fervently and greedily, one moment taking her mouth in an all-consuming embrace and the next moment pressing loving taps over her lips and face and neck. Her skin felt seared where he touched her. The clean smell of his skin and breath and even his saliva was absorbed by her skin and nostrils and tongue with relish. Her fingers dug into his flesh as she clung to him, and a low moan escaped from deep within her.

The prince pulled away from his wife and looked down into her face. He studied her for a moment as she stared back at him wide-eyed. He had never seen her so aroused and receptive to him. She merely continued to cling to him, trembling. He considered taking her right then and there. But in the next instant he pulled her up and helped steady her. "I must go for now," he told her. "But I will finish what we have started here later this evening."

She was disappointed. She wanted the prince more at that moment than she had ever wanted him before. When he left a minute later she wondered dazedly, *Could the bubbles the wizardess gave him truly possess magic powers?* She had detected no scent at all—nothing but her husband's own freshly cleansed flesh.

The princess pondered this throughout her day, unable to think of anything but the way her husband had kissed her and how wonderful it had felt. She walked around in a kind of aroused stupor, anticipating how it would be with her husband later that night. As the day grew older she prepared herself for his return as if it were their first night together, grooming her body to perfection so that he, too, would find her pleasing to his senses. These preparations made her anticipation all the more intense. She reminisced about the eve of their wedding, recalling her keen disappointment when he had come to her after a long night of eating, drinking and being merry, effectively burying the pleasures of the marital bed under an onslaught of odors and tastes that assailed her senses.

When at last the prince arrived home that evening the princess was far past being ready for him, but of course she was determined to hold out a little longer in order that he could bathe in the magic bubbles.

The prince, too, had been anticipating this evening with his wife. The wizardess's words, instructing him to "use the liquid to wash any part of you that you wish to make irresistible" kept repeating themselves in his brain. He lathered the liquid generously between his legs, fully covering every inch of flesh throughout the area. He imagined his wife's lips in the places he washed and his body hardened at the thought. He rinsed the bubbles away thoroughly and repeatedly, for he did not want his wife to become unwell from the taste of them.

Next the prince used the two-sided brush with the magic bubbles, thoroughly scrubbing his teeth, gums and tongue. His mouth felt tingling clean when he finished and he liked the feeling.

When at last husband and wife faced each other, unclothed, they were both fully groomed for the other's enjoyment. Their grooming activities had the added effect of giving them time to anticipate the other's response to their efforts, and so each approached the other desiring, as well as desirable. This was, then, half the battle won already.

Now that they stood before each other, the prince and princess paused for a moment to appreciate the other's appearance. The prince noticed his wife's shimmering smooth legs topped by her delicately trimmed curls. His body surged forward, growing painfully hard at the sight of her. The princess noticed his response and could actually smell his desire, pure and achingly potent. The scent drew her toward him, even as she felt the moisture growing between her legs. She wanted to put her lips and tongue all over him.

As she approached her husband, Princess Hygenia's face opened and lifted to him. His arms came around her as his mouth hungrily captured hers. Their tongues fused together, caressing and tasting each other's flesh and breathing each other's breath. Princess Hygenia was dizzied by the intoxicating aroma of her husband—or was it the magic bubbles? She could not say. She pressed herself against him, wanting more.

Without breaking the kiss, the prince lifted Princess Hygenia into his arms and carried her over to the bed. He laid her down and hovered over her, careful not to lean his full weight on her. He continued to kiss her, delighting in the way she was responding to him. She had never accepted his kisses with such eagerness before. She seemed to be sucking him farther into her mouth with her lips and tongue as if she could not get enough of him. If it was the wizardess's magic bubbles that caused this change in her he could not wait to see how she responded to the other parts of his body where he had also washed with them.

It was as if Princess Hygenia read his mind, for she pushed her hands against his chest suddenly, compelling him to lie on his back on the bed. As he rolled over she turned with him, so that now it was she who was lying on top of him.

The princess continued to kiss her husband, moving over his face and lower, spreading kisses over his cheeks, neck and shoulders. He closed his eyes and allowed her to have control as she explored his body with her mouth.

Princess Hygenia was lost in the pure masculine scent of her husband. She pressed her lips over his skin feverishly, breathing deeply as she traveled the length of his body. His aroma acted as an aphrodisiac, opening all her senses wide to him. Her tongue darted out to lick at his nipples and navel. As if she were under the influence of a drug, she fervently moved her lips over him, kissing and licking him all the way down the length of his body until she reached his deliciously hard shaft. She had no qualms whatsoever about putting him in her mouth now, but even so she delayed the moment of tasting him, to rub her face and cheek lovingly over and around the area, inhaling the fresh and heady fragrance of his arousal. She found that she adored the way his testicles felt and buried her face shamelessly in their softness. She felt dizzy with lust and suddenly she was sucking lovingly on the tender lobes, moaning softly.

The prince nearly flew off the bed. He had never in his wildest dreams expected the magic bubbles to have this effect. His wife's reaction took him completely by surprise. He had known that she was sensitive to smells, for he had seen her become excited by a fragrant flower, or utterly repulsed by day-old garbage. But the magic bubbles seemed to have caused her to lose control of her senses. She appeared to be on the verge of swooning, she was so taken by his scent. And her response was bringing him near the edge of swooning, as well.

The princess continued her suckling, completely unaware of the effect she was having on her husband. All she knew was that the real, genuine smell of her husband—the smell that drove her wild—was strongest here where his manhood was the most potent. She breathed deeply as she sucked on him.

The prince could stand no more. He must at least reciprocate so as give him something else to think about besides what she was doing, or else he would likely shame himself with a complete lack of control. He sat up and looked at the princess. She was still sucking hungrily between his legs, unaware of his plight. He picked up her legs carefully in each of his hands and pulled her lower body upward, until his face was level with her hips. Now he had something worthwhile to keep him busy!

Although Princess Hygenia had not used the magic bubbles, she was fastidious about her own personal care, and the prince loved nothing more than the smell and taste of her. He had never experienced one incident with her where he was given any little unwanted reminders of the other functions this part of her body performed—reminders that might have inhibited his enjoyment of her to some degree. Now, as he opened her legs wide to bury his face in between, he was doubly pleased by the look, as well as the smell and taste of her. Her hair was trimmed perfectly so that the area he liked best to taste—and indeed, the area she liked best to be tasted—could be enjoyed without a single distraction. He dipped his tongue into her moist slit and groaned loudly at the pleasure it gave him. The skin around it felt like silk without the coarse little hairs covering it. His tongue circled round and round, wanting to feel it again and again.

The princess suddenly came out of her dream. Her body felt so much more sensitive without the extra hair. His tongue was devouring her while the heat of his breath was scorching her. The pleasure was so intense that it made her body ache. She loved what he was doing but needed the relief she could only get from being rubbed in one place in particular. She was so aroused that she forgot her inhibitions and took his head in her hands as she adjusted her hips over his face just so, so that his tongue was touching that place. With a half laugh, half growl, her husband got her message immediately, and took up a slow, firm circling of the tender little bud of flesh that was trembling with need.

The princess opened her mouth wide now and at last slipped her lips over her husband's hardness, taking him all the way into her mouth until she could feel him against her throat. She heard his moan with a little thrill of delight as she circled her tongue round and round, simultaneously bobbing her head up and down, up and down over the length of him; not too fast, but at the speed she saw from his reactions that he liked best. Meanwhile she continued to move her hips over his mouth, guiding him as he pleasured her.

As the prince worked his magic with his tongue he grasped his wife's hips, fiercely enough to send thrills through her but not so much so as to prevent her ability to keep moving them over his mouth. He wanted to give her pleasure, not keep it from her. He dug his fingers into her flesh to let her know how much she was pleasing him.

The feeling of her husband's fingers pressing into her fleshy hips sent the princess over the edge. She loved displays of passion, especially when they had their origin in violence. The violent eruptions felt to her like evidence of strong desire, while a constrained control of them she knew stemmed from love. This combination of violent passion and loving control left her feeling well and truly cherished.

Her mind registered all of this without really even thinking of it, so that all she was really consciously aware of was that her husband's hands were holding her with enough force to remind her that he was a strong man who was fighting to control his passion for her at that moment. This ignited her own passion and she went suddenly still as waves of pleasure rushed over her. Before she could grasp hold of them they were gone.

The prince released her hips and pulled her beneath him. His passion was now at his highest and she reveled in his strength. She opened herself happily to him, embracing him with eagerness, and with every part of her being.

The princess had always imagined and longed for a mating where kissing was the most intimate part of the taking. She had built the kiss into every fantasy ever since she was a little child, hardly aware of intimacies other than the kiss. The kiss of her dreams would last throughout the lovemaking; really it would be one very long kiss, that at some moments would brush over her lips in a tender, warm breath and at other moments would savagely plunder her mouth and shatter her senses. Perhaps these dreams promising the magic of such an intimate kiss were part of her profound disappointment when she had first discovered that she did not enjoy her husband's kisses.

Now, as she opened herself to her husband, this time taking him with her mouth, as well as her body, she finally realized her dream. The kiss was all she had ever hoped for and much more. In her dreams she could never quite capture the feeling; here in reality it assailed her senses. This night her husband kissed her in exactly the way she had imagined her true lover would, with a passion that bordered on violence. Then, in intervals, he would hover over her lips for a moment, singeing her tender skin with his heated breath until his lips dipped lower to take her all over again. While he kissed her he thrust himself in and out of her violently, yet still short of hurting her. She clung to him with renewed desire. Her passion was satiated but something else within her, something entirely new, was being awakened. How strange, she thought, that it should take magic bubbles to bring about his newfound intimacy.

When at last the prince thrust himself into his wife for the final time, shuddering, she, too, shuddered with an emotion that she could not identify. Nothing had been different for the prince except his wife's response, but that had made everything different. He felt he had gotten closer to her than he had ever been capable of getting before. And all because of a little bottle of magic bubbles!

The next morning the couple awoke to find that for the first day since they were married the princess's shoes were not worn out in the least. The prince used the magic bubbles each and every evening and, in fact, discovered that he enjoyed the clean fresh feeling that he got from them. But more than anything else he enjoyed his wife's response to him after he washed with them. The new intimacy that had started to develop continued to grow stronger. And the princess discovered that she did not feel the same need to scrub and scour her house all hours of the day. They both marveled again and again that a small bottle of magic bubbles could have accomplished so much.

But ere long, the prince came near the bottom of his bottle of magic bubbles. He was suddenly alarmed. He could not go back to the way things were with his wife. He simply must have more bubbles! All of this came to the prince's attention on the very night of a rather important dinner feast at the castle of the king. The prince would simply have to approach the wizardess at the feast, and get her to supply him with more bubbles.

That evening, when the opportunity arose, the prince approached the wizardess sheepishly. "I'm afraid I'm nearly out of the magic bubbles you gave me," he said with a self-conscious grin.

She leaned closer to him in order to whisper in his ear. "Any good soap will work as well."

He was stunned. "Do you mean to say——?"

"What I mean to say is that the magic you are looking for is already within you. You merely need to clean everything else away more thoroughly so your wife can find it."

What a revelation this was for the prince! But of course it made perfect sense. His wife was fastidious in all matters and quite sensitive to unpleasant odors. He had been careless and inconsiderate of her feelings. But how could she not have told him?

He went to where his wife stood at the festivities to immediately communicate his displeasure with her over the matter. From now on, he swore, he would know sooner—and from her—when she was unhappy with him.

He grasped her arm gently but firmly as he politely—from all outward appearances—led her onto the dance floor. Only she could tell by the pressure of his fingers that he was not taking her away merely to dance. She could tell he was angry and was immediately concerned. He took her in his arms, holding her very close on the dance floor and causing her heart to beat more quickly in spite of her apprehension. She looked up at him.

"Why didn't you tell me that you were not happy with me before the wizardess gave me the bubbles?" he asked her.

She stared up at him. It all seemed so long ago now, like nothing more than a bad dream. "I suppose I was embarrassed," she replied finally.

"Why should you have been embarrassed?" he asked her. "It is I who was the unwitting fool!"

"Oh," she said, dismayed. "I am truly sorry."

He held her more tightly. "If we are going to be happy together you will have to be honest with me," he said. "I must know if there is something bothering you. Especially something that can be so easily remedied." He sighed in exasperation.

"How do you mean?" she asked him.

"I mean the bubbles are not magic at all," he told her.

She stared at him in shock. Then she smiled. "I knew it," she said.

"You knew I was an awkward dolt, do you mean?"

"No," she laughed now. "I knew it was you that I loved, not the bubbles. I knew it was *you!*"

He continued to look at her, confused.

"That smell that drives me wild," she explained. "It worried me a little to think that it might be magic that caused my sudden response to you. Remember, it started when you used the magic bubbles?" She laughed again, and he smiled, too, getting the point at last. "Now I know that what I am really attracted to is the natural, clean smell of you."

"Well, since you put it that way I will forgive this time," he said. "But the next time something is bothering you, you had better tell me right away, agreed?"

"Agreed!"

And with the problem so well resolved, and future problems so neatly foiled by their new agreement, there was nothing more but for the prince and princess to wear out their shoes on the dance floor.

PRINCESS ORA

Princess Ora came back to the present with a start.

"What?" she said, staring wide-eyed at her husband.

"You've been daydreaming again," her husband teased, wrapping his arms around her lovingly. "You haven't been listening to a word I've said."

It was true; she had not even heard him come into the room. The warm suds on her hands as she washed the dishes had lulled her into exotic visions of steamy baths and pink, flushed skin that became buoyant and bouncy in the water. Being alone with her thoughts was what she liked best; real life could be so unendurably boring. Each thing you contemplated before the fact turned into a poorly done reproduction by comparison.

How long, for example, had she dreamed of having her own prince, and all the wonderful and mysterious things they would do together? But alas, nothing they had done together had come close to the things she had imagined. And love her husband though she might, she could not find a way to stop comparing him and the things he did to the images she produced of him in her mind's eye. She never mentioned these thoughts to him for fear of ruining them altogether.

And anyway, if he truly loved her, shouldn't he have been able to guess her wishes in these matters? So the poor princess continued in silence, and lived her life flitting unhappily between her imaginary world and reality.

"I was asking if you knew when the wizardess was going to arrive," the prince repeated.

"Oh," replied Princess Ora absently, pretending to have been considering this. "As I remember it, the wizardess did not set a time. She will be here, I suppose, when she can fit us in between my sisters." She was slightly irritated to have been disturbed from her erotic daydream to answer mundane questions about tedious daily activities.

The prince had come up behind her and he began kissing her neck and shoulders as he wrapped his strong arms around her, behavior that could become something very exciting in her mind, but which she knew from experience was not likely to turn into anything terribly exciting in real life. Perhaps she would consider the possibilities later when she had a moment alone, but for the present she nudged the prince gently away from her.

"In case she comes sooner, rather than later, I must get this mess cleaned up," she said.

The prince sighed and stepped away. Oh, the things he would love to do to her! It seemed his life had turned into one never-ending exercise in self-control. Even when the princess opened herself to him she seemed distracted and disappointed in the things they did, and these were very tame. Surely she would leave him if she knew the things he longed to do to her. But he shook these thoughts from his mind; his wife was a woman to be treated with respect, not some trollop without any restraint.

They both jumped at the sound of the doorbell interrupting their thoughts. Princess Ora quickly dried her hands and rushed to greet the wizardess.

Harmonia immediately picked up the strange tension in the air as the princess led her into their kitchen. It was so palpable, in fact, that she actually looked into the air all around her, as if it might be visible. "My goodness!" she exclaimed.

But Princess Ora was too preoccupied to notice this outburst. She appeared, in a way, to be of a separate world entirely, thought the wizardess. And of course, she had identified what ailed the princess.

"Yes, my goodness indeed," said the prince to be polite, though in truth he had no idea what the wizardess meant by her outburst. Perhaps, he mused, all women were absentminded and abstract. He thought it best that he lead the group toward the point of their meeting. "Would you like anything to drink before you begin the interview?" he asked the wizardess.

"Oh, this interview is quite finished," replied Harmonia with a slight chuckle. She fished through her overstuffed bag and retrieved a little golden pen. She handed it to Princess Ora.

"Use this as needed each and every evening," she said.

The princess stared at the pen for a moment before accepting it. Then she examined it as if she had never seen a pen before. "A pen?" she asked.

"A *magic* pen," corrected the wizardess as she made to leave.

"But," the prince interjected on behalf of his wife, "What exactly is she supposed to *do* with the pen?"

"Why, she's to write with it, of course!" replied the wizardess. And as quickly as she had come in she went out.

"My goodness," said the prince again, hardly aware of what he was saying.

"Yes, my goodness indeed," replied his wife. She went back to the sink to finish washing the dishes. And it was not until their evening dinner that either one of them mentioned the pen again.

"What will you write tonight?" the prince asked his wife.

"What?" she blinked. She had been thinking about the whipped cream that was sitting atop her dessert.

"The pen," he reminded her. "What do you plan to write with it?"

"I hadn't thought of it," she replied. Where had she put the pen?

"Perhaps the wizardess intended for you to write about yourself, like in a diary," he suggested. He remembered hearing somewhere that this often helped people who were unhappy. Perhaps he should try it himself.

"Do you think so?" she asked offhandedly. She seemed so calm and unconcerned, as if it had nothing to do with her own interests. It was almost as if she were in another world, only half seeing and hearing what was really happening around her.

"Yes," he replied shortly. "I do." He found her cool disconnection to him and their life together irritating. It was becoming an effort to engage her in the simplest conversation. He rose from the table and left the room to prevent himself telling her what a dull, lifeless creature she was.

Princess Ora hardly noticed her husband leave. It was, in fact, a relief to be rid of his niggling questions. She did not want to discuss the pen or what she would write. No doubt he would expect her to write about doing dishes and cleaning his under shorts. She could think of better things to write about than those things. Suddenly she wanted the little golden pen, and she stood up from the table and looked around the kitchen. Finding the pen and a large notebook filled with paper, she took them outdoors to look for a quiet place to write. At length she wandered a small distance into the woods to a favorite spot of hers, and sat on a nearby stump. Her hand that was holding the magic pen twitched.

Princess Ora opened the notebook and looked at the blank page. Once again her fingers twitched around the pen. She put the point of the pen on the paper and all at once, and quite without effort, words began to appear. A story—*her* story—came pouring out onto the sheet. Or perhaps it would have been her story if she knew how to make it so. In the meantime, it would be her story on paper.

In Princess Ora's story there was a princess, much like her, waiting alone in the woods. She was waiting for her lover. Princess Ora paused in her writing every now and then to glance up and around, so that she might better describe the dusky woods and the surrounding shadowy places where the princess might be ravished once her lover arrived. She set the scene in great detail for her heroine's clandestine meeting.

Once the stage was set, it was time to at last introduce the prince who would ravish the story princess. He would, of course, look very much like her own handsome prince. But that was where the likeness to her husband would end. Her story prince would not act such the prim gentleman with his lover. No, this prince would hardly be able to control his passions for his princess. He would not make her suggest or seduce. Nor would he bore her with questions. Her absolute submission would be understood from her presence at this rendezvous, and he would need no further encouragement. Her commitment would be implicit and absolute.

While Princess Ora was busy in the woods writing her story, her husband became suddenly alert with a start. Strange words had begun to appear in his mind's eye and he could not, at first, make sense of them. At length he perceived he was seeing a story unravel in his head.

It was about a princess who was waiting for someone in the woods. The prince paced back and forth as he read about how the princess waited, so excited and hopeful about her meeting, which the prince quickly surmised to be with a lover. The anticipation with which the story princess waited left no doubt.

The real prince's curiosity was piqued when at last the story prince arrived, emerging from the thick forest and sneaking out to catch the story princess unaware. The real prince read on with interest as the story prince was described in great detail. All of a sudden he gasped. The story prince was no other than himself! But what could this mean?

The real prince could only continue to read the words as they appeared with startling clarity in his mind. A story was most certainly unraveling right before his eyes. But alas, the story prince was no respectable gentleman like himself. It was quickly becoming apparent to him that the character who had at first appeared to resemble him was, in fact, a cad. For this imposter prince came upon the princess in the woods like a panther, catching her quite unaware and, without so much as a word, reaching around her, grasping her breasts and pinching her nipples right through her clothing! The real prince gasped at the thought of such indecent and disreputable behavior.

But the story princess seemed delighted by this shocking disregard for her respectability. She reached her arms up behind her head to run her fingers through her lover's hair as he continued to pinch and twist her nipples sharply. Meanwhile, his roguishly hot breath and tongue caressed the back of her neck. Raising one hand to her head he seized a fistful of her hair and yanked it backward so that he might devour her lips. The real prince in the tower wondered to see such lewd treatment of a woman being narrated so clearly inside his head. Certainly he had never allowed himself to treat a lady in such a way. And yet, he could feel his body tightening with a strange longing. What kind of dream was this?

These ponderings were interrupted by the ongoing story in his mind, which was steadily accelerating in its debauchery. The woodland princess was now allowing her gown and under things to be torn from her body and tossed to the ground. Her lover picked up her naked form and laid her onto a nearby bed of leaves. She opened her legs wide to accept him into her body. He ravished her most thoroughly, pushing her legs up high over her head and far apart as he ground himself into her, his hot gaze taking in all of her openly displayed nakedness in the dusky light.

The real prince, meanwhile, was standing in his castle tower, staring blindly out one of the windows, but only seeing the story that was playing out in his mind. He reached between his legs to try and rub away the ache that was developing there. Absently his gaze fixed on a small figure far off in the distance, but he was so caught up in the narrative that he did not, at first, recognize it to be the form of his wife.

The story prince, meanwhile, in a swift and smooth maneuver, crossed his lover's splayed legs and flipped her over so she was on her knees. He did this without disengaging from her body and immediately resumed his pummeling thrusts with her on all fours on the forest floor. Under the influence of such unrestrained abandon, the story princess seemed to have forgotten all caution, allowing her body to be ignited from the violent passion of the prince. She thrashed about wildly, crying out as she thrust her hips up and down over her delighted lover. Still staring blindly out the window, the real prince read all this and imagined the scene well—for Princess Ora was quite explicit in her writing—and his own passions were also ignited to the point of burning out of control. Still, somewhere in the far back reaches of his mind, the prince wondered at the origin of these mysterious words, unraveling this most unusual scene right before his eyes. His gaze was still fixed on the little figure of his wife in the woods, but yet without recognition, as he simultaneously read the story of the ravished princess and rubbed his throbbing body for relief.

But all of a sudden the prince froze. His mind recoiled at the thought, even as it swiftly registered that the little figure hunched over in the woods was his wife and that she was the one responsible for the story of the ravished princess. Slowly, other realizations crept in, confirming this: the likeness of the story princess and her lover to Princess Ora and himself, the constant state of distraction in his wife, the magic pen. At length, the prince discerned that his daydreaming wife had secret passions that, for her own reasons, she had been too withdrawn to make him aware of. But now through the magic pen, the wizardess had seen to it that he found out.

The prince had not remained standing in the tower while having these revelations. Upon first realizing his wife was, in fact, the author of the amazing story, he had immediately descended the stairs of the tower with the intention of joining her.

It took no time for the prince to reach his wife's little hideaway in the wood, but he stopped for a moment a small distance off, thinking of how he should approach her. A slow smile crept over his lips as he watched her, single-mindedly bent over her little notebook, scribbling furiously. The words she wrote were still appearing in his mind. He struggled to clear the words and his thoughts so he could remember how the story had begun. Ah, yes, the story prince had come upon his princess in the woods and taken her by surprise!

It was still dusk as the prince stealthily crept up behind Princess Ora. His body was hard and alert and his heart was hammering in his chest.

Princess Ora dropped her notebook and pen when she perceived her husband's presence. He had come up behind her quite suddenly, grasping her breasts and pinching the nipples hard. She let out a little cry of surprise. He did not give her time to question or retreat; in her shock she was momentarily frozen so he continued to play his part, determined to let her catch up when she would. He knew she must be as aroused as he was after writing such a passionate tale.

With one hand still pinching and twisting one nipple, he raised his other hand to her head and clutched a handful of her hair, pulling it backward, just as the story prince had done. This brought her head back so his mouth could crush hers in a devouring kiss. A little moan escaped the princess's lips as her husband kissed her.

The princess's body slowly twisted around to face her husband's and, in spite of her shock, she wrapped her arms around his neck. Her mind was awhirl with sensations, and she no longer knew for sure what was real and what was fantasy.

The prince enjoyed their kiss thoroughly, unhurriedly demanding and taking everything from the kiss that it had to offer, but all the while mindful of the next stage of the story. While he kissed her he tore at the buttons of her dress. She gasped and drew her lips away from his when she realized what he was doing but he pulled her roughly back to him and resumed kissing her before she had an opportunity to speak. He had not even paused in the unfastening of her buttons during this little struggle, and so in very little time he managed to pull the dress off of her and toss it aside.

Next the prince removed his wife's under things, moving with swiftness and agility, and once again allowing no objections or discussion of any kind. Somehow, his lips never left hers long enough for her to speak. There had been no questions or speech in the story and he was determined to remain as close to the script as possible. In truth he had no desire to edit the story in any way.

Once the princess was fully undressed it took mere seconds for the prince to remove his own clothes. This, too, he accomplished while engaging the princess in a most passionate kiss.

Like the prince in the story, the real prince led his lover to a nearby pile of leaves, realizing with a little start that it was just like the one she had described. Had she imagined being led there and laid down, even as she wrote it?

The prince at last released her lips as he maneuvered the princess onto the leaves. He would have thought being laid out in such a way would be awkward and embarrassing to the cultured lady he had married, but she herself had heated his blood with the image and so, by god, he would see it!

He kissed her again as he raised her legs up slowly, parting them just as her story prince had while he pulled them up. She was wet— very wet—and he slid into her easily. Both the prince and the princess threw their heads back in ecstasy. It felt so good to have him inside her; it felt so good to be inside her.

Slowly the prince began pumping his body forward and back as his eyes roamed over his wife's body and looked their fill. Her legs were set up high and spread wide apart, with his hands holding them firmly by the ankles. He pushed them farther back, anchoring them in the soft leaves above her head as he gazed at her. Her face turned bright red, but she remained silent as she stared up at him. Her silence as she lay there, panting, ignited his passions to the boiling point. He thrust himself into her as violently as the

story prince had done, and found himself obliged to stop periodically, lest he end this fairy tale before it was destined to be
finished.

The princess cried out with delight. By now she had perceived that
her husband had somehow read her story and also that he was not
angry or disgusted with her. But the relief she felt from this realization was too mild to contemplate, for at the moment she was aware
of nothing except the fantasy and she followed breathlessly as her
husband took her there.

But the prince was moving ahead in the story still, and he crossed
his wife's legs in preparation for the next segment. The princess knew
her part, as well, and she prepared herself to be flipped over while
still impaled by his mighty shaft. She wondered vaguely what he
thought of her as he played out each and every little particular of the
story she had written. For him to act out her desires in such minute
detail seemed to her more intimate than even the things he was presently doing to her body, and it added an element to her excitement
that she had neither felt before nor imagined she could feel.

The prince managed the transformation flawlessly, and finding
herself on her hands and knees on the earth before her husband caused
Princess Ora to lose any remaining inhibitions or embarrassment she
may have had. The prince had never taken her this way before, and
she had never dared offer herself in this manner for fear of what he
would think. She had watched the animals in the yard perform this
ritual freely, without reserve, and always she felt a deep longing to
have her husband take her like that—and right in the yard, too! Now
at last she was experiencing that wish firsthand. Unable to restrain
herself any longer she pushed her buttocks up toward him, welcoming
his animalistic thrusts with little thrusts of her own.

But their passions were so strong that they had to reach a peak. Neither seemed to realize that this was where Princess Ora had left off in her story. Neither of them needed the story any longer as their bodies brought the tale to its only logical conclusion, with Princess Ora grinding and pumping her buttocks in the prince's direction, and her husband battering her flesh with his powerful thrusts. The woods stood silent and alert around them as they cried out their passion.

The next morning Princess Ora awoke with a start. She blinked several times to clear her mind. Had it been a dream? No, she realized it had been real. Her memory brought together the little pieces that made up the whole of the evening, ending with her husband carrying her home and up to bed. Her aching muscles gave her proof of their rough play in the woods. She blushed remembering.

She smelled coffee brewing below stairs and wondered what her husband was thinking this morning. Would he have changed his mind, having spent all his passion the night before? Would he think her debased?

She threw on her dressing gown and anxiously slipped downstairs. The prince sat at the kitchen table, reading. When he became aware of her he looked up and smiled.

"Good morning," he said warmly.

"Good morning," she answered, but her tone was reserved. She could not remember ever being so captivated by him. She was more aware of him than she had ever been, and even her trusty imagination could not take her mind off of the reality of him sitting there before her as she nervously wondered what he was thinking about the events of the night before.

"You're looking well rested," he remarked.

His small talk agitated her further. He must realize how embarrassed she felt and how much she needed reassuring; yet here he was pretending it hadn't happened. She decided she would approach the subject herself—on the defensive, of course. "I did not rest very well at all," she lied. Then she added pointedly, "I find it very disconcerting to think that I am being spied upon."

"Spied upon?" her husband repeated, shocked.

"You daren't deny it?" she challenged.

"I haven't any idea of what you are speaking," he said. So, he thought, she did not guess that the magic pen had exposed her secret. But on reconsideration he realized she could never have guessed such a thing. It had been hard for him to comprehend it even as he was seeing it right before his eyes. Even so, to accuse him of spying!

"So you deny you were spying on me last night," she said, wondering what other explanation there could be if he had not been looking over her shoulder, reading every line she wrote.

"Why do you even ask such a thing?" he replied cleverly. "What gives you reason to suspect me of spying?" He knew perfectly well why she suspected him, of course, but he also knew she would be hesitant to admit writing the story if there was any chance that he had not read it. He could tell that she was wondering if it were possible that he hadn't seen it. She was likely contemplating whether the magic pen had mysteriously brought her fantasy to life without him even knowing why. She seemed genuinely perplexed.

"I just found your behavior of last night...strange," she explained weakly.

He took her hand in his and rubbed the soft skin absently for a moment with his thumb. "I'm sorry, princess, if I acted inappropriately last night," he said with sincerity. "I vow, I think I went quite mad."

So! It must be the magic pen, she thought. Perhaps as she wrote her secret desires they became his, as well. She wondered if that was possible. Examining his face carefully she noticed a slight smirk of amusement, barely perceptible really, except that she had never before noticed such a look, or indeed ever had reason to suspect him of guile or trickery.

Princess Ora mused over the matter throughout the day, one moment convinced it was the work of the pen and the next certain that her husband must have, in fact, been reading over her shoulder. Upon further consideration, it occurred to her that the actions of her husband had not been so unusual. Certainly the events had been wild and exciting for them, but really, compared to things she had heard of and even imagined, they were pretty tame. Perhaps it had nothing to do with what she wrote. But then, ere long, her mind would once again review the events of the night previous and her suspicions about her husband would return.

By that evening, she had devised a plan to test the matter out. She would hide this time; somewhere deep in the woods where she could be certain her husband would not find her. There she would write something even more fantastic and see how it played out. She had lots and lots of fantasies, and was anxious to see if they would have the same effect on him if he were nowhere near her when she wrote them.

After dinner she sent her husband into the cellar on an errand and then very quickly, before he could come back to see which direction she went, she took her notebook and magic pen and flew out the door toward the woods. She hurried along a little path that her husband used for hunting, but after a while she veered off into the dense woods and finally settled herself in a truly obscure location behind a very large rock. *He will never find me here,* she thought.

Princess Ora sat down on a nearby stump and settled her notebook in her lap. Suddenly there was a rustling in a nearby tree and, startled, she swung around to find out what it was, half expecting to see her husband. But alas, it was only a mother bird, shaking her wings and fluttering about in an effort to become more comfortable in her nest.

Princess Ora stared up into the tree for a moment. It was remarkably tall—the tallest in the forest by far. She wondered how long it had been there. Her gaze traveled down the long, hard length of it. It had been there so long that its roots had risen high above the earth, becoming a part of the trunk really, but twisting and gnarling about in peculiar shapes around the base.

All at once she began writing. This time her story princess was being tied, naked, to the enormous tree, her fair skin being ravaged by the harsh, uneven bark. The story princess cried out and twitched about in agony. The birds in her story forest screamed out, sensing the princess's anguish. Wild animals of the story woods watched quietly from their hiding places.

Princess Ora's husband, meanwhile, had come back up the stairs to find his wife had disappeared. He immediately surmised that she must have slipped away to write again, and this brought a smile to his face. But the smile quickly faded when it occurred to him that she would likely have found a more private place to write this time. He suddenly realized with horror that he would not know how to find her if, as he suspected, she was hiding. Already, at the mere thought of it, his body had begun to tighten and harden. And no sooner had he come to these conclusions than, sure enough, the words began to appear in his mind, exactly as they had done the night before.

The prince read eagerly as the words appeared this time, groaning with a mixture of horror and excitement at what he was seeing.

Tonight's story began with the princess already naked in the woods. She was being tied to a tree! Her silky skin was chafed bright pink by the abrasive surface of the tree. The feel of the harsh bark against her skin made her thrash about in sweet anguish, titillating her senses with painful surges of awareness. Her captor pulled the knots tighter, aware of the delightful torture he was inflicting on her. When he finished, she was tightly secured over one of the gnarled roots that circled and entwined the tree in a seductive manner around the base of the trunk. Her upper body was curved around the biggest part of the root, which was the size of a medium-sized barrel, with her arms securely tied to another root that wound around above her head. Meanwhile her legs were spread apart and fastened to two more roots, with her knees resting comfortably in the earth in between the roots. In this position, her body was rounded and secured, so that her face and bottom were readily available to her captor.

The prince had been standing paralyzed to the spot while reading so far, but now he moved to collect some rope and go out into the woods in search of his wife. He was trembling with desire as he did these things, and all the while never skipping over a single word of the story that continued to unravel in his head.

The story princess was waiting in suspense while the cool breeze played havoc on her private areas, which were unused to the gentle teasing. Her captor moved leisurely about behind her, watching her as he prepared for his next move. The story princess felt him getting closer. Very subtly she perceived something pliant but still rather prickly touching her. She gasped at the sensation, all at once mild and abrasive. It tickled and pricked in one smooth, tantalizing stroke. Her captor applied the offending article, which she supposed was some kind of plant he had unearthed, over the exposed area between her legs, brushing it over the vulnerable flesh ever so slowly and gently, and causing her to jump and squirm as much as was possible within her constraints.

In the meantime, the real prince, who by now had reached the forest's edge, groaned as he read this. His eyes roamed over the forest floor keenly, wondering which plant had appealed to his wife, causing her to imagine it tickling her most tender areas. Several plants caught his eye as possible candidates for such a task, and he decided that when he finally found her he would try out each and every one of them. But at the moment, he could only continue to read helplessly as he searched the woods for her.

The strokes of the story princess's captor were coming faster and harder now, and she moaned and wriggled, obliged to make the most of whatever he gave her to endure. He seemed in no particular hurry, enjoying the pleasure of watching her reactions as he leisurely tormented her. He brushed his weapon across her flesh with precision and aim, purposefully landing the prickly whisk so that her body would move the way he liked best. He amused himself for quite a while in this manner.

Princess Ora was now as lost in her story as she was in the woods, forgetting her husband altogether for the moment as she let her imagination take hold of her uppermost thoughts. Her fingers moved the pen quickly and efficiently over the paper and her brow was creased in absolute concentration. She was so completely given over to her fantasy that it appeared to her more real than her husband, or the woods in which she sat, or even the notebook and pen she used to write it. It seemed that she could actually feel the brush of the woodland plant, as it thrashed gently against the story princess, causing a trickling wetness between both of their legs.

The prince stopped in frustration. In his hands he clutched the rope and various brush vines and plants that he had acquired along the way to use on the princess when he found her. But where the devil was she? He sighed impatiently, scanning his mind for any clue in her story that would lead him to where she was. It was not easy to concentrate when her words kept appearing in his mind, faster and faster, describing in great detail the jiggling movements of the story princess as she strained against the thrashing of her tormentor, and the stinging wetness that she felt as she awaited his pleasure in relieving her. The real prince could empathize well with the story princess's dilemma as he tried to ascertain his wife's whereabouts, almost too aroused to summon the full use of his brain. Even so, there was a nagging thought in the far reaches of his mind, insisting that he had overlooked an important detail in the story's setting. There had been something vaguely familiar before he had gotten caught up in the narrative. What was it? He made an effort to recall what his wife had written earlier; it was difficult with her words still coming at him so quickly, beguiling and tormenting him all at the same time. Quickly his mind went over the few details he could remember. She was being tied to the roots of a very large tree. All at once the prince threw his head back and made a sound that was half laugh and half roar. He knew the tree his wife described! By god, he would find her after all!

He changed directions immediately, running through the woods at full speed. He was startled that she would have gone out so far. But there was precious little time to consider these things, for he was reading as he ran, his body aching under the tireless persuasion of his wife's indefatigable imagination.

At last the prince approached the place where Princess Ora was hiding. Just like the previous night, she did not see or hear him approach. She was crouched down on the ground, sitting on her legs as she scrawled the words in her notebook. He stared at her a moment, fighting off a ferocious longing that bordered on madness. As if sensing this, Princess Ora looked up suddenly. She dropped the pen as her eyes took in the rope and the leafy branches in her husband's hands. Without a word he put down the rope and the branches and approached her. He turned her around and made a small, rather futile attempt to unbutton her gown, but in his impatience he ended up tearing the dress wide open with his hands and pulling it single-mindedly from her body. Just as quickly he discarded her under things, tearing them from her body even more violently.

The princess did not—could not—struggle against her husband. When at first she had seen him in the woods she thought she must have dreamed it. But the wild look on his face mirrored her inner feelings too keenly for this to be a dream. And besides, dreams did not impatiently rip the clothing from one's body.

It did not take long for the prince to figure out which root the princess had envisioned for her fantasy. It stood out among the others, rounded and fairly smooth, and as the prince deftly tied her to it he wondered absently that he had never thought of it himself. And as it happened, the princess had indeed assessed the area correctly; the dimensions were a perfect fit for her body and she settled comfortably into her new position, with her hands secured tightly to a root located in front of her and her legs tied far apart, knees resting perfectly on the ground in between. Her stomach straddled the largest root, with her breasts falling loosely just above where it curved around. She was short of breath from excitement, finding it hard to breathe in and out. She was excited to the point of fainting.

The prince was suffering, too, but he was determined that he play his part correctly in his wife's fantasy. He chose a branch covered in leaves that were slightly prickly all around the edges, and he moved it ever so slowly over the area between his wife's open legs. She moaned loudly as he did this, straining her hips against the tantalizing leaves in an attempt to get more of them. The feathery light touches were as exciting as she imagined, but they were equally distressing. It was only enough to tease and not nearly enough to please. As the strokes came firmer and faster, she moved her hips in time with them, at moments trying to get as much pleasure as she could and other times trying to avoid the harsher strokes that stung her flesh. She delighted in her husband's patient torment of her, and wondered if he enjoyed watching her wriggle and move as much as her story captor had.

The prince was enjoying watching his wife immensely, and he played with and pleasured her for as long as he could, until at last he could take no more. Her bouncing hips were driving him wild. He threw down the branch and approached her. Her flesh was swollen and pink. She was moaning quietly. He reached between her legs and stroked her with his hand. She was open and wet. He worked his way into her right then and there, taking her while she was still tied to the tree. He had not allowed her to finish her story before interrupting her, so he was not entirely sure how she would have ended it. However, he had a few ideas of his own that he thought were not half-bad.

He recalled that she had chosen this particular root because it left the story princess open "at both ends." Perceiving her reason for this, he planned to make use of the other end in due time, but for now, he reveled in the feel of her lower body engulfing him in its silky softness.

He took her with long, easy strokes, pausing now and then to control his passions so that she would have ample time to take pleasure in their activities. He was astute enough to grasp from her stories her longing to enjoy more from their intimacy than merely reaching a climax. She wanted to experience everything that the act could offer, and he, for his part, was fully willing to oblige her. Perhaps in the process he, too, would learn to get more out of it.

With this in mind he teased, tantalized and titillated them both for as long as he was able. Light was quickly leaving the forest and he still had more ground to cover. He eased himself out of her. She moaned in resistance. They still had neither spoken a single word.

The prince came around to the front of his wife now, holding her head gently for a moment before filling her eager mouth. The barrel shape of the tree root now came to be most useful, for it made it quite easy for him to reach between her legs as she sucked him. He approached this, too, teasingly, leisurely massaging her back and pink buttocks with his hands before reaching between her legs and stroking her there. With the greatest care he searched for her most receptive spot and lovingly rubbed and caressed her until her hips began to move in time with his fingers. She sucked him enthusiastically as she moaned and ground her hips. He let her set the pace, watching her like he would an outstanding performance, enjoying the show as much as he was able whilst struggling to maintain self-control.

Princess Ora closed her eyes tight, but for once it was not in an effort to imagine something more exciting than what she was actually experiencing. She was overwhelmed by the many sensations taking over her mind, and did not know whether to focus on her husband's fingers between her legs, or the harsh ropes around her wrists and ankles, or even his rock solid hardness penetrating her mouth. Her thoughts drifted from one very exciting sensation to the next, causing a sharp thrill to trickle over her anew with each tantalizing contemplation. Finally she struck upon the perfect combination of sensations that sent rivers of pleasure throughout her. While her whole body shuddered, she kept her eyes shut tight and her lips still sucked on her husband unconsciously.

Princess Ora's reaction was duly noted by the prince, and his body responded immediately. He made to pull himself out of her mouth but she surprised him further by clinging to him with her lips. His roar of pleasure seemed to reverberate off the forest trees, going on and on, much like his release. He was delighted to discover that his repeated efforts to hold off had had the effect of making his orgasm last longer and come over him with much more intensity. He had nearly seen stars!

Princess Ora was in a daze. Her husband had fulfilled her darkest desires every bit as well as she could have done.

But the next morning Princess Ora was once again anxiety-ridden. What must her husband think of her, really, even in spite of the pleasure they both had shared? What should she say to him? As before, she dealt with these doubts and fears with anger. How had he known where to find her? It was quite disconcerting. And yet, now and again, little remembrances of the events of the night before sent shivers clear through her, and she found herself quite confused indeed, feeling one moment distressingly aroused and the next feeling violated and enraged.

Her husband, when she met him downstairs, once again acted the perfect gentleman and was quite cavalier, it seemed, about the evening previous. She tried to mirror his manner but failed. At length she said, "Dare you deny yet again that you were spying on me?"

"Indeed I know nothing about it," he replied simply, daring her to say more.

She fumed inwardly but held her tongue. She did not have proof, yet how else could his behavior be explained? His actions were, verbatim, what she had written. Once again she wondered about the magic pen. Was the pen causing his behavior to mirror what she wrote on the pages of her notebook? She did not want to admit that she was the instigator of the fantasies if they were, in fact, caused by the magic pen. She tried to casually inquire about it, but it caused her much embarrassment to broach the subject.

"Last night you...how did you find me?" She blushed profusely at the mention of it. *Really,* she marveled at herself, *after the things you did with him!* She thought about the wanton way she had moved her hips over his prying hands.

"For last night I can do no more than beg your pardon," he said evasively. "I'm sure I don't know what came over me—stumbling upon you in the woods like that made me lose control!" And so, once again he effectively thwarted her efforts to solve the riddle.

That evening the princess left their house before her husband arrived home from work. Determined to see if the magic pen really gave her power to control his behavior, she slipped out early and went even farther into the woods this time, to a place she was certain he could not "stumble" upon her. Furthermore, she would write a story that even he could not act out! It would have to be bizarre and outrageous. She thought about the possibilities as she traveled farther and farther into the woods.

As Princess Ora contemplated these matters she wandered from the path she had intended and at length she was in a much denser forest, with a more primitive terrain. So deep in thought was she that she did not even notice this change until she stumbled into a large puddle of mud. She struggled a moment to regain her composure before losing her footing completely and falling facedown in the mud.

The princess let out a little scream of indignation. Suddenly she noticed the area around her and realized with horror that she had no idea where she was. Furthermore, she was covered in thick muck from head to foot. She tried to brush it off of her but it stubbornly clung to her in small clumps all over. *Well,* she thought, *I wonder what my husband would think if he saw me like this!* But her next thought was one of exclamation: *that was it!* Suddenly her fingers itched for the pen and she searched all around and in the puddle until she found it and the notebook, which she promptly opened and set out before her, right there on the forest floor. She was dirty already and so she kneeled over the notebook and gave in to her overwhelming urge to write.

Now we shall see, she thought, as she began to pen the outrageous tale. Her story princess would also be lost in the woods, and she, too, would have fallen in the mud. But in her story, the puddle was cursed by a woodland fairy and the earth within it would have the power to transform whoever touched it. Princess Ora absently tugged at the muddied collar around her neck as she contemplated how this puddle might transform her characters.

The prince, meanwhile, who had been riding home on his horse stopped abruptly. "What the…damn!" He swore. She was at it again! She had apparently left their castle before he could set a trap that would make it easier for him to find her. Instinctively his body began to tighten up in anticipation, even as his mind wondered in apprehension where she had slipped away to this time.

He quickly perceived that his wife had once again wandered off into the woods. Perhaps she, like her story princess, was lost. As he read the words that appeared in his mind, he could scarcely believe what he was seeing. Where was she coming up with all of this? He wanted to throttle her, right there in the mud...in the mud where the story princess was tearing her clothes off because she was changing. *My god,* he thought, aroused but also alarmed. Was it possible that his wife was really in some kind of trouble? He thought about the landscape in her story as he continued to read. Surely she had not wandered off so far that she could have reached the mudlands?

The story princess was now fully unclothed and rolling around in the mud, massaging the thick, black clumps into her skin. The prince pictured the black mud all over his wife's delicate skin and groaned.

Princess Ora tugged once again at her dress as she wrote. The mud caused her skin to itch where it was drying, and it scraped her skin where it had already dried on her clothes. She sat up a moment, thinking. *Way out here,* she thought, *who would know if I were to remove my dress so that I could shake the mud off it once it dries?* The dress was becoming too uncomfortable to remain on her body at any rate. She removed it hastily and hung it on a nearby branch so that she could resume her writing. It was time to bring her prince into the story.

The real prince was unsure what to do next. Should he go to the mudlands to see if Princess Ora was there? He felt it was extremely unlikely that she had gone that far. The story prince was faring better than he, however, for he was just coming upon his princess as she rolled in the mud, grunting happily as she covered herself in the sloppy rich soil. The story prince realized immediately that his princess had fallen under the spell of the woodland fairy and perceived that she was changing. Such was his love for her that he tore off his own clothes and joined her in the mud, resolving to change right along with her.

It appeared to the real prince as he read all this that the prince and princess in the story were changing into some kind of wild animal, perhaps swine. It was outrageous, but he could not get the images of the two characters, which he had by this time come to think of as Princess Ora and himself, out of his mind. The thought of his wife's body covered in slick mud appealed to him. The thought of himself rolling around in the mud with her was enticing. Some of what she wrote appalled him as much as it thrilled him. As the characters continued to change, their behavior became more animalistic. The story prince grunted as he sniffed between the legs of his transformed princess. She allowed him to sniff her but she bit him when he tried to mount her. Undaunted, they continued their mud play, until at last he got the better of her, triumphantly pressing her face into the mud as he mounted her successfully this time.

The real prince could not believe what he was reading. He rushed blindly through the woods toward the mudlands now, but was still a far distance off. He was tired and sweaty from the work he had done that day, but even so it was as if he had fire running through his veins. Each step he took toward the mudlands seemed to mingle with every word he read, and the fusion of the two was like gasoline on a fire. He was panting as he traversed the woods, looking this way and that, searching for his wife with only his instinct for a guide. He couldn't get the image of her mud-covered body out of his head. He knew he would be mounting her in the mud, just like the characters in her story, once he found her.

The princess, too, had been affected by her own story. She suddenly ached to feel the mud all over her skin. She had given up, by now, on the idea that the pen was affecting her husband's behavior, or that he was going to appear suddenly in these isolated woods. He had simply been looking over her shoulder on the two evenings previous. Being truly alone in these woods, she could easily slip off the rest of her clothes and have a healthful mud soak. On her way home she would bathe in the river. It was still quite warm and little rays of sunshine managed to slip through the branches of the dense forest trees. A few minutes later she was fully nude and wading in the puddle of mud. She sat down in the center of the puddle, and began to spread the slop over her torso and breasts with her hands. It felt cool and tingly and forbidden. It aroused her to feel it seeping its way into the pores of her flesh.

Princess Ora's husband was alarmed. The words had stopped coming. Had something happened to his wife? Random images lingered in his mind, turning his anxiety into fancy. Had she realized he could see what she wrote? Had she written the bizarre story to alert him to something that had happened? He tried to remain calm and rational as he tore through the woods in search of her.

A languid feeling of arousal permeated the princess. She loved the way the mud made her body look and feel. She could not take her eyes off her breasts as she rolled around shamelessly in the black mud. It seemed that the mud brought a tingling sensation to every pore. She fancied she could even feel it in the hairs upon her head. She knew it was wicked but she could not help but touch herself between her legs. She rubbed herself tenuously with her fingers, slowly giving in to the enticing feel of the mud. With no one to hear her in her isolation, she moaned loudly while she titillated herself.

The prince was becoming frantic. Too many minutes had passed and still no word had appeared in his mind. He tore through the woods in haste, panting like an animal. Suddenly he paused. He could hear a strange moaning sound that did not sound quite human, but nor could he identify it as that of an animal. He followed the sound toward the mudlands, convinced it would lead him to his wife, but not daring to guess that it was his wife.

He stopped short when he spotted her. She was lying on her back in a puddle of black mud; her legs bent and spread apart, her hair caked in the mud while she pleasured herself. The loud moans were hers. Her hips rose up and down as her fingers worked at her arousal. At the sight of her the prince felt a mixture of outrage and passion. His passion quickly overpowered everything else, and he swiftly and silently stripped down and approached her as lithely as cat.

When Princess Ora caught sight of him she froze. Every part of her was covered in the black muck except her face. She shrieked at him in outrage and embarrassment. She was so angry all of a sudden that she actually shook. How dared he? She took a handful of the mud and hurled it directly into his face. It hit him on the cheek and nose with a loud thud. She noticed with a small amount of satisfaction that he, too, was quite aroused. At least he had not been turned off by catching her at what she was so obviously doing. That would have been unpardonable.

Her attack seemed to have no effect on him. He continued his approach and bent down to grasp one thoroughly mud-coated breast. From the moment he first glimpsed it he knew he would touch it. She struggled to get away from him, tossing mud at him whole-heartedly now. He did not seem to mind this, either, but kept stroking her slickly coated body, completely unmoved by her struggles. She rolled onto her knees and tried to get up. The mud made her limbs heavy and awkward. The prince held her down easily, even slipping one hand over, around and between her buttocks leisurely as he did so. She kept flinging mud at him and struggling to stand up, but he easily held her down.

The prince knew his wife was embarrassed by the way he had found her and this was the source of her struggles. He also remembered that her story princess had struggled against her lover, too. She had written the script and he intended to play his part to the letter. He would do so with relish, in fact.

Without difficulty the prince grasped his wife's slick hips and dropped to his knees in the mud before her. She squirmed and tried to wriggle away, but she still uttered no words; only grunts and gasps and moans escaped her lips. She seemed to be struggling inwardly more than out. But the prince was merely playing with her through these struggles, and enjoying the sport. He would mount her when he was ready, just as the prince in the story had done to his princess, although they had been under a spell. But he, too, felt that he was under a spell, and he luxuriated in every single detail of their interplay, from the mud clinging to his wife's curves as she fought him, to the animal sounds that escaped her lips. He somehow managed to stroke himself while he held her.

At last he jerked her hips closer, forcing her legs wider apart with his knee. She struggled harder but he still managed her easily. He jerked her hips up roughly, causing her to lose her balance and fall face-first in the mud. She gasped in outrage even as he slid into her slick, waiting body.

They both fought to keep their balance as the prince ravished the princess right there in the mud puddle and for all appearances they might really have been two animals mating. The princess was subdued for the moment and thrust her muddied hips greedily up to meet her husband's. She could not seem to control the frenzied passion that had taken hold of her. She thrashed and moaned in full abandon, wanting nothing but a release from the pent-up desire she felt. When at last that release came to her she screamed out her pleasure, reveling in her absolute loss of restraint. She had truly let go of every last vestige of her self-control. Furthermore, she had exposed her most concealed and frightening secrets to her husband.

The princess's loss of control had the effect of further inflaming the prince. His cry that followed hers was a loud roar that sent echoes reverberating through the mudlands.

The princess's mind whirled. How could she face her husband after she had behaved in such a debased manner? She was almost glad that the mud still covered her face as she tried to move away from him.

"I have something I want to say to you," he told her firmly. She remained silent so he continued. "The next time you use that damned pen I want to know where you are so I don't have to search everywhere for you!"

"The pen!" she exclaimed.

"Yes," he admitted at last, kissing her muddied lips and cheek and neck. "Every single thing you write with it appears in my head."

"Oh!" she exclaimed. So that was it! "I shall never touch it again," she swore.

"The hell you won't," he said, surprising her. "I cannot live without your stories now that I have gotten a taste for them."

"Oh, but I was…I mean, today…that was not really…"

"Don't you dare apologize for anything you have written," he told her. "I'm here, aren't I?"

"Yes, but, well…"

"I don't care what comes into your mind as you write or why," he assured her. "The last thing I want to do is censure you. I just want to share it with you."

Tears came suddenly to her eyes. "Really?" she asked, not quite able to believe what he was telling her.

"Really," he said solemnly.

But it was impossible to remain serious while they were covered in mud. They found themselves chuckling joyfully as they tramped through the woods, stopping to wash in the lake on their way home. The princess was contented, for the time being anyway, and the new intimacy that began that day allowed her to always share her new longings with her husband.

And although the princess's shoes were caked in mud the following morning, they were not completely worn through.

PRINCESS RESENTTA

PRINCESS RESENTTA PACED BACK AND FORTH OVER THE LIVING ROOM floor as she waited anxiously for the wizardess to arrive. She had planned out over and again what she would say, even though she doubted that the wizardess would really be able to help her. It was one thing to recognize a person's unhappiness, but quite another to make it go away. And anyway, the princess reflected, her distress was not something that came from within herself. She had been a perfectly happy person until her marriage.

It was *him* who caused her discontent. She had tried and tried to make things pleasant between them, but it was impossible to keep trying when you were dealing with a tyrant. Everything always had to be done his way. Princess Resentta had ideas of her own about how they should live. But somehow, these ideas never got incorporated into real life.

This latest dispute between them was, she felt, the final straw. After months of pleading with her husband to make improvements to the castle, he at last agreed to take time away from his dragon fighting to do so. But instead of the greenhouse she had been pining for since the first day they came to this dreary castle, he had decided that they should build a tower. A tower! So now the horrible man could fight at home, as well as when he was away. And even worse, he always had everyone, including her own father, convinced that whatever he wanted to do was right.

She must speak to the wizardess first, she decided, and alone, before her husband could argue his points on castle safety and protection. If she could get the wizardess to advocate a greenhouse, then perhaps the prince would be obliged to do it under order of the king. And wouldn't it, in fact, be just the cure to fix what ailed them, if Princess Resentta could, at last, have her way on this one point, and get the greenhouse that would bring her so much happiness? She was certain it would. She glanced up the staircase anxiously, hoping upon hope that the wizardess would arrive before her husband should come down from upstairs, where she assumed he was studying the blueprints for his project. But alas, when Princess Resentta heard the door, she turned to see no other than her very own husband, the prince, escorting the wizardess into their castle.

The sight of them together enraged her, but the princess forced her lips into a stiff smile of greeting.

"I see you've met my husband already," Princess Resentta said sweetly enough, but the wizardess detected the bitterness behind the words and looked sharply at her.

"Indeed I have had that pleasure," Harmonia replied, watching the princess carefully as she spoke.

"Well, then," was all Princess Resentta said, but she glanced at her husband as she said it as if to add, "Score another point for you!"

This little exchange was all that the wizardess needed to see the matter clearly. Theirs was a common enough problem. It was, in fact, one that every new couple was obliged to face. And it seemed that

Princess Resentta and her husband were having no small amount of difficulty with it.

Harmonia opened her bag and pulled from it a mask. The mask flopped feebly in her hand, being feather light, extremely supple and flexible, and so translucent as to be nearly invisible.

"This magic mask will help you both," she said, looking from the princess to the prince. They both stared at the flimsy mask as it flopped about in the wizardess's hand for a split second before simultaneously reaching out for it. The wizardess suddenly pulled it away from them.

"Listen carefully," Harmonia told them. "The mask is hardly felt or seen when worn, but it carries enormous responsibility. The wearer of this mask will have complete and absolute power and control over the other." She paused a moment to allow Princess Resentta and her husband to absorb this. Then she continued, "The mask holds its power by day and by night. Whoever wears it by day loses their power at nightfall and whoever wears it by night loses their power by day."

Now the wizardess held the mask out once again. It dangled ominously from her fingers.

The prince and princess looked at each other. The prince could see by his wife's expression that she was itching to get her fingers on the mask. He shuddered to think of how thoughtless and impractical her decisions might be if she were allowed to have the full power by day. There were so many important things still yet for him to do to protect them and their castle and she had nothing in her head except flower gardens. She would probably plant a row of pansies all around their borders in lieu of soldiers.

But in the very same instant the prince imagined himself having the mask by night, with all the power it promised. He was getting mighty sick and tired of the princess controlling that part of their lives—or lack of it these days. If everything did not go exactly her way she froze herself against him. No doubt her idea of evening pleasure would be to have him bow down and kiss her feet. It would be nice to have the power to show her how a wife should treat her husband in an evening after he has worked all day.

However, the prince decided quickly and regretfully, it was not to be. He could not risk his and the princess's safety simply for a few nights of pleasure. He reached out, before his wife could do so, and took the mask from the wizardess. Immediately upon doing so, he felt a strange surge of power shoot up his arm.

The princess stared at her husband in horror. "Dear," she said, trying to sound civil, and only for the wizardess's benefit, "shouldn't we let the wizardess decide who gets to wear it first?"

"I cannot decide that for you, princess," Harmonia interjected. "I am leaving now, so the two of you can settle the matter between yourselves." And at that the wizardess walked out the door, glad to be away from the unpleasant couple, and with a number of important things to do still in front of her.

Meanwhile, the princess—even before the door had completely closed behind the wizardess, in fact—had whirled around to face her husband. "Give it to me!" she demanded.

"I don't think it would be wise for you to wear the mask first," her husband replied calmly. "You're currently too excited to be trusted with this kind of responsibility."

The princess tried to grab the mask out of his hand but he quite easily jerked it out of her reach with a little laugh. "You should see how ridiculous you look. You are acting just like a child."

"And you are acting like a bully," she retorted, her voice rising.

"Look," he said in an aggravatingly reasonable tone, "you can have the mask tonight, after you've calmed down." His condescending tone and cool assumption that he was perfectly entitled to make the final decision enraged her even further.

"Why do you even need the mask?" she screamed. "You always make all the decisions anyway."

"As usual, you're getting too emotional to discuss what needs to be done in a rational way," he said in a tone that indicated he had not only made up his mind, but that his decision was flawless.

"And as usual," she replied, seething, and deliberately emphasizing every word, "you're too *un*emotional to realize that I *hate* you!"

He ignored this and looked at the mask in his hand. It was as thin and colorless as to be nearly transparent. He tentatively placed the mask over his face. At the first touch it immediately adhered to his skin perfectly and completely, without any further effort necessary. He felt an instant surge of power flow throughout his body, but after that he felt exactly as he had before. He looked at his wife.

Princess Resentta had watched resentfully as her husband placed the mask over his face and it became one with his skin. Now, as she looked at him, she was filled with strange new emotions. All the anger and resentment of only seconds before were washed from her mind. She suddenly felt a strong admiration for him, combined with a compulsion to please him. She was all at once reminded of earlier days, when she still felt these things for her husband, and she smiled at the memory.

The prince could not remember the last time his wife had smiled, or more especially when she had smiled at him. His whole body reacted to that one little smile, and all of a sudden the things he had planned to do that day seemed not so urgent. Here was his wife, who had shunned him in their marital chamber for months, under his power to succumb to anything he desired. He felt that he ought to take every bit of what he had been denied—and then some.

The prince approached his wife and took her face in his hands. She allowed him to lift her face and even opened her mouth willingly for his kiss. He moaned out loud at her eagerness to kiss him. Was this his angry little wife? Where was all the resentment of a moment ago? What was she thinking at that moment? He decided he would not question the magic of the mask, but simply enjoy it for as long as he could. He lifted the sweet acquiescent Princess Resentta into his arms and carried her up the stairs to their bedchamber.

The princess clung to her husband. She was filled with a desire to please him and sat eagerly awaiting him on their bed where he had placed her. Just seeing her there, waiting for him, warmed his heart, but he, too, had some resentment stored up from the past months of her abuse. He had a desire to test the limits of the mask, and see just how willing his wife would be to honor his wishes.

"Come here, wife," he said. She instantly rose from the bed and came to stand before him. He felt another surge of power rush through him, and he found it even more satisfying than the first.

"Remove all your clothes," he continued.

Once again she complied fully with his request. He watched in utter shock, hardly able to believe what was happening.

"Now, take off my pants." This, too, she did willingly and efficiently.

He was standing, and in the course of lowering his pants down his legs, she was obliged to bend and kneel, so that she could better undress him. Once this was completed she began to get up, but he stopped her with a hand on her shoulder.

"Stay there," he said. She looked up into his eyes and it was as if she could read his thoughts. While he still held her eyes with his, she reached out to wrap her arms around his hips and she clasped on to his manhood with her lips and tongue. She immediately took to the task at hand with eagerness. She sucked and licked diligently as she moved her head to and fro, trying to take more and more of him with each forward thrust of her head as she perceived he wished it, according to his moans and movements.

As the princess was giving her husband this pleasure, her mind reeled in confusion. She almost felt that she had never before caressed her husband in this way with her mouth and tongue, or tasted the wonderful flavor of him. Certainly she had performed this act on him, before she had begun to dislike him, but that had been different somehow. It had satisfied her to please him back then, but it had not actually given her pleasure. Now, her whole body quivered with a fierce longing and desire to give her husband the most intense pleasure she could supply; indeed, it appeared that she could feel each and every little ripple and wave of exquisite sensation that coursed through him when she sucked hungrily at the tip of him, or lapped her tongue along the length of him. It was as if in pleasuring him she was pleasuring herself. She almost felt as if she could not endure it if she did not make the experience better than any he had had before, and make it one that she alone could provide. She struggled harder to take him deeper with each stroke of her head, sucking more and more vigorously with her lips as she drew them over his flesh. It was as if she was starving for him, gasping and choking as she struggled to please him and her both.

The prince stared in stunned amazement at his wife. Her naked breasts bounced and bobbed against his legs as she franticly worked on him with her lips and tongue. Her hands clung to his hips for support, and her knees were set apart for stability. She was wild to please him, but it was not only him. He could hear her little moans and cries as she sucked and licked at him furiously. He could see her hips moving more and more frantically, as if she were trying to find something right there in midair that might give her relief. He had never seen his wife so aroused without even being touched. He didn't want her to stop what she was doing, but he could not stand to watch her hips bouncing aimlessly in the air, untouched, either. He wanted to give her the same pleasure she was giving him.

With effort, the prince took his wife's face in his hands and pulled himself out of her mouth. She looked up at him, questioning, panting, whimpering, wanting…and he almost lost himself then and there. He picked her up off the floor and placed her on the bed, filled all of a sudden with the same strong desire to please her that she was consumed with to please him, but it was still mingled with pent-up anger from months of neglect. He would please her, of course, but it would be on his terms.

The prince positioned himself over his wife, facing in the opposite direction, with his legs spread wide and his knees settled on either side of her head. He kept his hips raised for the moment, and the princess felt a yearning desire as she stared up at her husband's manhood bobbing directly over her face, hard with anticipation, a little bead of excitement escaping from its tip.

Meanwhile the prince took his wife's ankles in each of his hands and pulled them forward and apart, causing her knees to bend and her legs to spread wide apart as they were pulled up toward her body. He loved having her opened to his view like this. He stared at her lustfully for a moment, recalling how she would often hide herself from him. The bad memories caused him to pull her legs even farther apart, forcing her to become even more exposed to his hot gaze than before.

Wanting to keep her open to his view, the prince carefully and deliberately positioned his arms under and around her upper thighs to fasten her legs wide apart while giving him the full use of his hands. Again he recalled how she tended to censor his view of her and he instinctively tightened his elbows around her legs, opening her even wider yet.

The sight of her legs spread so far apart, and all the little parts and pieces of her anatomy popped right up toward him, almost reaching for him, softened his heart. Very gently, with the tips of his fingers, he pulled apart her little private lips and looked at the soft, pink glistening flesh inside. He touched it with his fingers, delighting in the silky wetness. Mesmerized, he rubbed his finger deeper into her and then circled it around the outside, and continued for a moment, massaging his fingers gently in and around her soft opening. Wishing to taste her, he lowered his head and dipped his tongue deep into her softness, while his fingers pried her open to receive him. As he did this, he lowered his hips toward her face and felt himself being instantly received by her warm, wide-opened mouth. It caused another surge of power to flow through him to have Princess Resentta accept him in her mouth so eagerly, and yet, he, too, was eager to give her pleasure.

With this in mind, the prince's fingers began carefully exploring his wife as he continued to lap at her with his tongue. He felt all around the area just above her opening with his fingertips, looking for the little mound of flesh that he knew he would enhance her enjoyment further. She moaned when he found it. He became keenly aware of her responses as he massaged the spot, anxious not to rub too hard or too fast. By carefully noting her reactions, he was able to massage the little swollen nub with exactly the correct precision and timing and pressure; all the while licking and swirling his tongue deeper and deeper into her, tasting as well as feeling her pleasure. In short time the princess's hips were moving in perfect harmony with his fingers and tongue; and he delighted in the knowledge that he was truly mastering her at last!

In the wake of the prince's expertise, the princess had temporarily forgotten her desire to please him, and was now completely unconscious of everything but the prince's fingers and tongue. She seemed to be traveling through a long, dark tunnel that absorbed all of her thoughts except those that concerned her present obsession for that which she single-mindedly sought after. As if on cue, she followed the perfect motion of his fingers with her hips. She sucked him absently, without thought for how or what she did, but rather, only as it enhanced her own pleasure to feel the length of him inside her mouth.

The prince did not mind, or in truth even notice, the princess's present lack of effort on his behalf, for he was fully absorbed in pleasing her. His whole being swelled and delighted in the knowledge that he could give his wife so much pleasure with his touch. He wanted to make her cry out. He needed to feel and taste it when he satisfied her.

The prince continued to caress and lick his wife patiently, unconsciously moving his hips up and down over his wife's eager mouth as he did so. Every now and then he would dip a finger deep inside her and shudder when he felt how warm and swollen and wet she was. Afterward, he promised himself, he would delve all the way into her and enjoy the warm silkiness to the fullest extent, but for now, he continued diligently, careful not to rush, or rub too hard, or to do anything to prevent his wife from finding satisfaction.

In due time the princess's body stiffened as she was swept over with waves of rapturous pleasure. The prince noticed this and could not resist sliding one finger all the way into her body to feel firsthand the little quivers and contractions of her orgasm. It seemed that he could feel her little spasms of pleasure throughout his own body, as well as around his finger.

Now the prince had been truly patient throughout this encounter so far, enjoying each and every moment for the poignant and delightful sensations that they brought him. But now all he felt was his own need to be satisfied. He turned himself around abruptly to face his flushing wife and spread her legs wide. She cried out as he entered her, but not in pain, for she was well prepared to receive him. The prince, feeling the wet evidence of his wife's pleasure on his body as he took her, was brought to a passion that bordered on violence. He grasped her by the hair as he crushed her lips with his. This seemed to bring his wife back to life again and she moaned and wiggled beneath him. Her hands reached around him to pull his hips farther into her. This action inflamed him further, and he grasped both her hands and forced them high above her head, holding them firmly in place. Once again, his forcefulness acted like a fan to her flame and her whole body began to writhe and thrash about beneath his. Again and again, her responses repeatedly inflamed him, until he was no longer conscious of his actions as he took her with a blind fury.

The princess clutched the prince with her legs, since her arms were still stretched high above her head in her husband's viselike grip. Her whole body was shaken by the passion she witnessed in her husband. She was again obsessed with the desire to please him, and aware that he was now in that same tunnel where she had previously been, insensible to everything around him except his pleasure. She opened herself up to him completely as she clung to him, reveling in his strength and power and passion as she felt his whole body tighten and convulse.

Afterward they clung to each other; the prince basking in his wife's soft openness and the princess trembling in the aftermath of surrender. Both had completely forgotten about the mask.

The prince was the first to come back to the present. The memory of the mask came back to him in a rush, and he sighed. It was not really his princess but the mask that had given him pleasure. And yet, he could not help but wonder if it were possible to make his bride respond this way without the mask.

He looked into the face of his princess. She was still under the influence of the mask quite obviously, for she returned his look with no embarrassment or pride, but with real pleasure on her face. How long had it been since she looked at him like that? He thought that perhaps this was his best opportunity to get through to her, while she was so receptive. He could try to get her to understand why he made the decisions that he did. He knew that she was particularly upset with him about his newest project, the tower, and thought this might be the perfect time to take her out to the project and show her how important it was.

The prince got up from the bed, pulling the princess up with him. "Come," he said. "Get dressed. I have something to show you."

The tower, when completed, would be taller than any other structure in the kingdom. The prince had designed it himself. It would house many weapons, and many soldiers when necessary, so that from within it they could protect their royal castle and the surrounding community. A spiral staircase up the center of the tower was added to carry soldiers to varying heights and positions along the fighting wall, and give them the greatest advantage over any foe at almost any distance. The tower was still in its early stages, but even so, it was an impressive sight. The prince approached it eagerly with his wife beside him, while workers buzzed all around, taking the fortress farther and farther into the sky, with masses of rocks of all shapes and sizes, laid together in such harmony that it appeared as if they were made for each other.

The princess gasped at the sight. She had always been so consumed with resentment over her husband's lack of consideration for her that she had never really paid attention to what it was he was actually doing. All she had been able to think about was that he was doing what *he* wanted, without regard for her wishes. That what he did was significant or impressive moved her not; it was already tainted for her by the way in which he had decided to do it.

Thus it was that now, for the first time since their marriage, the princess was able to look upon her husband's proceedings without bitterness. And the princess was genuinely impressed.

And so the day continued most pleasantly, with the prince supervising the construction of the tower and the princess watching everything, awestruck. He took her by the hand and showed her each and every detail, encouraged and delighted by her approval of what she saw. The day passed very quickly indeed, with the prince certain that he had finally gotten through to his wife.

However, only with nightfall would the moment of truth arrive. The time was quickly approaching for the prince to remove the mask; indeed, he could already feel the power of it wearing off. He could almost see the exact moment when it became ineffective, for in that instant he saw in the princess's face such a look of loathing that it took his breath away.

The princess was staring at her husband with pure hatred. All the events of the day rushed through her mind from her perspective as it was before he had put on the mask, and all her bitterness and resentment came rushing back in a startling wave, filling her with such a powerful surge of anger that she thought she might actually strike him.

How dare he? She actually blushed when she remembered how he had taken advantage of her that morning when she first came under the influence of the mask. The mask!

She held out her hand to him, trembling with rage.

"Now, husband," she said in a low, menacing voice, "it is my turn. Give me the mask at once." For the first time in their marriage she could tell him what to do. For the first time in their marriage he would have to listen to her!

"I think we should talk about this before——"

"Give it to me!" she screeched.

"I can't give you the mask when you are like this," he said calmly. "You might do something we'll both regret."

"You should have thought about that before you put the mask on this morning," she railed at him. "You don't think I regret that?"

"I'm sorry to hear that you——"

Once again she cut him off. "You're not sorry about anything. You think you don't have to keep your end of the bargain——not with the mask and not with our marriage." To her dismay, tears started to come to her eyes. Quickly, she buried the hurt, as was her habit, under her anger. She looked at her husband more calmly.

"Well, husband," she said in a challenging tone. "Are you going to honor the arrangement and give me my turn with the mask or not?"

The prince looked at his fierce little wife. He felt no small amount of trepidation over the irrational things she might do with the power of the mask while in her emotional state and, yet, how could he possibly deny her? He sighed. He could not renege on their arrangement. He had had his turn, and now it was hers. Whatever she did with her share of the power, he would just have to undo later. He took off the mask and handed it to his wife. Strangely enough, he felt a small but pleasurable relief as he gave over the mask. What was the worst that could happen?

The princess's fingers snatched up the mask from his hands before he could change his mind. She looked at it with something akin to madness, so excited was she at the thought of having some power at last, even if it was only temporary. She trembled as she brought the mask to her face. When it touched her skin, she felt such a surge of authority and power that she was nearly lifted from the ground. She heard a small cry escape her lips.

The prince watched this phenomenon with a mixture of horror and amusement. He still felt apprehensive about what his wife might do, but he could not help smiling at her trembling excitement over the opportunity to have the longed-for power. The look on her face was priceless, making it difficult for him to dwell on what such palpable happiness might cost him. In short, the prince found himself quickly coming under the charm of the mask.

Now you might think that the princess, as her first order of business, would immediately force her husband to return to the tower to tear down all his efforts of that day. But as a matter of fact, her first act of power was to gather together a group of workmen, that the aforementioned demolition might be done more quickly and efficiently.

Upon arriving at the tower, however, the princess realized that this first impulse would not be in her best interests. For one thing, she had formed a genuine, if grudging, admiration for the workmanship and beauty of the tower as it stood. And for another, she was not so silly and naive that she did not recognize the necessity for a tower to protect their castle. She was in favor of this protection. But more than anything else, the princess realized that if she destroyed all of her husband's efforts, she would be no better than he. And even worse than that, she would prove his theory that she was not to be trusted with authority.

Therefore, she quickly formulated a plan that would incorporate her aspirations into his existing project. Once she had made up her mind to work within these boundaries, it became quite simple to implement her additions. Indeed, it almost appeared that her embellishments to the tower had always been part of the plan; they fit so neatly into what her husband had already done.

When the prince learned of his wife's ideas, he was filled with admiration for her. Why hadn't he thought of this? Why hadn't she mentioned it before? He immediately began ordering his men this way and that, offering triple wages if they could make the princess's creation come to life that very night.

Much later, near morning, the princess threw herself down on their bed, laughing. She had never known such joy. The tower was truly magnificent. It would now bring beauty and life even as it sturdily protected them from harm. She should have been exhausted but she wasn't tired in the least. She felt her husband crawl into the bed next to her, and she looked at him curiously. He was smiling at her now, but she felt a sense of dread for when she would have to remove the mask.

The prince stared as his wife in amazement. She was so sweet and soft; it had never occurred to him that she could also be practical and clever. But then, he realized, he was perhaps too quick to generalize people and things. Who would have thought, for example, that a tower could bring pleasure and beauty, as well as protection? Her ideas had turned their fortress into a haven. During times of fighting, there would be warmth and comfort present to keep the soldiers reminded of what it was they were fighting for.

He wanted her. But more than that, he wanted to please her. He remembered earlier that morning, how she had surprised him by enjoying it when he became a little rougher with her, and he pulled her to him just as he had then—except that now he did it to please her and not himself. He put his fingers in her hair and felt at the plush softness for a moment before grasping a handful of it and yanking it back gently. When her face and lips were just where he wanted them, he searched her eyes for a moment before crushing her lips with his. His heart delighted to hear her little gasp of excitement as he kissed her.

And the prince ravished the princess, using the same procedure as he had that morning. Only this time he used his power and force only as he knew it would please her. This time, when he pulled her hair, or pinned her arms to the bed, or even experimented with new ways of making her submit, he did it all for her pleasure. That it pleased him beyond his wildest dreams was outside of his consciousness for the moment. He was single-mindedly preoccupied with the new knowledge he was gaining about his wife, and how he could use it to bring her pleasure.

But alas, the pair slept, and morning was already upon them. The power of the mask had mysteriously gone from the princess during the early morning hours and she woke suddenly to face her husband's disapproving glare.

"Tell me it was only a nightmare." He spoke slowly, in a danger-ously calm tone, directly into her blinking visage.

"Oh, no," she murmured, disheartened. But the old familiar anger was already beginning to creep back into her consciousness, waking her up with a jolt.

"I knew I should not have trusted you with the mask," the prince con-tinued in the same, nerve-rackingly calm tone. "Conniving little—"

"How dare you!" the princess interjected with authority. "I had every right to do whatever I wanted." She raised her head a notch as she faced her husband. "And furthermore," she added smugly, "when I had the power I considered your ideas and thoughts more than you have ever considered mine."

The prince ignored this comment entirely. He put out his hand with authority. "Hand it over, princess," he demanded.

The princess hesitated. How she hated the thought of losing the delicious power of the mask! She was suddenly filled with regret. She had tried to be responsible and thoughtful in how she used the power, and this was the thanks she got. She was seized with such a sense of injustice that for a moment she thought she might actually really hate her husband, and she wished spitefully that she really had done some-thing terrible with her power the night before, so that at least she would have deserved this denunciation.

But more than anything else, she dreaded the thought of giving her husband the mask.

"Do you promise not to change anything I've done?" she asked him.

"Do you dare to make stipulations to me?" he asked, his eyes burning fierce, his voice raised so that all his strength and authority were visible to intimidate her. He was incensed by her audacity. For her to have interfered in *his* project while he was under a spell and thereby helpless to stop her—and now this? He took a step toward her and said in a low, menacing voice, "Give me the mask or I will take it from you."

Princess Resentta felt a strange tingling sensation course through her when he said this. She wondered how it would go, if he decided to "take it" from her. Would the forcefulness of the ensuing struggle bring about any other emotion in him besides his insatiable lust for power?

Her hesitation while she considered these impudent thoughts gave him a jolt. She actually seemed to be mulling the threat over with amusement. His body tightened as he watched her contemplate, actually *contemplate,* his challenge! He believed he might be losing control of her, even as he felt a strange new admiration and anticipation over what that might mean. He truly didn't know what to do next.

But luckily, his wife gave in without him having to take any further action. She removed the mask and placed it into his hands with a little sigh. Then she silently watched him as he placed it over his face. The alterations to her perception of him were almost impalpable, but ere long, she once again felt the familiar sense that she was absolutely and thoroughly in her husband's power. However, it no longer bothered her. She marveled that she could still feel any desire to please him.

At her changed expression, the prince felt the slightest, almost imperceptible loss, but he did not stop to consider it. That he had possibly enjoyed that little rebellion of his wife's was probably no more than a momentary recurrence of the strange malady he had suffered last night while under the influence of the mask. But he could not afford to give in to it. He would reclaim his authority here and now.

But alas, the confused prince could not so easily brush aside his newfound desire for his wife. His mind worked diligently to push the errant thoughts out of his head, thinking he should not reward, but punish her. He fought off the aching tightening of his body, determined to prevail against it.

The princess, meanwhile, approached her husband and took his hand in hers. She looked up at him meekly.

"I want you to understand something," he began sternly. "This is not a joke. I have to make decisions every day that affect our lives and our livelihood."

"I know that," she said.

"Someone has to take charge and manage the day-to-day responsibilities," he continued.

"You're perfectly right," she responded.

He had a sudden impulse to take off the mask, but he resisted it.

"If you really believe somewhere in that mixed-up little head of yours that I am right, then you should try to show support for what I am doing instead of always trying to criticize and manipulate every task I take on," he persisted.

"Is that what you think I'm doing?" she asked innocently. He looked at her face. It was free of guile.

The prince had had enough. He tore off the mask. "Now tell me what you think!" he yelled at her.

She stood silently stunned. But in a moment she recovered.

"I think you're a beast and a bully," she told him.

"What happened to 'you're perfectly right?'" he asked.

"I was wrong," she said.

"Do you believe anything you're saying, or just speaking to hear yourself talk?" he queried her.

"I don't have to listen to this," she said, and turned to walk out the door.

"Oh, princess," he called out to her sweetly.

She turned and started at the sight of him. He had replaced the mask over his face. The confusion she felt lasted less than a moment and then all of a sudden she was falling for him all over again...or the mask—she hardly knew which anymore. She blinked the tears of confusion from her eyes.

"I only wanted to please you," she whispered.

"It would please me to beat you right now," he replied. "What do you think of that?" He saw her shudder and realized with a faint twinge of revulsion that the idea excited her, and it also excited him. Suddenly he realized he would beat her.

"Come then, and lie down on the bed for me, princess," he said. When she did this, trembling, he turned her facedown and lifted her nightgown so that she was bare from the waist down. She lay motionless, except for the trembling, which he knew was caused by the excitement of what was about to happen. He picked up his belt.

"I will beat the truth out of you," he told her as he flung out his belt so that it caught her sharply across her buttocks. She jumped and cried out. He sent the belt flying across her skin again, and then again.

"Oh, enough," she cried out. She began to rub her reddened bottom with her hands. "I only wanted a taste of it," she admitted.

"But I am not finished yet," her husband informed her, taking her hands and deftly tying them to the bedpost with a stray stocking so that she could no longer rub the soreness away. "I intend to punish you until I am satisfied that you have told me the truth."

"No, no, please," she cried, squirming. "I have had enough of this."

"You seem to believe that you should be in charge of everything," he said, as he flung his belt out at her reddened buttocks again. "Isn't that what you want?" And he followed this with yet another lash of the belt.

"I only want the same thing you want!" she cried.

"Oh," he prompted. "And what might that be?" She was silent a moment and he let the belt fly out at her again. She moaned and wriggled. She started to cry. He sent the belt across her flesh again. And then, after a moment of further silence, he hit her again.

"Power!" she cried out at last.

The prince finally stopped, dropping the belt. "You have too much power already," he murmured, staring at her steaming red buttocks. Suddenly his hands were caressing her skin, inflamed and tender beneath his fingers. He tried to soothe her burning flesh with his hand. She moaned and opened her legs to him. He bent his head between them and began to devour her.

The princess's hips rose up off the bed from the force of her husband's sudden change in behavior. He continued to delve between her legs with his tongue even as he caressed her swollen buttocks gently with his fingers. She allowed her hips to be maneuvered up high in the air and her legs spread far apart, leaving her body exposed to his mouth absolutely as her tearstained face rested on the bed. She lay there in utter abandon, with her hands still tied to the post beyond her head. She was once again lost in the tunnel, and surrendered entirely to her desire to find the release.

The prince continued his efforts on his wife, using his fingers and tongue expertly and patiently. He had forgotten his anger momentarily, as he observed her hips moving to and fro, bright red from his spanking, with the flesh shaking and wriggling against his hands and lips as he caressed her so very carefully. With every movement of her hips, and each moan from her lips, the prince could feel himself getting harder and harder, until his desire was at last painful. He reveled in the pain, even as she had herself reveled in the pain he had inflicted on her.

The prince felt her shudder and stiffen, and he coaxed every last shudder from her before he let her go. Then he suddenly took off the mask and untied the princess. He turned her over to face him. "What say you now, princess?" he asked. "Will you please your prince willingly?"

"Yes!" she cried. And she continued to repeat the word over and over, even as he savagely took her, and each "yes" from her lips acted as gas to a fire, to further incite him and her. The surrender made her feel like she was flying. And it finally occurred to him that the power she had been given was what was allowing her to surrender to him without the mask. Then he could think no more.

When he was once again able to speak, the prince said to the princess, "You will not need the mask again." He saw the disappointment in her eyes and he kissed her.

"I did not say 'you could not have' the mask," he explained. "I said you will not *need* the mask."

The princess got up on one elbow and searched her husband's eyes for his meaning. She was so hopeful that she didn't dare speak.

The prince could not help but laugh at her expression. He pulled himself up from the bed and her with him.

"Come, princess," he said. "Let us go and admire what you and I have accomplished together." The princess gaped at him in surprise.

"And let us never forget *how* we did it, either," he added.

And the tower was indeed magnificent, and became a legend that people came from miles around to admire. On its outside wall there stood level upon level of battlements and ammunitions; while on the other side, facing the castle, there were built-in levels of flower gardens, all encased by windows to let in the light. It took a full hour to reach the very top of the tower, and climbing up the delightful staircase was from that day forward the only thing that caused wear to Princess Resentta's shoes.

PRINCESS TARTIA

Princess Tartia hummed cheerfully as she powdered her nose. It was getting later in the day and she could hardly wait for the wizardess to arrive. A real wizardess, coming to see her! She was intrigued. If the wizardess truly had magic powers this could most certainly work out to her advantage. The wizardess had already foretold her discontent with her marriage, so it would stand to reason that the wise lady would know how to fix it.

She prepared certain phrases in her mind, little hints that she intended to drop in order to help the wizardess use her magic in the most useful way. She would naturally have to mention those things she believed to be the cause of her discontent, like the heart-shaped diamond bracelet she had received when she had specifically asked for the tear-shaped one, or the dress that should have had the gloves and stockings to go with it. These little inadequacies in her husband's gift-giving abilities drove her to distraction. It wasn't as if they were genuine gifts, after all, for didn't she make every effort to compensate him for each and every present? It's not as if he weren't always trying to get something from her, too. There had to be something in it for her, didn't there?

Once the wizardess was made aware of these things, the princess was certain she would put a spell on her husband that would help him behave in a more generous manner toward her. That would most definitely solve the problem with her discontent, and put an end to her little shoe problem. And really, didn't the wizardess have as much to gain in this matter as she herself did?

The princess assessed her image in the mirror. She looked demure and sensible, just as she had intended. She did not want to appear extravagant.

She went down to wait for the wizardess and was surprised to find her husband waiting there, too. She gave him a questioning look.

"I would like to hear what the wizardess has to say," he explained with a shrug. He had caught all her insinuations that his presence was neither necessary nor welcome, but he had learned from experience that her discontent often led to his own, so he had a vested interest in what the wizardess might recommend.

"I will fill you in later," Princess Tartia assured her husband. "I'm sure you have things you should be doing."

"Nope," he said casually, giving her a stiff smile. She returned his smile with a frosty one of her own. *Well,* she thought, *this will put a crimp in things!*

And with her usual impeccable timing, Harmonia rang their doorbell at just that moment. She greeted the princess and her husband cheerfully, assessing the situation all the while.

"I think the wizardess might like some refreshment," suggested the princess. "Darling, would you be a dear and fetch her something?"

"I would, my love," he replied smoothly, "but I fear that eating at this time of day may ruin her dinner."

The princess bit her lip with another frosty smile. "Always so thoughtful!" she murmured. He gave her a genuine smile at that, crushing her to him and landing a loud kiss on her forehead. She forced the smile to remain on her lips even though they felt as if they might crack.

"Perhaps something to drink then," she continued, determined to get him to leave the room for a moment so she could speak to the wizardess alone.

"Don't you remember?" he said, looking her straight in the eye with an expression of determination that she didn't like at all to see. "We are completely *out* of things to drink."

"Perhaps some water..."

"I am neither thirsty nor hungry," interjected Harmonia at last. Indeed, she was quite befuddled by the pair. Certainly there was a power struggle between them, but what was the source of the problem?

Not to be thwarted, Princess Tartia tried a different tack. She took the wizardess by the arm and led her into the sitting room, saying, "Look at the beautiful bracelet my husband gave me the other day." She twisted her arm this way and that as she displayed it for the wizardess, adding in as casual a tone as she could muster, "I had wanted tear-shaped diamonds at first, but my husband chose the heart-shaped ones instead. I think they're nice, too. What do you think?"

Harmonia thought the princess was a brazen little hussy but she said, "I think it's quite lovely. And if you'll forgive me, I don't think I'll sit. There's too much to do and I'm afraid I must be off." With this she dislodged her arm from the princess's grasp and began to fish through her large bag.

"Oh, but I have so much I would like to talk to you about," insisted the princess. "Surely you could sit for a moment or two?" She gave Harmonia her most disarming smile.

But she might have spared herself the trouble because Harmonia had not even looked up from her bag. "Aha," Harmonia said with satisfaction. "Here it is." She drew from her bag a little black jewel box. This caught the princess's attention.

"What is that?" she asked, itching to open the box.

The wizardess answered her, but unfortunately handed the sleek little black box to the prince. "Inside the box is a magical golden eel and a ring," Harmonia explained. "The golden eel is for you and the ring is for your husband."

The prince opened the box and the princess gaped at its contents in wonder. "A magical golden eel," she repeated, wide-eyed. She was already affiliating it with the golden goose of fairy tales, and imagining an unlimited supply of desirable things coming her way.

"What do we do with them?" her husband asked.

"Once you put on the ring you will know what to do," Harmonia assured him.

The princess was so happy she impulsively embraced the wizardess. The wizardess's words confirmed her guess; now her husband would know instinctively which gifts she wanted simply by wearing the magic ring.

"Thank you," she gushed. Harmonia chuckled in spite of herself.

"It is my pleasure," she said with meaning, and without further ado she left the young couple alone.

Princess Tartia looked at her husband. "Well," she prompted him excitedly, "put on the ring!" He was rather curious over the matter himself and so he slipped the ring onto his finger. He didn't feel any different, and yet, he suddenly knew how the ring and the eel were meant to be used. He looked at his wife doubtfully.

"Well?" she said again.

"You have to wear the other part," he began.

"Of course!" she said eagerly. "That makes perfect sense." She put out her hand for him to give it to her.

"It's rather, er...delicate," he warned.

The smile left her face. "What do you mean, delicate?" Why was he acting so strange?

"You wear it *inside* you," he said.

"Inside?" she repeated, and then seeing his expression her eyes widened in shock. "What?" she expostulated. She wished she had asked the wizardess where she was going next in the event they had difficulties. This could not be right.

"It's true," he said, reading her thoughts from her incredulous expression. "It is the only way it will work. I am certain of it."

She hesitated another moment. There was a certain logic that suggested the magical golden eel could communicate her wishes best from inside her body. Still...

"Very well," she agreed at last. "Give it to me and I'll put it in."

He smiled. "It has to be me who places it there," he told her. To the look she gave him he put up his hands, saying, "It will all become clear afterward."

"Oh, all right," she said. *This better pay off,* she thought. She pushed up her skirt and pulled down her undergarments.

The prince went down on one knee, holding her hips steady with one hand while he inserted the little golden eel with the other. The moment the eel was exposed to her fleshy softness it suddenly came alive and disappeared inside her of its own accord. The prince looked up at the princess.

"Do you feel anything?" he asked.

"I don't feel anything at all," she replied. They stared at each other for a moment, waiting for something to happen. She began to wish fervently for the little tear-shaped diamond bracelet she had been pining over as she stared intently at him. However, he didn't seem to be receiving the communication she was trying so hard to convey.

"Is there something you're supposed to do to make it work?" she asked.

He sighed. "Actually, it is working."

"Well?"

"Well, what?"

"Do you have the urge to do anything for me?" she asked him with a sly smile, thinking over and over in her mind: *get me the bracelet…get me the bracelet…get me the bracelet.*

He smiled, genuinely amused by her childish self-absorption. "I have a few ideas," he remarked suggestively. "But before you say any more, princess, I ought to warn you…"

"You aren't seeing an image of anything all sparkly in your head?"

"Look," he said. "I don't know what you think is supposed to happen here but the ring and the eel…"

"Something sparkly and *tear*-shaped?"

"Don't say any more until you hear me out," he warned.

"Are you or are you not going to buy me the tear-shaped diamond bracelet?" she whined in exasperation.

"Princess!"

"Oh, just tell me what I have to do to get my bracelet."

Fully exasperated, the prince suddenly touched the little golden ring that was on his finger and in the next instant Princess Tartia felt a piercing sting between her legs, causing her to cry out. It was as if the little eel he had placed inside her had come alive, sending a stinging shock between her legs that reverberated outward through her entire body. It shocked, then stung, then smarted and finally ached and throbbed, leaving her tender and tingling in the lingering aftermath. It took, however, several minutes for her to reach the tingling aftermath, and she could not guess how long that part would last. It felt as if the entire area between her legs was swollen and tender and pulsating. She stared at the prince, dumbfounded. She had completely forgotten about the bracelet for the moment. She was angry and terribly, horribly, *painfully* aroused.

"Now do you see?" he asked her.

"I...don't understand."

"The eel is not a means to get what you want," he explained. "It is a behavior modifier."

"A...what?" It was impossible to grasp what he was telling her while it felt as if her heart was pounding between her legs.

"A behavior modifier," he repeated patiently. "From now on, when you try to negotiate marital intimacies in exchange for gifts, the eel will help me to modify your behavior." *Boy, do I owe the wizardess for this,* he thought.

"From now on...?" Just those first three words were enough to fill her with dread.

"Well, until you have no further need of it," he amended. He moved closer to her but she backed away from him. She felt an unwelcome yearning for him.

"Negotiate marital intimacies...?" She was starting to comprehend the situation now with a mortification that teetered on horror. Was this what he thought of her?

"Yes, you know...the little tricks you dole out in order to get the things you want."

"And just how is this supposed to change all that?" she asked, hating him and the wizardess. She wished fervently that she would make the throbbing between her legs stop.

"That remains to be seen," he replied.

"I will take it out," she decided.

"I wouldn't try it if I were you," he warned.

She lifted her skirts, ignoring him. She pushed a finger into her body, feeling around for the eel. "Ah," she exclaimed, but the second she touched it, it seemed to disappear from her reach while simultaneously sending out another stinging shock. She cried out again, yanking her finger out as if it had been burned.

Princess Tartia went through the agonizing chain of sensations all over again, and when at last the smarting and aching subsided a bit, leaving her with only the throbbing, she looked at her husband desperately. "Help me," she begged him. She felt as if there was nothing else in the world besides the aching hole between her legs.

The prince realized that this was the moment of truth, when he could restore sexual balance between them, not only by reclaiming some of the sexual control but also by helping his wife salvage her own sexuality. He used her own words to do this, saying, "What's in it for me?"

She stared at him as if he slapped her. "I thought this was what you always wanted," she whispered.

"Well," he remarked coolly, "wanting can be subjective. I think your situation is more urgent than mine at the moment. Therefore, I would like *you* to show me how much you want *me* this time." While she had never put it quite so callously, it was certainly the way she had always made him feel.

"Please," she whispered. She never thought she would see the day when *she* would be begging *him* for sex.

"How badly do you want it?" he asked her.

"I...I don't know," she answered honestly.

"Let's see," he said, unbuttoning his pants. "Last time I wanted you to take me in your mouth you felt I should prove to you how badly I wanted it...to the tune of a lovely green stone ring, I believe."

She just stared at him in silence, wondering how he could be so cruel as to withhold the relief she needed so badly.

"Well?" he challenged, baring his hardness to her. She approached him finally, realizing that she had no choice but to give him what he wanted.

"Wait," he said. "First take off your clothes. I want to see your body."

She did this quickly, watching him as he watched her. Her eyes never left his, even when she went to her knees and took him into her mouth. She began the task rather resentfully but ere long she decided it was not so bad. She used her tongue and lips as deftly as she could to please him. "That's it," he murmured, causing her aching flesh to throb even harder. "Take it deeper."

She suddenly needed to make him want her as badly as she wanted him. She gave all she had to the task at hand, trying to gain back a little of the power she had lost. And she was actually enjoying it!

"That's enough," he groaned suddenly. He pulled himself out of her mouth. She moaned in anticipation as he pushed her down on all fours.

"Touch yourself," he told her, hovering close behind her open legs. He wanted to see how she found satisfaction. He had always wondered if she did, and he was certain that she had never been completely honest with him about it.

She put her hand between her legs and began to stroke herself while he watched. She rubbed herself self-consciously, obviously in an effort to entice him, spreading the little lips and opening herself to him. Although it pleased him to see it, he preferred at the moment to see what it took to bring *her* pleasure and satisfaction. He was beginning to wonder if she even knew.

"I need you," she murmured anxiously.

"I'm not convinced," he replied. "First show me where you like to be touched."

With her finger she pointed to her opening. "I want to be touched here," she moaned. "Please!"

"I want to see you satisfy yourself first," he insisted.

"What?" she asked, incredulous.

"Surely you must know how to give yourself satisfaction?"

She just looked at him. He was genuinely shocked.

"Lie down on your back," he said after a moment. She immediately obeyed.

"Now open your legs. Yes, like this." He maneuvered her so that her legs were parted comfortably, bent at the knees. Using the tips of his fingers he carefully felt around between her legs until he found the small nub of hardened flesh that sat just above her opening. Pressing one finger firmly but tenderly on the hardened tissue on top of the little nub, he slowly moved his finger back and forth over it. Princess Tartia gasped.

"That's it," he said. "Now just relax and enjoy it." Princess Tartia sat back in stunned silence. His rubbing seemed to be easing the tension even as it increased it. His fingers soothed her; yet they afflicted her, too, escalating the pressure, and driving her closer and closer to she knew not what.

In no time at all the prince had her hips bucking and thrashing about, assisting his fingers as they kept up their gentle but firm rubbing, urging and encouraging of her. She had never been this aroused before in her life and had momentarily forgotten the disdain she had felt for this kind of lack of sexual restraint. Her need was so great and the pleasure his hand was giving her was so intense. But just as the pressure was nearing its peak he abruptly stopped.

The princess looked up at her husband in horror. She wasn't exactly sure what had just been about to happen, but she knew it would have been incredible. "Don't stop," she cried.

"There is something I want you to do for me, too," he said. "Press your breasts together."

She groaned, hating him. But she pressed her breasts together for him. "You will please me while I please you," he explained.

She held her breasts together for him as he rubbed himself back and forth in between them. She remembered vaguely how she had laughingly offered herself in this way to him in exchange for…what had it been? She could no longer remember. His fingers had begun their delightful caress yet again, and all of a sudden taking him between her breasts did not seem so disagreeable. She liked it, in fact. It was exciting to watch his arousal moving so close to her face. His fingers forced her to feel what he was feeling with a steady stroking that caused her own hips to move back and forth, back and forth, faster and faster, just as he was moving his hips. She watched him, fascinated as he pummeled her breasts. She recalled suddenly how she had demanded an extra gift from him once for allowing his pleasure to erupt over her face but now it seemed like the most erotic thing she could imagine. She opened her mouth to tell him so, but only got so far as to cry out loudly. The mere thought of such decadence brought her over the edge from arousal to a pulsating explosion of pleasurable sensations. Her whole body shook with the impact of her release. Her response brought an instantaneous reaction from the prince and he pressed forward one last time, spattering hot liquid all over her face, just as she imagined seconds before.

The shock of the eel was at last subdued. But the princess was far from reconciled with all that had occurred. She had been shocked in more ways than one. She had always thought her husband selfish in his desires, never guessing that she would ever feel those same desires herself. She wondered if he felt the way she just did when he wanted her all those times; that aching, painful desire that separated everything from your mind except the need to be satisfied. Furthermore, why had no one told her that she, too, could get this kind of satisfaction from these intimacies?

The hardest thing of all would be letting go of the power she had gained from their previous arrangement. What now did she have to bargain with? In truth, she did not really enjoy lording it over him in that manner. Thinking back, she realized she had started using sex as a weapon shortly after their wedding night, feeling justified by her anger that he got more pleasure from the marital acts than she did. Instead of talking to him about her feelings—or working on them—she began withholding and trading favors. At some point that part of her life had become a task and her feelings for her husband became more like those for an employer.

That evening, Princess Tartia prepared a sumptuous dinner for her husband.

"I want you to take the eel out," she told him once he had eaten his fill.

He looked at her skeptically.

"I have learned my lesson," she said solemnly. "I have thought about this all day and I understand now how you must have felt when I have manipulated you...in that way."

He was astounded as well as pleased by this confession, but even so, he wasn't convinced. "Does the eel bring you discomfort having it inside you?" he wanted to know.

"Well, no," she admitted. "But I hate it. I'm afraid with it inside me."

"What have you to fear?" he asked. "If you have truly learned your lesson, as you say, the eel remaining inside you for a few days more should give you no cause for fear."

"But it does give me cause for fear," she insisted.

"Perhaps it is that you do not like the way in which the tables have turned," he deduced. "Perhaps you fear I shall be as cruel as you have been in the past."

This had indeed occurred to her and she remained silent.

He chuckled, and then continued in a scolding tone of voice, "I promise not to abuse you, princess. I will use the eel with discretion."

This statement enraged and thrilled her and, unable to manage the conflicting emotions, she abruptly stood up from the dining table and fled the room. The tables had most definitely turned against her, just as he surmised, and now it seemed that she would be obliged to await his leisure in resolving the matter.

Later that evening, when her husband joined her in their bed, Princess Tartia shivered with a mixture of anxiety and anticipation. She wanted him to do to her what he had done earlier that morning, but she was not sure how to ask. There was a much milder sensation of desire growing within her now than there had been then, but even so; it wore on her nerves to have to wait for it to be appeased.

The prince leaned over his wife in their bed. He brushed her hair away from her face in a gesture that was both loving and tender. "Are you feeling better?" he asked her in a husky whisper.

"I want you," she blurted out. He took a sharp intake of breath, searching her eyes to see if he heard her right. Satisfied that he had, the prince took her face in his hands and kissed her very affectionately. She embraced him, wanting a more passionate kiss and getting it. When the kiss was broken they were both breathless.

"You see," she told him candidly. "I really don't need the magic eel anymore."

At this the prince's expression turned cold. "So," he said in a scathing tone. "You've changed, have you?"

"Wh-what?" Princess Tartia stammered. What had she done?

"You are still the scheming little shrew," he stormed. "You seduced me most convincingly just now, but you still have to learn not to be so quick to name your price!"

"Oh!" she cried. "That was not at all what I meant." Tears came immediately to her eyes, but unfortunately, those, too, had been used too often to move him. Before she could stop him he had touched the magic ring.

"No!" she screamed. But it was too late. The shock pierced her with an intensity that nearly lifted her off the bed. She squeezed her thighs together in an effort to quiet the horribly intense sensations that followed. It felt like pins and needles were oppressing and tantalizing her most vulnerable and private area and she reached her hand down to rub the place where her husband had touched her earlier. This brought some small measure of relief but she still needed more.

"Oh, no," she heard her husband say, grasping her hands and pulling them up over her head as he flung her down on her back. "You will not get relief until I permit it."

Tears continued to stream down her face as she cried, "I'm sorry, I'm sorry," over and over again. She struggled beneath him, but it was not in an effort to escape him but rather, to rub against him in an effort to somewhat assuage the incredible need between her legs.

"Little vixen," he murmured, kissing her tears away in spite of his anger. "I think you need to learn how it feels to want." In fact, his body was aching nearly as much as hers, but he felt he should really make her suffer this time.

"Please listen," she implored.

"Do you want me to satisfy you?" he asked.

"Yes," she whispered, closing her eyes.

"Will you pay my price for satisfaction?" he continued.

"What is your price?"

"Will you pay it, princess?" he asked her again.

"Yes, anything," she swore.

But he loved her still, so how could he make he suffer?

"Then my price is that you satisfy me, too," he said at last. She opened her eyes and looked at her husband. Tears filled her eyes again, but this time they were tears of joy.

"Just tell me how you want me to do it," she said with a sniff.

"Surely you know what I like best?" he reminded her. Of course, she thought, shamefaced—and isn't that how she got the biggest presents from him!

His benevolence motivated her to make up for past hurts by giving him her best effort at his highest pleasure. She positioned herself carefully over him, settling her hips over his chest to cuddle his face between her legs while simultaneously leaning forward to grasp hold of him in her hand. She stroked the bottom half of his shaft with her hand in the way she knew he liked best while she massaged the upper half of him with her lips and tongue. She leaned the heaviest part of her weight on her legs and belly, so that he could enjoy her in absolute comfort. She moaned in relief to at last have his tongue soothing the nagging ache, even though the raging fire was still burning hot within her.

They both caressed and soothed each other exactly in the way they knew the other liked best. The pleasure was doled out in even parts, stroke for stroke, and as each partner became more impassioned, they struggled to give as much pleasure as they received. Pretty soon, their bodies were guiding the pleasure giver, so that all they really needed was the friction that person provided against their writhing bodies. The princess knew they would reach their climax here and now; for this was the prince's favorite thing in the world, to have his face buried deep between his wife's legs while she swallowed all of him down her throat. Each and every time they had done this in the past, the princess had walked away with a very special trinket, but this time she did it purely for the pleasure it gave her. She could tell the moment when he was ready to release himself in her mouth and found herself longing for the taste of him. At last when she felt the hot liquid erupting over her tongue and the inside of her mouth, her own body shuddered with a magnificent release of its own.

In the afterglow she could have shouted. Giving her husband pleasure had brought her satisfaction! She felt that she was at last really and truly a wife.

But in the morning it still plagued and worried her to be fettered with the eel, although she refrained from mentioning this to her husband. Aside from that, she felt very happy and contented, and found that she enjoyed her husband's company more than she had realized. She sought him out later that day at lunchtime so that they might dine together.

Now Princess Tartia dearly loved to shop, as you may already have surmised, and there stood in between the town's various restaurants several of her favorite stores. As she walked along the street with her husband she spied, in one of the large shop's windows, such a fabulous pair of ruby earrings that she momentarily forgot herself. With only the exquisite earrings on her mind—and how they would look in her ears—she immediately reverted back to her old ways.

"Oh, my," she cried suddenly, squeezing her husband's arm. "What I wouldn't give to have those!" She turned to punctuate this statement with one of her most suggestive looks, and without her even thinking about it automatically slipped her tongue out to play along her lip. But when she saw her husband's expression her tongue stopped short and her look turned to one of dismay. It was now on the tip of her tongue to apologize for this slip but the prince had already touched the magic ring.

To her utter disgrace, the princess was struck with the piercing sting of the eel right there on the public street! She grasped her husband's arm in her absolute misery, trying to hide the tears in her eyes as much as the stinging epidemic between her legs. Seeing her discomfort the prince led her into a dark alley between the buildings. By the time he got her into the most isolated part of the alley, the smarting had subsided to a pulsing ache, and the princess reached between her legs. But the prince grasped her hand and held it cruelly behind her back. She cried out with frustration.

"Do you still want the earrings?" the prince asked her.

"No!" she cried.

"You wanted them a minute ago," he reminded her.

"Yes."

"But now you want something else?"

"You know what I want now!"

"Yes," he said. "And the price for what you want is the same as the price of those ruby earrings!"

"I...I don't understand," she said.

"You don't remember the going rate for a pair of gemstone earrings?" he asked mockingly.

She tried to concentrate. Yes, she did recall another similar pair of earrings. Suddenly she gasped. Her face turned bright red, remembering what she had offered him for them. The thought of it aroused as much as it horrified her. "Please," she begged.

"Right here and now," he told her. She looked around. There was no one else in the dark alley but she still didn't think she could do it.

"If you will just...help me through this little problem now, I promise I'll do that for you when we get home," she told him.

"I find I want satisfaction now, too," he persisted.

"You can't be serious," she objected. "Someone might find us."

"No one will find us," he assured her and, indeed, the alley was quite dark and uninviting to visitors.

The throbbing between Princess Tartia's legs was becoming intolerable. "And you will...help me, too?" she asked him.

"After you have satisfied me, yes."

He released her then, and Princess Tartia nervously lifted her skirts and slipped down her undergarments. There was a wall nearby and she leaned on it as she bent over, still holding up her skirt. Her backside was fully exposed to her husband.

When he addressed her his voice sounded different. It was husky and low, sending titillating thrills through her. "Open your legs more," he told her. She complied and at length she felt him prying her open from behind, in that forbidden place, where she remembered with shame having offered herself to him for the more expensive gifts that she desired. Now she was bending for him, accepting him there so that he might later give her pleasure in return. She moaned as he pushed his way into her backside.

She had always disliked doing this for her husband, for there was a sharp discomfort involved in having him fill her that way. But on this occasion the discomfort inflamed her, making the throbbing ache she already suffered from multiply in its intensity. It did not come close to satisfying her; it solely had the power to antagonize and exacerbate her frustrated condition. She moaned her distress, swinging her hips to the agonizing thrills that rocked her body. Every thought that crossed her mind, along with every sensation that she experienced, tormented her more: the dark alley where at any moment someone might come upon them...perhaps someone was watching quietly, at that very moment, in one of the dark shadows...the steady pounding, pounding, pounding of her husband as he thrust himself into her...teasing and antagonizing her with his own pleasure while she suffered...even the feel of the cold wall on her hands as she bent before her husband had the power to send new waves of painfully strong desire pulsing between her legs.

The prince was enjoying his wife's submission immensely but at length he became aware of her dilemma. He was in no hurry to finish, preferring to have her for as long as possible while also hoping to give her something to think about when she felt the small twinges of tenderness he left behind after he was done with her. Yet he was keenly aware that she was suffering severely with her need, and he knew only too well how frustrating that could be.

"Reach your hand down between your legs, Princess Tartia," he instructed her.

She obeyed him unquestioningly. "Yes?"

"Find the place above your opening where I touched you yesterday," he continued.

"Yes, I have it," she said.

"Now rub it like I did." He reached his hand around to where hers was and showed her. "See," he said. "Like that." They rubbed her together for a few minutes.

Princess Tartia leaned her face against the cold wall of the alley as she rubbed herself vigorously with her hand. Her hips rocked back and forth in perfect time with his thrusts, thrilling both her and her husband with the delightful motion. In his excitement he ravished her behind all the harder and faster, and this excited her so much that she suddenly slipped over the edge, freezing her rocking motions suddenly in the intensity of her long-awaited release. It seemed that every minute of her delayed longing had added one decimal of strength to her orgasm, and when at last it came she felt that she would surely collapse.

As would become the rule, seeing his wife climax was the ultimate trigger to initiate the prince's own explosive release. He threw himself into her one last time with a yell, and she was still affected enough by the overwhelming pleasure she had received to feel a delighted thrill from his satisfaction.

Afterward, the princess felt quite shaken by the experience. She trembled awkwardly as she pulled on her undergarments and readjusted her skirt.

"I want to go home," she told him.

"Let's have lunch first," the prince insisted. She acquiesced, although she remained feeling awkward and uncomfortable. Her initial fear of the eel had by now metamorphosed into a total feeling of vulnerability that left her quite disturbed. They sat silently in the dark restaurant for several moments before either of them spoke.

"I was going to apologize," she blurted out suddenly. To his look of confusion she continued, "When I slipped up on the street with the earrings...once I realized what I was saying I was going to apologize."

"Why do you do it?" he asked her.

"I don't know," she admitted.

"I mean, if you want something you can simply ask for it or, better yet, think of a way to get it yourself," he continued. "How can we change things so you can get the things you want without having to...make deals?"

"I'm beginning to think that it isn't about things I want," she told him truthfully.

"I enjoy pleasing you, you know," he told her then, sliding a small gray velvet box across the table to her. She opened it to find the little ruby earrings inside.

"How did you...?"

"I am capable of things you haven't even thought of yet," he said with a grin.

She smiled, but she closed the little gray box and slid it back over to him. There were tears in her eyes. "I don't want them," she said. "But thank you."

"I want you to keep them," he insisted. "I want you to think of today when you wear them."

"Is there anything else you want?" she asked him teasingly.

"I want you to enjoy being my wife."

And then and there, with those words, Princess Tartia realized that she loved her husband. She did not want their relationship to be based on an exchange of gifts and favors. And she, too, wanted him to enjoy being her husband. She told him so.

Now Princess Tartia and her husband were able to begin their lives anew. Their problem was for the most part solved, and so from that day forward the princess's shoes remained quite pristine. Even so, it took another three days before the prince would agree to remove the little golden eel. But by that time, the princess had changed her mind about it, and for all I know she wears it to this day.

PRINCESS TOILLA

PRINCESS TOILLA PUSHED THE LAST HAIRPIN INTO PLACE AND TURNED HER head this way and that to evaluate the overall effect. As desired, her hairstyle made her appear quite cosmopolitan. It was the fourth time she had adjusted her appearance that day. Her gaze moved from her hair to her eyes and she paused, uncertain. Always she tried to hide her innermost fears and failings from the world, presenting the image of a sophisticate, but perhaps she should not try so hard to achieve that effect today, when the wizardess was visiting. Perhaps she should allow the wizardess to see her as she really was. But which hairstyle successfully represented the sexually challenged individual, who was able to lust and crave, but not able to find satisfaction?

Tears welled up in her eyes and she blinked rapidly to avoid them spilling over and spoiling her expertly painted features. Perhaps if she were honest with the wizardess, that wise lady would be able to help her. Hadn't she already inadvertently touched upon the truth when she made her claim that the princesses were "discontented" in their marriages? Princess Toilla could remember well how her cheeks had burned while she listened to the wizardess's speech, and how she had wondered if anyone, particularly her husband, had ever guessed her secret. She had been terrified to even look at him at that moment, lest he guess that she had deceived him all this time.

Princess Toilla sighed yet again. How unfair it all was! The same doubts that overwhelmed her each and every night rushed through her mind again now. Was she doing the right thing, pretending to be fully satisfied with her husband's lovemaking? It was, after all, her own inadequacies and not his that kept her from finding satisfaction. He always waited until she made her little counterfeit sounds of pleasure before he concluded his own pleasure. On the other hand, she felt his constant readiness and waiting for her to be somehow a part of the overall problem, but she could hardly fault him for that, either; for if he were not so aroused by her she knew that would cause her anxiety, too. It seemed that her body was simply unwilling to cooperate, and she doubted that even the clever wizardess would be able to help her solve this problem. And to make matters worse, she felt too much shame to admit her secret failure to anyone, even the wizardess.

The ringing of the doorbell drew her out of her revelry, and she suddenly regretted this last change in hairstyles. However, there was no time to remedy this. She made a few final adjustments to her appearance while her husband, unaware of his wife's inner torment, greeted the wizardess below stairs.

Harmonia was fully disarmed by the charming husband of Princess Toilla. He showed no discernable signs of conflict whatsoever and was attentive and loving to his wife as she entered the room, looking for all the world like the most contented wife in the kingdom. The princess greeted the wizardess with a welcoming smile that seemed quite genuine, and then looked at her husband with such love in her eyes that the wizardess blushed.

Harmonia felt a moment's discomfiture. Usually these things were so easy for her to identify. As she watched the two lovebirds in their living room she could find nothing more than love and goodwill between the two. And yet, there remained that morning's worn shoes, which was proof positive of a conflict. Suddenly Harmonia gasped aloud. Princess Toilla and her husband stared at her.

"Is anything wrong?" asked the princess.

"No, dear," replied the wizardess, recovering herself quickly. She smiled at the princess with a mixture of sympathy and admiration, marveling at how kind and loving she must be to so unwaveringly hide her own unhappiness for the sake of her husband's. She seemed to have none of the usual resentment that was quite normal for a woman in her position. Nevertheless, her sacrifice was completely unnecessary, and the wizardess was delighted to think that the princess's suffering would soon come to an end. "Just a little hiccup," she added with a chuckle. "I will write down your remedy presently and then be off."

"But...!" The princess was shocked. She turned to her husband, who merely shrugged his shoulders, looking equally baffled by the wizardess's announcement. To the wizardess's questioning look she paled. Should she speak now or forever hold her peace? But she knew that she would never be able to speak about her secret and so, with the familiar disappointment of anticipated failure she pushed her agony aside with a sad little smile. Her inadequacies were not the wizardess's problem any more than they were her husband's. "I am just surprised by how quickly you have..." The princess paused, blushing, before she finished with, "Diagnosed me."

"Oh, there is nothing wrong with you, my dear," Harmonia assured her. "All will be well, you'll see!"

Presently she scribbled on a sheet of paper and handed it to the prince. Princess Toilla waited expectantly for one of her own, but the wizardess stood up and was preparing to leave. Tears gushed forward with such force that the princess had to blink rapidly in order to stop them. She was profoundly disappointed but somehow managed to play the perfect hostess until the door closed behind the wizardess. Then she made to leave the room with a casual air, as if she had something important to do, but her husband called out to her.

"Aren't you curious about what it says?" he asked, waving the little sheet of paper.

"Not really," she replied with indifference, and for once she wasn't hiding her true feelings. She truly felt that whatever the wizardess had written on that paper had no bearing on her at all. How could it? The wizardess knew nothing of her secret. Apparently she had leapt to her own conclusions from meeting her other sisters, and had simply doled out the same cure for each of them. But from her own conversations with her sisters she knew that, whatever their problems were, they were not the same as hers. She walked out of the room, leaving her husband staring after her in surprise.

The prince turned to the instructions the wizardess left him. He read them with no small amount of shock, and then read them several times over again. He could scarcely believe his eyes.

But by later that evening, the prince had quite recovered his shock, and was, in fact, quite determined and prepared. Meanwhile, Princess Toilla seemed to have forgotten that the wizardess had even visited them.

The prince entered their bedroom and found his wife sitting forlornly at her dressing table, brushing out her hair. Though it was not part of the wizardess's instructions, he went up behind her and took the brush gently from her hand. Then he carefully resumed the brushing of her hair, looking at her face in the mirror as he did so. They smiled at each other as he leisurely performed this service for her.

The prince brushed Princess Toilla's hair until it sparkled and snapped, then he bent down and kissed her cheek, whispering, "Come to bed, darling."

She followed him to the bed with a small, almost imperceptible sigh. Her husband caught the little sound and smiled. He lifted her gown over her shoulders and tossed it onto a nearby chair.

"Lie down, close your eyes and relax," he instructed her, adding, "I have a few things to do before I join you."

She glanced at him when he said that, but then shrugged and lay upon the bed. As always, she felt a tingling pleasure throughout her body from simply being near him. She closed her eyes and sighed again, more deeply this time. How was it that she could feel such a strong longing for her husband only to have it dissolve into nothingness when she held him?

The prince had returned to the room, but he busied himself with lighting candles all around. The princess noticed immediately that there was something different about the candles. These candles, when lit, caused strange shapes to appear on the walls all around her. She stared at the odd shapes curiously as they flickered and moved throughout the room, and a slow dawning crept over her that they were actually graphic depictions of an intimate nature. She gasped when she realized this, and turned her head to look directly at one of the candles on a nearby table. The candle itself was quite ordinary, but it sat inside a metal container that had miniature cutouts of the images on the wall all around it. This then, was the trick that caused the shadowy graphics to appear and flutter all over on the walls. The effect was quite remarkable; Princess Toilla was amazed and aroused by the sight, and suddenly she found herself interested and wondering about what it was exactly that the wizardess had put down on that little piece of paper that she gave her husband.

"Keep your eyes closed and relax," the prince told her in a teasingly authoritative tone that simultaneously caused a thrill to course through her and a nervous giggle to burst forth from her lips. There was something very exciting in simply lying nude and waiting for what might happen next, but she found it hard to keep her eyes closed with the wild images flickering over the walls all around her. She couldn't keep herself from peering through her lashes at the images.

The next of her senses to be assailed was her hearing, as a low, pulsating beat began to reverberate in her ears. It was music she had never heard before, strange and provoking in its nature and intensity. Mingled within the throbbing tension of the instruments were other sounds she could not identify…perhaps they were voices? Yes, it seemed that they were voices, alien and unidentifiable, and yet…there was an overt sensuality in the general tone that she could detect. Or was it just her imagination? She wasn't certain, but the combination of imagery and sound was certainly enhancing her state of arousal by fixing her consciousness on the erotic messages that were being entered through her senses. The voices in particular kept her attention riveted, as they seemed to change in tone and substance, so that just when she began to believe they were chanting something indecent it would suddenly appear that they were perhaps whispering restlessly instead. The pictures, too, seemed to change all around her, so that one moment they appeared to be shadowy lovers and the next they appeared more like wild creatures. All of this had the effect of holding two of her five senses hostage to the tantalizing arousal that was building up within her.

Her husband approached her at last, reminding her to relax as he began touching her gently, moving his hands over her shoulders and breasts, and leisurely caressing her skin and curves without regard for time as his hands traveled the length of her in an exploratory manner. Now her sense of touch joined her other senses in escalating her desire to a point it had never before achieved. When the prince's hands reached in between her legs, the voices in the hypnotic music seemed to be chanting for her to "open" again and again, and at length she complied with the compelling directive, opening her legs wide for her husband's gently prying touch.

The prince's fingers prodded and pressed her flesh, massaging their way in between her little lips and into her wet opening. He slipped one of them all the way in and she gasped. A low moaning followed, but she could not tell for sure if it was her or the music. The voices now seemed to be moaning in time with her own pleasure as her husband touched her. Her breathing went in and out in perfect harmony with the instruments, even as her heartbeat began throbbing in time with the drumbeat.

A new voice pierced her consciousness and she had to concentrate for a moment to realize that it was that of her husband.

"I want you to grasp my finger," he said.

With effort, Princess Toilla tightened her body around his finger as instructed.

"That's very good," he praised huskily, causing a thrill to shoot through her. "Now release it." She did this, too.

"That was perfect," he told her. "Now tighten up again...that's good. Now release." The prince had her tighten and release like this many times. Each and every time she responded to his instruction he praised her, and with each little bit of praise she felt yet another painfully exquisite thrill stream through her. And all the while the voices and images continued to entice her, until she trembled with excitement and hardly knew which sensation to focus on next.

"I want you to do these exercises every night before you come to bed," he told her. "Just like brushing your hair."

"Hmm," she murmured, still clenching and unclenching her muscles over his finger.

"Tell me you will do the exercises," he insisted.

"I will do the exercises," she vowed eagerly. "But will your finger…?"

He laughed, a deep resonating sound that delighted her senses more than the music. "If you want I will help you with my finger."

Another thrill titillated her with this husky reassurance from her husband. But he slipped his finger out of her then, causing her to feel a terrible loss.

The prince picked up a glass and slipped something from it into his mouth. He then lowered his face between Princess Toilla's legs and gently began licking her wet opening with a very cold tongue. She gasped and her hips involuntarily rose up off the bed. Her husband grasped her hips with his hands, effectively holding her in place as he slipped something hard and cold—ice—into her body and pushed it in as far as it would go with his tongue.

"Oh!" she cried out loudly. The sensations were alarming. Piercing, sharp, icy stings awakened the interior walls of her body as she struggled to move her hips—not to escape her husband or the excruciating cold—but simply because it seemed she had to move. Indeed, it seemed that the music and images were telling her to move, and she wanted to obey. "I cannot bear it," she cried as her hips bounced up and down upon the bed. Her husband's husky chuckle antagonized her even further, making her need so great she felt almost desperate. It felt as if the music was now coming from within her, not without.

But alas, the frozen chip had melted, leaving her aching for something more.

"Do you want more?" her husband asked, perceiving her loss.

"Yes! Oh, yes!" she cried.

He had been licking her all the while but now he slipped another chip into his mouth and then with his tongue once again pushed it far up into her. Her head moved back and forth on the pillow as she endured the tantalizing sensations all over again.

"Oh, surely...?" she moaned, thinking there must be a way to harness this pleasure.

"Yes," he answered her. "We will get to it...just slow down."

His voice, so calm and low and delightfully reassuring, instructing her in this way was having a strange effect on her. She listened through the music, waiting restlessly for his next directive. But presently his tongue was busy licking hungrily at her trembling little opening. He stopped again for a moment to slip another ice chip into her. She cried out with excitement as she received it.

Now the prince, perceiving Princess Toilla's readiness, slipped his fingers up over the top of her and began searching for the small, cartilage-like knob of flesh that sat directly over her opening, about a half inch up, right in the center. Just as the wizardess had predicted it sat there swollen and quivering, never having been fully awakened from its overlong slumber. He settled his finger over the top of it, applying a small amount of pressure as he gently moved his finger back and forth and around it. His wife's hips stopped moving suddenly, and she lay as if paralyzed by his touch.

"Does that feel good?" he asked her.

"Yes," she sighed, unable to collect all of her strength or find her voice.

"Tell me you like it," he insisted, wanting to keep her fully focused on the activity so as to maximize her excitement and further ensure her success in finding satisfaction. As he rubbed, he picked up another little ice chip with his other hand. He would indeed keep her focused on the task at hand!

"I like it," she whispered obediently. She was beginning to get lost in her desire again, for the music had never stopped, nor the images, nor his finger, nor his instructions, nor even the tantalizing stinging of the ice, as he slipped another chip far up into her, causing her to moan loudly.

"Say, 'I want you to keep touching me.'"

There were so many erotic sensations fighting for her attention, between the music and the images and the piercing cold and his deep voice issuing instructions, she could hardly think. Mostly though, there was his finger massaging her in that place where everything came together. She was terrified that he would stop. She mechanically obeyed him, crying, "I want you to keep touching me." The voices in the music seemed to be echoing her cries. The drums continued to pound out the rhythm of her heart. Her hips had started to move again, and now she was rubbing herself against his hand, for her instinct had finally kicked in and she knew that somehow that little place he had discovered was just like the magic genie in the bottle, and that with enough rubbing something very magical would surely happen. She moaned in delighted agony as she struggled against his hand.

His sexy deep voice was saying, "Just relax and enjoy the sensations…we have all night. I love touching you." Or was it the voices in the music? She wasn't sure. Her head swam in time with the erotic images on the wall. She wanted him inside her and she told him so.

"No, not tonight," he told her, not without difficulty.

She became upset by this. "But..."

"Maybe afterward then," he assured her to quiet her agitation. "But only if you try hard and you're very good." This seemed to bring her back on track so he added, "You are going to try very hard, aren't you?" She moaned loudly, grinding her hips even harder into his hand.

"Tell me you're going to try very hard," he continued, seeing her excitement over this type of questioning.

"I will try," she moaned. She closed her eyes but her mind seemed to conjure images that were more graphic than those on the wall. She tried to push the images away, but they persisted. Her imagination was running away with her and she began to visualize things she had never thought of before, things that surely were not natural or done. Was it the music that put those images in her head? Her hips moved furiously against her husband's hand.

"Tell me you're going to try very hard," he persisted, slipping in another chip of ice with his free hand.

"I will try very hard," she cried out, moving her hips faster with each question he put to her. Several times already she had reached the brink of something only to get too excited or afraid, and lose it completely. She could feel it coming upon her again, and once again her mind seemed to want to change directions and revolt, but she squeezed her eyes shut and forced her thoughts to remain with the images—the very worst ones, in fact—where in her mind's eye she was doing unspeakable things that perhaps her husband might not even approve of. The music helped to push her along as she dwelled on the forbidden images, murmuring all the while, "I will try, I will try."

"That's it, princess," her husband coaxed her, amazed by her efforts and how much it aroused him to watch her. He slipped yet another ice chip into her quivering hot opening.

She was still chanting, with eyes squeezed shut, "I will— Oh!" The ice pierced her flesh just as her release came upon her, so that the effect was intensified and lengthened. Her hand flew down to where her husband's hand stroked her and she held it still, trying desperately to hold on to the incredible waves of pleasure that tickled their way through her body, seemingly meandering through her very veins.

The prince watched with delight as his wife was consumed by the pleasure. Her eyes were still shut tight and her body was rigid and tense. But at length she relaxed and lay still and limp.

The prince was on fire.

Princess Toilla was soft and trembling as she wrapped herself around her husband. The wizardess had recommended that he focus solely on her that first night, so that the princess might learn to find pleasure without worrying about his pleasure, or him waiting for her, but how could he help it, with her so warm and willing, and especially after he promised to take her if she tried hard, which there was no arguing she most certainly had?

So he slid gleefully into her, and neither of them had realized it could feel so good. For him to be inside her when she was so wet and well satisfied was indeed an amazing thing. His body shuddered violently as he struggled to hold off his own release so that he might linger in the sweet, tender folds of her swollen flesh for as long as humanly possible. For her, feeling him inside her softened body brought delicious little ripples of pleasure that, although not as strong in their intensity as her earlier pleasure, brought tingling little reminders of what she had just enjoyed. Suddenly she felt that she was truly making love, and she marveled at the glorious feeling.

The next day was a long one for the princess, spent in anticipation of what was to come. She felt like this was her real honeymoon. The night came at last with the same measures of lights, music and touching. The princess had rushed to their bedroom, and by the time she was bathed and naked upon the bed she was already in a state of arousal. She approached the marital bed with anticipation instead of anxiety, and she was amazed to find that this had a huge influence in her ability to enjoy what followed.

This time, when the prince perceived her readiness, he instructed her to lay on all fours on top of him but facing opposite him, resting her head on his stomach with her forearms and knees resting on the bed on either side of him. In this position, her hips were spread wide open and high in the air…and positioned directly in front of her husband's face. But shyness was not her problem, especially while such wild images flickered over the walls and the low, throbbing music filled her mind with ideas that seemed to come directly from the suggestive voices of the musicians. Furthermore, this position forced her to be fully aware of her sex. No sooner had she settled herself on the bed over her husband than she was tingling and wet.

She forced her head to remain rested on his stomach as instructed, even though she knew he was hard and aching to be touched just inches away from where she lay.

He began much like the night before, moving his hands over her and caressing the shape and feel of her. Soon his finger slipped into her wetness and she began the little exercises that strengthened her awareness as much as they strengthened the little muscles that contracted with her pleasure. All the while he encouraged her like before, stroking her backside with one hand while he monitored her progress with his finger. She found she was much more easily excited now, and her hips rocked with the music while she obediently kept up with his orders to tighten and release. Indeed, it had by now occurred to her experienced mind that this exercise actually mimicked the contracting of her muscles that occurred during her orgasm, except that she was doing it much slower than when passion brought it along of its own accord. Was this exercise helping her then? It certainly seemed that the simple act of doing it made her more aware of the capacity for pleasure that always waited, dormant, between her legs, until such times she decided to awaken it.

"Take your time," she heard her husband tell her in his deep, reassuring voice, but the music seemed to be whispering for her to move faster, so she did, wiggling her fanny with delight as she imagined her husband's eyes watching her. After she finished her exercises he rewarded her with his tongue, wiggling it deep inside her while his hot breath scorched the tender skin on the outside.

She could hear the rattling of a cup and knew that he was collecting an ice chip for her. She began to whimper in anticipation, causing him to laugh.

"Do you enjoy the ice chips?" he asked her.

"Yes!" she was forced to admit.

"I think you should earn them," he teased.

"No!" she cried. She could feel her labia lips trembling, reaching and grasping for the ice of their own accord.

"Bring your hand down between your legs," he ordered.

She hesitated only a second. Maybe it would not be so bad. She reached her hand down and felt around for the place he had discovered the night before.

"There's my love," he encouraged, and she once again thrilled in the knowledge that his eyes were watching her from his perfect viewpoint. He took her hand with his and helped her. She shuddered at the utter delight in having him instruct her this way. Each time she followed his directions he would slip in another little chip of ice, so she had double the incentive to perform well. Her eyes, meanwhile, were grafted to the wall, taking in the erotic imagery while she listened attentively to his instructions through the pounding music, and massaged the magic little button for her and her husband's pleasure. And all the while the voices continued their encouraging chants.

The prince watched with fascination from his incredible vantage point, tormented by the sight of her hand caressing herself and her hips bouncing erotically, mere inches from his face. Every time she pleased him he slipped in another chip of ice, causing her hips to jump and dance even more delightfully. He knew it was impossible, but it seemed that her little lips would reach out for the ice when his hands approached them with it, sucking it up into themselves hungrily— only to have it dissipate all too quickly into mere wetness. He licked at the little lips when this happened, kissing away their disappointment. Meanwhile her hand continued diligently rubbing between her legs. She realized she was able to perform this service on herself even better than her husband had done and, what's more, she loved having him watch her do it.

But now the voices seemed to be moving the princess toward something new. As if in a trance she lifted her head and stared at the throbbing flesh that stood up fiercely between her husband's legs. Instinctively she slipped her mouth over him and began moving her head up and down to the same rhythm that her hips moved back and forth to. Now she felt in sync with the thrilling music, but still the voices seemed to be calling out for her suck harder and deeper. Her husband moaned loudly, thinking it was all really too much, having her most private area wiggling in his face while she was stroking him with her mouth. Just who was supposed to be learning about pleasure here?

But it was true—in the past two evenings he had felt more intense pleasure than he had ever felt before in all of his life. And all from trying to bring pleasure to his wife, who deserved it after giving him so much without ever asking for anything in return. But, oh, how delightfully it had all turned out! All the little recommendations that the wizardess had given him to awaken his wife's senses had awakened his, as well. The images playing over the wall and the erotic music with the sensual chanting had delighted his senses as much as hers. He had learned to savor pleasure, whereas she had learned to find it.

The prince perceived that his wife was reaching the proximity of her release and to spur her along he slipped another ice chip deep inside her, pushing it all the way in with his finger and then leaving his finger inside her to relish the silky wetness of her.

Now the princess knew that she only had to give herself over to the passionate images and sounds and sensations to once again feel that wonderful vibration run through her. Her mind still hesitated, but she did not give in to it. Rather, she gave over her will to her senses. She sucked her husband harder and better than she ever had before, until she heard—or imagined that she heard—the voices applauding her efforts. Her hips moved in wild abandon as she sucked her husband with all her might and rubbed herself furiously. His hips were also moving as he stared helplessly at her shaking hips. With effort he reached for another ice chip. He felt drunk.

Suddenly the princess was nearly toppled off the bed as her husband moved from beneath her to behind her in one quick maneuver. She stayed on her hands and knees and resumed caressing herself, realizing instantly that he was going to take her from behind.

The prince deftly slipped an ice chip inside the princess and ground himself into her behind it, stuffing the ice deeper and deeper with each thrust. She cried out loudly as the ice again caught her in the middle of her release, extending and magnifying it for her and the prince both—for her release had set his off. And all at once the prince realized why Princess Toilla liked the ice so much!

The wizardess had recommended that the prince continue these sensation awareness exercises with his wife each night for as long as it was needed, but long after Princess Toilla's shoes ceased appearing mysteriously worn through in the mornings, the exercises continued. And for all I know, they practice them still.

PRINCESS WEARIA

PRINCESS WEARIA ROLLED OVER AND GROANED. IT WAS LATE IN THE DAY, she knew, but she didn't feel like leaving the comfort of her bed. She made a silent wish that the wizardess would be kept longer with her other sisters so that she would have additional time to make herself and her house presentable, but even as she wished it, it registered somewhere in her consciousness that no matter how much time she had she would not likely trouble herself too much anyway.

Why, oh, why did her father have to expose her to the pestering wizardess in the first place? Who cared if her shoes wore themselves out while she was sleeping? It wasn't as if they couldn't afford new shoes!

She yawned petulantly, looking around her. Her husband was long gone from their bed, she wasn't sure where, but that was not unusual; he always rose from their bed in the mornings. She, on the other hand, often slept late into the afternoons if left unhindered. But it seemed that too often there arose some irritating task of mundane proportions that she had to attend to. Why must she bother? Her lethargy quickly turned into resentment. However, in Princess Wearia's case, resentment proved to be a useful emotion that actually acted as a cathartic, giving her the power to haul herself out of her bed at last.

She stared at herself in the mirror for a moment, wondering over the image she saw there. She reluctantly acknowledged the little evidences of neglect and excess, and made herself a mental promise that she would attend to those matters sometime near in the future. Somewhere in the far back reaches of her mind, buried beneath many such promises, rested the realization that these daily pledges were nothing but fluff, created for the sole purpose of making the moment more tolerable, but as always, at the forefront of her mind she felt satisfied that this time she would achieve success where before she had failed.

The princess wandered over to her wardrobe and browsed absently through the clothes, somewhat discouraged by the challenge of transforming herself into something that was fit to be seen by a wizardess. There were a few items that brought out the best in her, but upon closer inspection she realized that they were in dire need of ironing. This was a sufficient obstacle to eliminate them from her options. Next she spied a large, flowing dress that, although not very impressive, would most certainly fit and did not require any preparations. She quickly plucked it from the wardrobe, quieting her outraged subconscious by arguing the import of this day. Why should she dress for some aged wizardess? The wizardess would likely be removed from their kingdom by the end of the week anyway, for the princess was certain the woman would fail. She was the only one of her sisters who had not acknowledged any truth in the wizardess's assessment that the princesses were "discontented" in their married life. She had, in fact, been outraged that the wizardess would dare to even suggest such a thing.

The princess thought about her husband as she dressed. He was so handsome and kind, never pressuring her about "her ways" as her father used to do while she was growing up. Her husband seemed content to let her live her life as she wished, without expecting her to constantly put forth effort to do more. She could not imagine herself being happier. Oh, to be sure, they were not honeymooners anymore, but that was to be expected. Married couples did not share intimacies all the time. She tried to think of the last intimacy they had shared, and her mind couldn't locate the memory of so much as a kiss. Oh, well, her husband was busy building their legacy, and once this was accomplished they would, quite possibly, take a second honey-moon.

Princess Wearia went to her dressing-room table. Her hair, which used to be her crowning glory, lay in disorderly clumps all around her head. Just looking at it made her blanch. As she pulled it back into a tight knot, she reasoned that she could either dress her hair or straighten up downstairs—she did not have time for both. If her con-science had not given up so long ago it might have pointed out that she was not likely to be doing much downstairs, either. Oh, well, she sighed again as she looked at the pitiful creature staring back at her, she was not so shallow a person that she concerned herself with what other people thought of her!

Princess Wearia went down the stairs to find that the wizardess had already arrived and was, in fact, waiting for her. She was seated opposite the prince, speaking to him in deep, low tones. As the princess approached the two noticed her.

At the sight of Princess Wearia, Harmonia gasped. Her preliminary impression of the tardy princess was none too flattering of course, having been made to wait around with so many things to do and so much at stake, and especially after having learned from the prince that his wife was detained for no better reason than that she was a "late riser" by nature. But she had expected to lay eyes upon a perfectly groomed prima donna, imposing from outward appearances at least. The wizardess stared, open-mouthed, at the slovenly creature that stood before her. This case would require the most drastic measures available to her.

Harmonia turned back to the prince and put out her hand to him. "Thank you for keeping me in such charming company," she said, effectively dismissing him.

The prince was a bit surprised by this, for he had thought his presence would be required in this matter, but he good-naturedly took the hand she offered and rose up to leave, replying gallantly, "The pleasure has been all mine."

Once the prince had gone from the room, the wizardess took a deep breath and faced the princess. "Come sit beside me," she said as kindly as she could manage; the princess seemed incapable of the simplest courtesies of a hostess. The princess slumped down next to her obediently.

"Do you really have magic powers?" she asked the wizardess.

"Oh, yes!" exclaimed Harmonia without hesitation. "I daresay my powers have already benefited your sisters." She paused for a moment and then realized how she might turn the princess's interest in her wizardry to her advantage. "My specialty is in predicting the future," she remarked casually, setting the bait.

"Indeed," remarked the princess, coming suddenly alert. "How do you do that?"

"I can read everything about a person from simply looking into their hand," she said. "All the events of a person's life are written in a secret language on their palms. One hand carries the past and the other carries the future." She was embellishing a bit, for although our stories are written on our palms, they are rather oblique sometimes, even for a wizardess. However, it suited her purpose—and would ultimately suit Princess Wearia's, too—to deceive the princess for the time being. She took up one of the princess's hands and peered at the palm with interest. "You see," she said, pointing to one of the lines on the girl's hand as if to prove her point, "it says here that you took a terrible tumble from a horse as a little girl."

The princess gasped. It was true!

The wizardess quickly pointed to another line on the same hand. "You were also once very musical," she said with a strange little knowing smile.

The princess gasped again. She had indeed studied music but the wizardess's self-satisfied look clearly told her that she was referring to her naughty exploits in the music room with her instructor. She yanked her hand away from the wizardess's grasp. "How fascinating," she murmured uncomfortably. A slight blush rose up along her neck.

Harmonia restrained a laugh. The girl's reputation had preceded her, but the real puzzle was what could have caused the girl of those renowned exploits to become the blob she was today. The correct pattern of things dictated that life become more remarkable and eventful with the passage of time, but in Princess Wearia's case, her past was markedly more intriguing than her present. Where once there was an abundant zest for life there now appeared to be none at all.

Harmonia, undaunted, raised her own hand, palm up, to the princess. "The other hand," she continued, ignoring the princess's embarrassment completely, "shows us what lies ahead of us." Using an old trick she had learned as a child, she caused an unusual line to appear on her hand. "This is the most important mark of all," she said in a confidential tone. "It is our life line. It shortens as we approach death. When death is upon us, it disappears entirely. Mine, as you can see, has quite a length to go."

Just as the wizardess expected, the princess began to search her own hand for her life line. She looked up at the wizardess when she could not find it.

"Let me see," Harmonia said casually, taking the princess's hand in hers. She prepared herself for the performance she was about to give; it must be absolutely convincing.

All of a sudden the wizardess became quite pale and serious as she pretended to search the princess's palm for her "life line." "But it must be here," she murmured.

"Unless..." began the princess in horror.

The wizardess abruptly dropped the princess's hand and attempted to change the topic. "Perhaps we should get on with the purpose of my visit," she said shakily.

"No!" cried the princess. "We must find my life line!" She continued to search frantically the area of her palm.

"Perhaps in your case..." Harmonia paused a moment, seemingly alarmed and at a loss for words. "Perhaps your life line is different than others'."

"Perhaps I am going to die, you mean!" The princess grabbed the wizardess's hand again and searched her palm. "Where did you say it was?"

The wizardess caused the little line to appear on her hand again. It stood out clearly on her palm.

"Oh, dear, oh, dear," repeated the princess as she searched her hand yet again. Harmonia felt a touch of sympathy for her. But really, what else could she do? The truth was that nobody's life line was written in stone; lines appearing on the skin were always subject to change. More importantly, she was not about to allow this lazy princess to jeopardize her ability to successfully solve the riddle when all she needed was a little jolt to get her back on track.

The princess looked up at the wizardess, and their eyes locked. Harmonia's eyes were very solemn and sympathetic. The look accomplished what words could not and Princess Wearia burst into tears.

"Please tell me the truth, wizardess," she sobbed. "How long do I have?"

"It could be any day," Harmonia told her after a long pause, which she used to give the impression that she was reluctant to admit it. She consoled herself for this misrepresentation to the princess with the fact that what she said was, at least in part, the truth. "Suffice it to say," she added with a sad little sigh, "when my own week is up it appears that you, at least, will not be wearing out any more shoes." This, too, was an honest statement; for if her wizardry worked, this princess would be cured of her discontent and the worn shoes would indeed stop appearing each morning. But for the misguided princess, the wizardess's words in this context had their intended effect. Her cries turned into wails.

"Oh, my poor girl," encouraged the wizardess.

"Isn't there anything I can do?" she asked the wizardess when her cries at last died down to hiccups.

"Well..." mused the wizardess, pretending to consider this.

"Oh, please, wizardess," the princess implored. "You *must* tell me."

"Well, I can't say for sure that it will work, but I suppose anything is worth a try." She paused again, pretending to think. The princess sat very still and hopeful, waiting. Harmonia continued, "I have heard rumors that some have defied the life line with denial."

"Denial?" asked the princess.

"Yes." Harmonia now grasped the princess's hands in hers and looked into her face. "You must try this method," she insisted. "There is no other hope."

"What…what do I do?" asked the princess, her lips quivering.

"You must first and foremost never mention a word of this to anyone. Not a soul! Not even the prince. To do so would be to bring death closer through acceptance. You must deny its existence by not speaking of it to anyone—not even to me."

"Yes," agreed the princess. "I will not speak of it to anyone."

"Very good," said Harmonia. "Next, you must deny death itself with life. You must live your life so well that death would not dare to touch you."

"How…?" queried the princess.

"That is for you to say, not me," replied Harmonia. "Is there anything you have wanted to do that you have put off?"

Was there anything she wanted to do that she *hadn't* put off? That would have been easier to answer. Indeed, where could she begin the list of things she had put off?

"You must do as many of those things as possible," continued Harmonia. "That is your only hope."

The princess's mind was racing.

"Well, I must leave you, I'm afraid," said Harmonia. She took the princess in her arms and hugged her. Then she blessed her and wished her well three times with tears in her eyes. Anyone could clearly see she was offering a final farewell. The princess choked back tears as she watched the wizardess leave. Even after she was out the door, Harmonia stopped and looked back toward the princess dramatically a number of times, presenting, without a doubt, the saddest farewell any princess has ever witnessed.

Long after the wizardess was finally out of sight Princess Wearia continued to stare out the open door. Tears threatened to well up again but she choked them back. She must defy death.

She looked out at the field in the distance and saw in it spots of color she had not noticed before. When had the flowers begun blooming? She loved the feel and smell of flowers and suddenly it became the most important thing for her to go and get a closer look at them. She rushed out through the doors, and ran feverishly toward the field. It was filled with colorful wild flowers of blue and pink and yellow and red. She bent down to smell each and every one of them as she came upon them. Their smell intoxicated her. Why did she not do this every morning? She walked, and then ran and sometimes skipped through the field for a quarter of an hour. Here and there she would stop where she spotted a flower struggling to bloom among the weeds, and she would pluck out the weeds with her fingers, giving the little bud space to flourish. She mused that if she came out to do this every day these gardens would indeed be impressive.

But at last, the quiet beauty she had taken in had kindled a small fire in her that forced her to move on to other things. On her way back to the castle, she collected flowers of every color and variety to take home with her.

Inside the castle the princess placed the flowers carefully in water. She had become quite overheated from her exertions and aside from that, she no longer was content to go through what may be the last day of her life looking the way she did now. She tore the hideous dress from her body, tossing it contemptuously into the garbage and prepared herself for a luxurious bath.

Into very warm water she poured bath bubbles from a little jar that had sat in her cabinet for years. She was not sure why she had not bothered to use the bubbles before this; she loved the way they smelled and made the water feel. She had been saving them for something but at the present moment she could not recall what. In fact, she dumped the entire contents of the little jar into her bath.

Princess Wearia removed the rest of her undergarments and slipped into the warm bath before it was even filled. She could not wait to feel the deliciously warm and gently scented water on her skin. She rested her head against the rounded back of the bathtub and closed her eyes. She thought about what the wizardess had said. She must think of a way to live in defiance of death. She must do all of the things she had been meaning to do. But there were so many things she had meant to do. Meaning to do things was, it seemed, her most practiced activity. As she thought about this her hand absently stroked her skin. The bath bubbles added an unusually silky quality to her flesh that was hard to resist. At length her hands wandered between her legs.

Often of late, when she looked at or touched herself there, she would think, *someday I should like to experiment with the styling of it;* for she had often heard mentioned, in hushed voices of the women's cafés and salons that it was the exciting and fashionable thing to do. She had always put the experiment aside for a better time but, given the circumstances, it seemed that there truly would be no time like the present.

She picked up a razor and looked down at the little patch of curls critically. She liked the way they looked overall; it was the little stragglers that offended her. Also, she remembered how it had excited her once to hear of a certain notorious hoyden who had removed all the hair around the opening, leaving nothing but a curly triangle above. This appealed to her now as much as it had then, so she set off to work at once. Within minutes she could feel the luscious softness of the skin that had been buried beneath the coarse curls until that moment. The newly smoothed skin, after mingling with the bath oils, felt like the finest oriental silk. She wondered what her husband would think, and this started yet another little fire inside her to get up and go, quickly, at once, and find him.

The princess rinsed and dried and dressed, more carefully this time, with an effort to please, but periodically pausing for a single moment in which to touch her newly shaved flesh. The silky feel of it excited her to no end, and she wondered why she had put the pleasing task off for so long. What other things had she been missing out on because of her procrastination, always pushing things off to another day?

She thought of one thing in particular and her pulse raced at the thought of seeing her husband. She put on her prettiest dress, which fit her well and brought out the color of her eyes. This time when she looked at herself in the mirror she mused that the ironing of her dress had been well worth the few minutes it took. She intentionally omitted wearing undergarments—another thing, as it turns out, that she had always wanted to do but never found the right time for. But there was no more perfect time than after her bath, and she could feel the mingling sensations of air and moisture between her legs as she rushed from the house to seek out her husband.

Princess Wearia's husband was building a great bridge that would eventually become the main entranceway to their castle. It was a lofty project that occupied the majority of his spare time. He was sculpting the bridge from rocks of all shapes and sizes, arranging them just so with his hands to create, not only a strong throughway that would last for generations, but also a work of art from the depths of his imagination.

His hands were rough, rutted and misshapen from the ongoing project, as if the rocks, too, were sculpting him. Little droplets of moisture trickled down his neck as he stopped for a moment to study the large pile of rocks, searching for one that was just the right size and shape.

When Princess Wearia first discovered her husband at his work she stopped for a moment to quietly watch him. She had somehow managed to forget how handsome he was. She slipped up closer to him as quietly as she could manage. But all of a sudden he became aware of a presence behind him and turned. There was a look of surprise on his face when he saw her.

"Well!" he exclaimed, obviously pleased by the sight of her. "What brings you out here?"

"I should have come sooner," she admitted, glancing at the massive structure which, even being only half-finished, was quite an impressive sight. "It's beautiful," she breathed.

"Still," he said, standing up and dusting off his hands, "it's a dirty place for a beautiful princess in such a pretty dress."

"Actually," she admitted, "I was just thinking the opposite—that such magnificence makes everything else seem rather ordinary by comparison."

He was deeply pleased and flattered by this remark, but he replied, "I assure you I do not find your appearance to be 'ordinary'." He realized that there must be some reason for her to have come all this way from the castle in search of him. Perhaps it had something to do with the wizardess's visit. "How did it go with the wizardess?" he asked.

"Oh," she said absently, with a little wave of her hand, "it was nothing." She was still taken aback by the beauty of the wall and the sight of her husband working out here all by himself in the midst of nature.

But why had she come then? wondered the prince. He looked at her expectantly. When she noticed his confusion she blushed. "I feel silly," she confessed.

"Silly?" Why, this was indeed unusual. His wife, here? Behaving timidly? He was completely disarmed. "Why should my wife feel silly to come and see me?" he asked her.

Her blush deepened, but she decided to tell him the truth. "Because I came out here to show you something that I think is not so impressive, after all," she confessed.

He was intrigued. "What did you come out here to show me?"

She bit her lip. "Honestly, I don't think I would rather, now." She looked again at the half-built bridge. Why had she never come to see it before?

The prince took her face in his hands and forced her to look at him. "Tell me," he demanded gently.

"I...it's just that..." she stammered. "Heavens, it's really rather embarrassing now that I think about it. I wish I hadn't said anything about it." Her heart was suddenly pounding and her face burned.

Her husband held her flushed face determinedly in his hands and looked at her with puzzled eyes. "Tell me," he insisted a little more firmly.

She realized suddenly that there would now be no way to avoid telling him what brought her out there, short of making something else up, and anyway, she had never wanted him more than she did at that moment. Perhaps it would not seem quite so trivial a thing to him after all. He might at the very least find it an amusing interruption in his otherwise difficult workday. With a ragged sigh she took one of his hands and brought it down the length of her dress, reaching beneath the hem and then traveling back up again, this time with his hand traveling along her smooth, bare leg. She watched his shocked eyes as she placed his hand between her legs. She laughed low and breathy, and blushed even harder, saying, "I told you it would seem rather silly."

The prince was speechless. He touched her soft, silky wetness tenderly as he attempted to rein in his emotions. His senses were scattered in all directions, thrilling each to its own preference—the way she looked and smelled, the shy expression on her face, the fact that she came to him wearing nothing at all underneath her dress, but more than anything, the way she felt between her legs, so silky and smooth. Each and every one of these stimulants assailed his brain and left him reeling. Even so, he wanted to add yet another enticement into the mix. He wanted to see her.

The prince tore off his shirt and laid it down on a more level area of ground beneath a nearby tree. "Come, princess," he said in a teasing manner, but quite determined, too. "Let me have a good look at this thing you came all this way to show me."

The princess trembled at the thought, but allowed her husband to lead her to the tree and seat her down upon his shirt.

The prince took the skirt of her dress in his hands and raised it slowly to her waist. "Ah, yes," he breathed. He stared speechless for a moment and then whispered, "Open your legs wider for me, princess." She did as he told her, trembling with exquisite pleasure as she opened her legs as wide as she could for him. She had never felt so alive. "Yes," the prince murmured again and again as he looked at her bared loveliness.

The prince leaned in closer and his senses were once again assailed by the freshly bathed smell of her. He reached below her and grasped her buttocks, and then in the next instant he buried his face between her legs, lapping at her like a starving animal. The princess could do little more than sit there, stunned and shuddering. There was a most delicious desire that had been growing inside her since her bath; now she had only to wait for the exquisite release to come. She was beginning to feel the agonizing little twinges of warning that preceded her release and, as if sensing this, the prince abruptly stopped tormenting her with his tongue. He straightened up and removed his trousers. Now it was the princess's senses that were reeling at the sight of her husband's hard body in the brilliant afternoon light.

Princess Wearia reached out for her husband as he came to her, leading him into her body. When at last he filled her, she cried out loudly with all of her unfulfilled desire. She loved the feel of her husband deep inside her. Why did so much time go by without them enjoying each other this way? But she was not able to dwell on this because she was obliged to concentrate all her efforts on satisfying her body. She rubbed her silky smooth skin against her husband in frenzied little jerks, and he, likewise followed the direction of his yearning body, driving himself into his wife vigorously. Both were too caught up in the intensity of their passion to notice any discomfort; his knees strained against the dirt and rocks to find leverage and her bared buttocks had only his shirt beneath them to soften the hard ground. They struggled together almost violently, panting and moaning, until the princess at last cried out, followed by her husband, who poured himself into her while she moaned giddily.

He was still confused when he looked down at her afterward. She laughed at his expression. Suddenly it seemed that life was terribly amusing. She remained basking in the afterglow while he got up and dressed. *Oh, how I would love to lie here and take a nap,* she thought. But then, in the next instant she said to herself, *there will be plenty enough time to sleep when I die!*

This thought prompted her to get up and dress also. She turned to her husband, a bit awkwardly. "I suppose I should let you get back to your work," she said.

"Shall I walk you home?" he asked her.

"Oh, no, please," she replied at once. "You mustn't let me disrupt your day." As an afterthought she added, "Any more than I have already, that is." And she realized with a shock that she was, for once, behaving like a wife.

The prince grasped her by the shoulders and kissed her. "I will see you tonight," he promised with meaning. She couldn't contain a little giggle of delight when he said this.

On her way home Princess Wearia pondered what she should do next. She felt happy and strangely lighthearted. Absently, she brushed her disheveled hair out of her face. She had been meaning to do something with the unruly mess, but it was always such a bother to take the time. And there, all at once, was her next project. She would have her hair cut, and perhaps styled in the manner that her husband had liked best when they were courting. Why had she stopped doing it, anyway? She struggled to recall when she had stopped fussing with her hair and it occurred to her with a shock that it was almost immediately after her marriage. And yet she could not recall why. Upon thinking about it, in fact, she realized she had stopped a great many things after her wedding day. This knowledge came to her with a rush of shame. How horrible it must have been for the prince to court one woman only to find himself shackled for life to a different one entirely. What had come over her to make it so?

Upon considering the matter in some detail, the princess acknowledged that she had become a bit disillusioned with her life. Her child-hood had been so full of delights under her father's loving care and supervision. Once it had come upon herself to take over the task it had been abandoned. Her husband was not her father, and he was not of the mind, as some men were, to offer guardianship. He seemed content to let her be herself. But who was that? It seemed that she had done nothing whatsoever with or for herself.

She hoped she hadn't pushed her husband too far with her apathy. She made a silent vow that she would be more like the person they both thought he was marrying for the remainder of their time together, short though it may turn out to be. But she would not think of dying. She had spent too long living as if she were already dead.

It took less than an hour for Princess Wearia to have her hair cut and arranged. But as oftentimes happens, such an elaborately adorned head called for something equally impressive to wear. With this in mind, the princess went into her favorite dress shop. She walked up and down the rows of dresses, looking for just the right thing. A few items immediately caught her eye but she dismissed these as not special enough for the evening to come. It might, after all, very well be her last.

Suddenly the princess fell back against the wall in a swoon. A wave of dizziness swept over her and she thought to herself, *this is it—I am dying!* The saleswoman who had been hovering about put her arms around her.

"Are you all right, princess?" she asked her, alarmed.

Princess Wearia put her hand up to her flushed face. Her gaze wandered, at just that moment, to an item that was hanging on a wall. It was a luscious gown of thin silk the precise color of her eyes. It would be perfect for that evening, if she lived that long. "I must sit," she murmured, her eyes never leaving the little silk dress.

The saleslady helped her to a nearby chair. "That dress," whispered the princess, still feeling rather shaky but nevertheless managing to point to the dress that hung on the wall.

"My goodness," remarked the startled shopkeeper, "but you are quite the dedicated shopper! Wouldn't you rather I fetch you a glass of water?"

"No, no," said the princess, feeling much better now that she was sitting. "What I would like is for you to bring me that dress in my size." Normally she insisted on a size smaller than her own, hoping the too-small item would act as an incentive for her to do something about her expanding waistline, but what would be the point of such an exercise now? She surely did not have time for these little delusions anymore. Heaven only knew if she would even be able to wear the dress tonight. She was still feeling lightheaded, and all at once she felt a fervent wish to live. She knew she could do a better job at living her life if only she were given a second chance. She anxiously looked into her palm to see if her little life line had, perhaps, reappeared. It had not, but here was the saleswoman, returning with the dress.

"Oh, yes!" exclaimed the saleswoman. "It is a perfect match for your eyes."

The princess took the gown and held it up, delighted even more by the feel of it. "I will wear it tonight," she decided.

Walking out of the shop with her dress, the princess was suddenly overwhelmed by the smell of fresh bread baking. Another surge of dizziness assailed her but this time she nearly collapsed from laughter. "Goodness," she exclaimed. "I have forgotten to eat!" And it was true that she had not eaten a single thing that entire day, in spite of her many activities, which had certainly been significant for her.

But to have forgotten to eat! Most of her days passed from one snack to the next. She did not miss this obvious solution to her dieting problems. Instead of living to eat she would start eating, when necessary, to live. How had she become so dull a creature that her daily activities had mostly been comprised of eating? However disgusted she might feel by this revelation, she could not linger long with it; for there was precious little time to waste now.

She went into the bakery to get something to eat—for sustenance this time—and a wonderful idea occurred to her. She would hire someone to come in for the evening and prepare a sumptuous dinner for her and her husband—and why not? She was not herself terribly talented in the kitchen—not that she would have wished to spend what was perhaps her last day alive cooking anyway—but she had always wanted to surprise her hardworking husband with a delicious dinner by candlelight. This would, at last, be the night she would do it.

The arrangements were remarkably easy to make and affordable, and the princess returned to her home, for once very excited about the evening ahead of her. Already, dusk was peeking around the corner, ready to chase away the last rays of light at any moment.

The first thing Princess Wearia noticed when she walked in the door of her home was the flowers. The smell had dropped from the petals and now lingered in the air all around. She stopped for a moment to breath in the heady fragrance. She vowed then and there that she would never let a day pass without bringing fresh flowers indoors.

Princess Wearia did not take time to dwell too long on the flowers but rushed around preparing things for the woman who would arrive any minute to cook and serve their dinner. How exciting it was! She had always loved having her dinners served to her when she was growing up in the castle with her father. She had believed that she would continue enjoying this luxury, if not all the time, then as often as her married budget would allow. But this was, in fact, the first time she had bothered to actually plan such an event.

The princess pulled some candles from a kitchen cabinet. There were many of them, of all lengths and colors, for she collected them. The sight and smell of candles burning caused her heart to flutter with delight. Strange that she could not remember actually burning any. She stood for a moment, trying to recall the last time she had lit a candle. But alas, she realized, she had only collected them. But what had she been saving them for?

"Well, I shall burn them tonight at least," she vowed. She placed them all about the dining room and adjacent sitting rooms in readiness, but walked away before lighting them, thinking they would last longer if she lit them when her husband arrived home. But before she had even made it halfway down the hall she stopped. "I've done it again," she laughed to herself, and went back into the dining room to light the candles at once. When she and her husband entered their dining room a little later, it would be cozier and more inviting to walk into candlelight.

The cooking woman duly arrived and, after settling her in the kitchen, the princess finally went to her chamber to dress for dinner. This, too, caused her to wonder—*when was the last time she dressed for dinner?* It had certainly been too long. Life was to be savored, she scolded herself. A romantic dinner for two should be treated as a party! This was how she wanted to live her life, although perhaps it was too late.

She primped and preened and did everything she could think of to improve her appearance, and her efforts had the desired effect. She even wore her most expensive jewelry, finding it tangled in a drawer untouched for many months. She put on her gown last, fully dressed now except for her undergarments. She reached down and touched herself between her legs as she contemplated this. The feeling of the smooth skin on her fingertips caused her to giggle. She would leave the undergarments off, she decided—perhaps forever!

At length she heard her husband come through the front door and she rushed down to meet him, breathless and excited. He stopped short when he saw her, staring at her open-mouthed.

She laughed, embracing him and placing a kiss on his lips like she should have—like she wished she had—every day since they were married. "I wanted to surprise you," she said.

"You did," he said, grinning.

"Dinner will be served shortly," she told him.

"I will make myself presentable," he assented. He, too, had become somewhat negligent in his manners of late, but then, the princess had not seemed to notice. He whistled as he prepared to meet his wife for dinner. It reminded him of their courtship days and he, too, felt a new excitement.

The princess took out two sparkling glasses and poured a little wine into each of them. She would normally have consumed more than both the glasses full by this time of day, she realized, for she had lost the ability to enjoy her evening drink, as well as everything else, it seemed. Instead of leisurely enjoying the wine, she misused it to drown her senses and quiet her aspirations. It was one more part of her life that she had greedily sucked the pleasure out of. She brought the glasses into the sitting room and took a small sip from her glass. Ah, the first sip of a glass of wine! There were perhaps four or five really agreeable mouthfuls, then, after that, one would simply have to wait until it was entirely out of their system before they could experience that pleasure again. But alas, she had always just kept sipping and then gulping, faster and faster, trying desperately to make it feel like the first sip once again. Princess Wearia tipped back her head and relished the delightfully mild, and utterly exquisite, feeling that came over her with that first taste of wine.

The prince walked into the room just then, stopping momentarily to admire his beautiful and contented wife, who was sitting demurely in the candlelit room sipping wine.

"Come join me," she persuaded him. He sat very close to her and picked up his wine. The princess noticed his clean, masculine smell and took a deep breath to capture more of it. She was agog for a moment, her senses overwhelmed by the intoxicating combinations of the heady wine and the smell of her husband. What had she been doing all those other nights? She could not remember what she had been doing—or feeling, for that matter. But she was certain she would never forget what she was feeling at that moment. Delight, exhilaration, excitement, anticipation—and so much more, too. She was feeling things she could not even name, and once again she felt, stronger than ever, that she wanted to live.

Suddenly Princess Wearia wanted to know more about this handsome, wonderful-smelling prince who sat beside her. When they were courting she asked only superficial questions, and since their marriage she hadn't asked any questions at all. Now she found there were all kinds of things that she wanted to know. She began by asking him how long he expected to be working on the bridge. This led to many more questions, and she was dismayed when the cooking woman interrupted them to say that dinner was ready to be served.

Walking into the dining room, the princess immediately commended herself for lighting the candles ahead of time. They had burned perhaps a half an inch, but the effect that half inch gave the room as they entered it was dramatic. She truly felt like the princess of her own castle as her husband pulled out her chair for her to sit down to dinner.

In fact, all of Princess Wearia's preparations that day paid off, so that the dinner was a fabulous event that would stay in both of their memories forever. Surveying her husband from across the table, she realized that if she did die, there would be many women who would be happy to follow in her footsteps. She allowed this realization to lead her thoughts even further in the same direction—and she found herself imagining her husband with another woman. Would he forget her quickly? Would he be glad to be rid of her? She nearly cried out at the thought. Oh, why had she taken him for granted? She must make it up to him. There simply must be time! She would try her best to give him memories to last a lifetime.

"My, but you have a serious expression on your face," the prince observed.

"I'm sorry," she told him. "My mind was wandering. Did you say something?"

"Well, I was about to ask you about something, actually," he replied with a partially teasing aspect. "You see, I had a dream this afternoon, perhaps it was heatstroke…" He raised an eyebrow and grinned charmingly.

Princess Wearia laughed. "Tell me about it," she encouraged him playfully. "What happened?"

"As I said, I'm not entirely certain anything happened at all," he went on. "I think I shall need proof in order to believe it was real."

"Proof?" she repeated. "Hmm, how could you prove or disprove a dream, I wonder?"

"Well, there was one very unique element to the dream which could certainly be put to the test." He was enjoying this little tête-à-tête immensely, and he could see by the rising color of her cheeks that his wife was, too. He moved closer to her, settling on one knee in front of her and placing his hand on her leg, just below the knee, and said, "But I'm afraid I'll need your help to test it."

"My help?" She was feeling giddy from the exciting little game. "What have I to do with it?" she asked in mock innocence.

"I'm afraid that's where it gets a little…sticky," he explained, still relatively straight-faced. "You see, you were there, in my dream."

"I?"

"Would you have me dream of another?"

"Well, but tell me more about the dream," she insisted, keeping her lips from smiling but not quite managing to keep them from twitching.

"There was something…different about you in my dream," he told her solemnly.

"Something different?"

"Yes," he replied. "Something rather…remarkable."

"I can't think what that might be," she lied.

"I thought not," he said. His hand had begun slowly, excruciatingly slowly, to creep up her leg, but at the rate it was going the princess felt she might expire before his hand reached its destination. "Still," he added nonchalantly, his hand continuing its maddeningly slow caress up her leg, "I wonder if you would be kind enough to indulge me whilst I investigate."

"Oh!" she exclaimed, trembling in anticipation. "Indulge you how?"

"By opening your legs for me," he concluded, having nearly reached the top of her thigh with his hand.

"Well," she said, faking contemplation, "if it would help you to resolve the matter."

"It most certainly would," he assured her. At this she opened her trembling legs for him. His hand lingered on her upper thigh. So far, his eyes had never left hers for a single moment throughout the questioning. But now he raised her skirt with his free hand and lowered his eyes to catch another glimpse of the perfectly trimmed little triangle between her legs. In truth, until that very moment he had not been entirely certain that the afternoon's events hadn't been just a dream. He took in his breath at the sight of her. "Ah," he groaned. "So it was true!"

"Yes!" she admitted at last.

"Did you do this for me?" he queried.

"Yes, for you my darling," she told him. "Do you like it?"

"Let me show you!"

He pulled her onto his lap on the floor.

"May I—" the serving woman had come upon them at that moment and paused midsentence in shocked surprise "—get you anything more?"

Princess Wearia had forgotten all about the hired woman. She struggled to get up but her husband held her down, laughing.

"That will be all for tonight," he told the woman in a relaxed tone. The woman murmured a confused answer and hastily left.

"Oh, you!" the princess whispered, trying hard to stifle her giggle.

But her husband laughed heartily and the sound of it took away her breath.

"How have I managed to stay away from you all these nights?" she murmured to herself really, but her husband looked at her as if she had been asking him.

"I guess I have never been as attractive as I am today," he joked. But they both knew that the real answer was that most nights she would have been passed out on the couch by now.

"I'm sorry," she told him, serious now. "I think I forgot to be a wife." *And a woman,* she added to herself.

He did not dwell on her confession or her apology, as some men might have been tempted to do, but instead took the more pleasant route for both of them by pushing her down on her back right there on the floor and asking her teasingly how she planned to make it up to him. And she was very delighted to show him.

But much later, after her husband was asleep, Princess Wearia stared up at the ceiling, wondering what would become of her. She did not want to die, but more importantly, she did not want to continue this living death, either. But perhaps it was not for her to decide. Perhaps she was already dying.

She sat up in bed. But of course she was dying! She always had been, hadn't she, ever since the day she was born? No one lived forever. The time for living was in each and every moment, and the next morning, when the princess noticed that her shoes were not worn she knew that she had lived well the previous day. And she determined to do the same that day, and for however many more days that she continued to wake up.

Well, and what about you?

EPILOGUE

AND SO IT WAS THAT THE MYSTERY OF THE TWELVE "DANCING" princesses, as they had come to be called, and their worn shoes was put to rest once and for all. One last great feast was arranged to celebrate the wizardess's success, and now the question on everyone's lips was what she would request for her reward. The king had promised her any single thing from his kingdom, and everyone wondered what that one thing would be. Would the brazen woman ask for the castle?

One day, while Harmonia was walking through the great gardens of the castle, the king walked out to join her, for they had become friends. While they were walking together the wizardess happened to ask him, "Which half of the kingdom shall be mine?"

The king stared at her, aghast. "I have dispensed with that old bargain, as you well know," he said at length.

"Dispensed with it?" she repeated. "Since when?"

"Since the night I accepted your challenge!"

"That is ridiculous!" Harmonia stormed, instantly outraged, and immediately on the defensive. "This is because I am a woman!"

"No," the king told her. "It is because I did not wish to put you to death if you failed."

"But I didn't fail!" she insisted.

And on the dispute went, round and round, until at last the king lost his temper, bellowing, "You may have any one thing from my kingdom. Take it or leave it!"

Harmonia was obliged to accept this offer, but she left the king in the garden and avoided him until the night of the feast.

When the night of the great feast arrived, which was in all respects Harmonia's night of honor, she found that she was in very good spirits. She prepared herself with care, slightly nervous but still terribly excited. She had learned many things from the inhabitants of this kingdom, and from the princesses most of all. In each of them she had detected characteristics she herself possessed, and this had helped her to understand herself better.

When she at last left her private room to join the king in kicking off the festivities, she was glowing with serenity and beauty. She greeted the king with a cheerfulness that he had not expected, but he was quickly captured by her mood and he, too, became more jovial as the night advanced.

As part of the celebration, the princesses had arranged a ceremony of sorts, where they could each express their appreciation to the wizardess by presenting her with a gift. Harmonia was delighted and charmed by the rare and distinctive treasures the princesses bestowed upon her. In addition to their gifts, the princesses each curtsied before the wizardess, offering their heartfelt thanks in words, as well.

There were also a few remaining questions for the wizardess to answer. Princess Wearia approached her first, to see what more she could learn of her precarious life expectancy. The wizardess bit her lip guiltily when she saw her, quickly explaining that she may have misread her hand. And sure enough, under reexamination, they discovered that the princess's life line, which was actually located in an entirely different place than where they were searching for it, was actually remarkably long. The princess found no reason to be upset with the wizardess over this mishap, and all other matters brought forth before her were settled equally satisfactorily.

At last the king motioned for everyone to be silent. He was impatient to hear what Harmonia would ask of him.

"I have inspected my daughters' shoes this very morning," he began. "And I am fully satisfied that the wizardess has indeed solved the mystery once and for all."

There rose a loud cheer to this declaration, and the king waited for the crowd to settle down before continuing. "The time has come to give Harmonia her reward."

There was complete silence throughout the feasting hall now as the king turned toward the wizardess. "Well?" he asked. "What will you have from my kingdom?"

Harmonia stood up and looked at the king a moment before speaking. At length she said in a clear but slightly trembling voice, "I will have...you!"

Everyone spoke at once. Women gasped, others cried out, some even had the presence of mind to deny their own hearing and ask, "What did she say?" The noise level rose to record proportions as the guests came to terms with the wizardess's announcement. But at length the crowd quieted, curious now to know how the king would respond.

The king was speechless. His first reaction to Harmonia's shocking declaration had very nearly been delight. He found that in the short time he had known her he had come to not only admire, but also to adore her. However, the thoughts that followed were much less pleasant, for he quickly realized that she must have devised this clever plan in order to obtain half of his kingdom in spite of their earlier conversation. He felt trapped—for what could he do? He had declared in front of his daughters and his entire kingdom that she could choose any single thing that she wished.

Everyone held their breath as they waited for the king to answer. He noticed that Harmonia's lips were turned upward on one side as she, too, watched him keenly. It was as if she were challenging him.

"So it shall be," he said at last, but it sounded more menacing than he had intended, almost like a threat. He noticed that his answer had caused the smile to fade from Harmonia's lips.

And now it was the king who avoided Harmonia while preparations were made for their wedding—for in those days that was what such a declaration denoted. In the meantime, the king thought a great deal about Harmonia. There was much he admired about her and he felt that she would indeed make a fine and clever queen. As for her person, he admitted to himself that he found her quite attractive and delightful on many different levels. It was, however, the way in which it had been done that angered him and damaged his pride. Furthermore, he feared that her inconsiderate behavior had tainted their marriage before it had even begun. It would not bode well for the future.

In spite of these reservations, the king appeared on his wedding day looking handsome and calm. Harmonia was beautifully dignified, and the king grudgingly admired her poise. He knew that he wanted her in spite of his doubts, yet they were no longer children to be ruled by passion.

When the priest asked him, "Do you take this woman?" he answered truthfully, meeting her eyes as he spoke the words, "I do."

But when her turn came Harmonia answered in a mere whisper, seemingly spellbound by the king's stare as she said, "I do."

"Then you may kiss the bride."

Harmonia raised her face to the king, now her husband, as he approached her. Her eyes were locked with his. With his fingers the king gently lifted her chin and held her face as he kissed her. Her lips were soft and inviting and his kiss was tender and lingering. It seemed to convey a promise of something to come—or perhaps it was only the possibility of something that could have been.

But all at once a cheer rose up and then there followed feasting and dancing for hours, until the moment when the king took Harmonia's hand and led her away.

At last the newly married couple was alone in their bedchamber and Harmonia's poise finally left her. She struggled to control her trembling. The king faced her with a mixture of feelings ranging from anger to desire. This made him belligerent.

"So Harmonia, my wife," he said, once again lifting her face and holding her chin so that she was obliged to look at him. "Now that you have gained half my kingdom, what have you for me?"

At his words her own anger flared, but with effort she forced it back down. As her eyes met his she mused that time was short, and they were both too old to play games. If she learned nothing else from the princesses, she had certainly learned that a lack of communication could rob a couple of happiness. She knew she must try to open the doors of communication between them, by empathizing with him and by being absolutely honest.

Queen Harmonia took her husband's hand in hers. "Please sit

Nancy Madore

beside me," she said in her warm voice. He was once again taken aback by her demeanor and calm, and he obediently sat on the bed beside her. Her eyes met his.

"I realize now that you were speaking the truth about the night that I accepted the challenge," she admitted. Her voice was soft and her tone was kindly. "At the time, I thought you were generously adding another wish to the existing gift of one half of your kingdom. I guess I did not understand at the time because I did not want to. Anyway, I want you to know that when I thought I could have half your kingdom plus one additional thing, the additional thing I wanted…I wanted…" She paused, becoming more uncomfortable. A blush rose up over her cheeks. "I wanted… you…then, too."

She rushed on, now that the difficult words were out. "I had planned to mention it to you in private first, to make sure that you wanted me, too, but then…well, I decided to take a chance. Perhaps I was wrong to do so. But I still want more than anything to be here with you and if we could just begin anew I will try to be a good wife to you." At this last there were tears in her eyes.

The king was shocked by her candor, honesty and above all, her humility. He was deeply touched. Her behavior was truly queenly, and he believed every word she said. There were tears in his eyes, too, as he assured her, "We will indeed begin anew." Their earlier attraction to one another was now joined with a newfound respect and trust. And from there they both realized something truly wonderful could develop.

Nancy Madore

Nancy Madore lives with her family in Newburyport, Massachusetts, where she operates a shoe store with her son. A former feature writer for some local newspapers, Nancy has a degree in journalism and finds every opportunity she can to write. She is currently busy working on her next collection of erotic short stories for Spice Books.

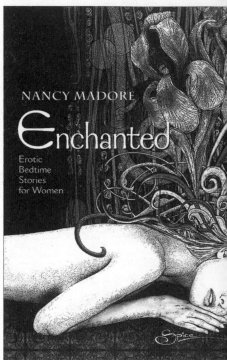

A One-Year Anniversary has never been this hot...

Celebrate the first anniversary of SPICE by indulging in the sexiest, most scintillating stories destined to ignite your senses!

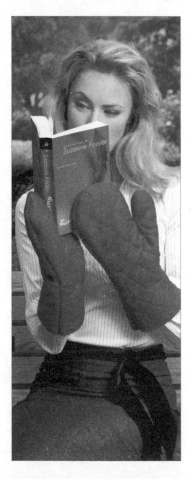

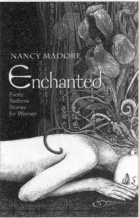

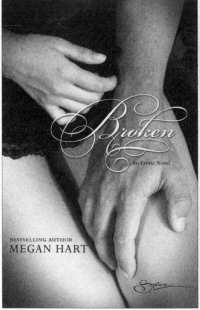